33.31

W9-BUI-667

THE KNITTING CIRCLE

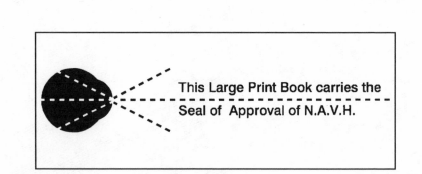

This Large Print Book carries the
Seal of Approval of N.A.V.H.

THE KNITTING CIRCLE

ANN HOOD

THORNDIKE PRESS
An imprint of Thomson Gale, a part of The Thomson Corporation

THOMSON
✳ ™
GALE

Detroit • New York • San Francisco • New Haven, Conn. • Waterville, Maine • London

THOMSON

GALE

™

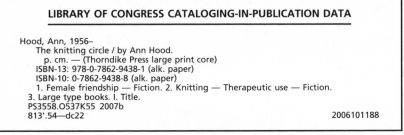

LIBRARY OF CONGRESS CATALOGING-IN-PUBLICATION DATA

Hood, Ann, 1956–
   The knitting circle / by Ann Hood.
     p. cm. — (Thorndike Press large print core)
   ISBN-13: 978-0-7862-9438-1 (alk. paper)
   ISBN-10: 0-7862-9438-8 (alk. paper)
   1. Female friendship — Fiction. 2. Knitting — Therapeutic use — Fiction.
  3. Large type books. I. Title.
PS3558.O537K55 2007b
813'.54—dc22   2006101188

Published in 2007 by arrangement with W. W. Norton & Company, Inc.

Printed in the United States of America on permanent paper
10 9 8 7 6 5 4 3 2 1

For knitters
For friends

PROLOGUE

Daughter, I have a story to tell you. I have wanted to tell it to you for a very long time. But unlike Babar or Eloise or any of the other stories that you loved to hear, this one is not funny. This one is not clever. It is simply true. It is my story, yet I do not have the words to tell it. Instead, I pick up my needles and I knit. Every stitch is a letter. A row spells out "I love you." I knit "I love you" into everything I make. Like a prayer, or a wish, I send it out to you, hoping you can hear me. Hoping, daughter, that the story I am knitting reaches you somehow. Hoping, that my love reaches you somehow.

■ ■ ■ ■

PART ONE:
CASTING ON

■ ■ ■ ■

To knit, you have to have the stitches on one needle. "Casting on" is the term for making the foundation row of stitches. Once you have cast on, you are ready to knit.

— Nancy J. Thomas and Ilana Rabinowitz, *A Passion for Knitting*

1
MARY

Mary showed up empty-handed.

"I don't have anything with me," she said, and she opened her arms to indicate their emptiness.

The woman standing before her was called Big Alice, but there was nothing big about her. She stood five feet tall, with a tiny waist, short silver hair, and gray eyes the color of a sky right before a storm. Big Alice had her slight body wedged between the worn wooden door to the shop and Mary herself.

"This isn't really my kind of thing," Mary said apologetically.

The woman nodded. "I know," she said, stepping back so that the door swung open wide. "I can't tell you how many people have stood right where you're standing and said that exact thing." Her voice was soft, British.

"Well," Mary said, because she didn't

know what else to say.

She never did know what to say these days, or what to do. This was in September, five months after her daughter Stella had died. That stunned disbelief had ebbed slightly, but the horrible noises in her head had grown. They were hospital noises, doctors' voices, and Stella's own five-year-old voice saying *Mama.* Sometimes Mary imagined she really heard her daughter calling out to her and her heart would squeeze tight on itself.

"Come on in," Big Alice said.

Mary followed her into the shop. Alice wore a gray tweed skirt, a white oxford shirt, a gold cardigan, and pearls. Although the top half of her looked like a schoolmarm, she had crazy-colored striped socks on her feet and pink chenille bedroom slippers with red rhinestone cherries across the tops.

"I've got the gout," Big Alice explained, lifting one slippered foot. Then she added, "I guess you know I'm Alice."

"Yes," Mary said.

Like everything else, Mary could easily have forgotten the woman's name. She'd written it on one of the hundreds of Post-its scattered around the house like confetti after a party. But, like all of the phone numbers and dates and directions, the paper with *Alice* written on it was gone. Outside the store, however, a wooden sign read *Big Alice's Sit and Knit,* and when Mary saw it she had remembered: Alice.

Mary stopped and got her bearings. These days this was always necessary, even in familiar places. In her own kitchen she would stop what she was doing and look around, take stock. Oh, she would say to herself, noting that the television was off instead of tuned to *Sagwa, the Chinese Cat;* the bowl Stella had made at Claytime with its carefully painted and placed polka dots was empty of the sliced cucumbers or mound of blueberries it used to hold; the cutout hearts with crayoned *I love you*'s and the construction-paper kite with its pink ribbon tail drooped. Oh, Mary would say, realizing all over again that this was how her kitchen — her life — looked now. Empty and sad.

The shop was small, with creaky wooden floors and baskets and shelves brimming over with yarn. It smelled like sweaters and cedar and Alice's own citrus scent. There were three rooms: this small one, the room beyond with the cash register and a well-worn couch slipcovered in a pink and red floral pattern, and another larger room with more yarn and a few chairs.

The yarn was beautiful. Mary saw this immediately and touched some as she followed Alice into the next room, letting her fingertips linger a bit over the skeins.

"So," Alice was saying, "we'll start you on a scarf." She held up a finished scarf. Cobalt blue with pale blue tassels. "You like this one?"

"I guess so," Mary said.

"You don't like it? You're frowning."

"I do. It's fine. It's just, I can't make it. I'm not good with my hands. I flunked home ec. Really, I did."

Alice turned toward the wall and pulled down some wooden knitting needles.

"A ten-year-old can make that scarf," she said, a bit impatiently. She handed the needles to Mary.

They felt large and smooth and awkward in her hands. Mary watched as Alice went over to a shelf and grabbed several balls of yarn. The same cobalt blue, and aquamarine, and mauve.

"Which color do you like?" Alice said. She held them out to Mary like an offering.

"The blue, I guess," Mary said, and the particular blue of Stella's eyes presented itself in her mind. When she tried to blink it away, she felt tears slide out. She turned her head and wiped her eyes.

"Blue it is," Alice said, more gently. She pointed to a chair tucked into a corner beneath balls of fat yarn. "Sit down and I'll teach you how to knit."

Mary laughed. "Such optimism," she said.

"A woman came in here two weeks ago," Alice said, dropping into an overstuffed chair and sticking her feet up on a small footstool with a needlepoint cover. "She'd never knit a thing, and she's made three of these scarves. That's how easy it is."

Mary had driven forty miles to this store, even though there was a knitting shop less than a mile from her house. As she navigated the unfamiliar back roads, it had seemed foolish, coming so far, to knit of all things. But sitting here with this stranger who knew nothing about her, or about what had happened, with these unfamiliar needles in her sweaty hands, Mary knew somehow that it was the right thing to do.

"It's just a series of slipknots," Alice said. She held up a long tail of the yarn and demonstrated.

"I was kicked out of the Girl Scouts," Mary said. "Slipknots are a mystery to me."

"First home economics. Then the Girl Scouts," Alice said, tsking. But her gray eyes gleamed mischievously.

"Actually, it was Girl Scouts, then home

ec," Mary said.

Alice chuckled. "If it makes you feel any better, I hated knitting. Didn't want to learn. Now here I am. I own a knitting store. I teach people to knit."

Mary smiled politely. Other people's stories held little interest for her. She used to like to listen to tales of broken hearts and triumphs and the odd twists of life. But her own story had taken over the part of her that was once open to such things. And if she listened out of politeness or necessity — like now — the situation begged for her to talk, to share. She wanted no part in that. There were times when she wondered if she'd ever tell her story to anyone.

"So," Mary said, "slipknots."

"Since you're a Girl Scouts–home economics flunkee," Alice said, "I'll cast on for you. Besides, if I stand here and teach you, I'll be wasting both our time because you're going to forget."

Mary didn't bother to ask what "cast on" meant. Like a magician practicing sleight of hand, Alice made a series of loops and twists, then held out one needle, the blue yarn snaking up it ominously.

"I cast on twenty-two stitches for you, and you're ready to go."

"Uh-huh," Mary said.

16

Alice motioned for Mary to come sit beside her.

"In here," Alice said, demonstrating. "Then wrap the yarn like this. And pull this needle through."

Mary smiled as first one stitch, then another, appeared on the empty needle.

"Okay," Alice said. "Go ahead."

"Me?" Mary said.

"I already know how to do it," Alice said, "don't I?"

Mary took a breath and began.

2
THE KNITTING
CIRCLE

Here was what Mary still found extraordinary: on the day before Stella died, nothing unusual happened. There were no signs, no premonitions, nothing but the simple daily routine of their life together — she and Dylan and Stella. Her neighbor when she'd lived in San Francisco, on a high hill in North Beach, had been an old Italian woman named Angelina. Angelina always wore a black shawl over her head, and thick-soled black shoes, and a black dress. "People should know you're in mourning," she'd told Mary. "When you wear black, they understand."

Mary hadn't pointed out to her that everyone wore black these days. She hadn't rolled her eyes or smirked when Angelina told her that three days before her husband died — and here she'd made the sign of the cross, spitting into her palm at the end — a dog had howled, facing their apartment. "I knew death was coming," she'd said. Also, two other men from the neighborhood had died in the past few months. "Death," she'd explained, "comes in threes." Angelina had a litany of signs, dreams of clear water, of teeth falling out of her mouth; a dead bird on her doorstep; goose bumps in still, warm air.

But Mary had none of this. No dreams or dead birds or howling dogs. What she had was a typical day. A good day. At five, Stella still drank a bottle of milk in the morning and one at bedtime, a secret they kept from her kindergarten friends. Dylan brought her, happily and sleepily sucking her bottle, into bed with them and they cuddled there, Mary and Dylan reading the newspaper and Stella watching *Sesame Street*.

They knew it was time to get up when Stella came to life. No longer sleepy, she would start to tickle Dylan. Mary wished she could remember what they'd had for breakfast that last morning together, what they talked about over Eggos or cinnamon toast. But so ordinary was that morning that she cannot recall such details.

She knows that Stella wore striped tights and polka-dot clogs and a jumper that was too long, also striped. But she knows this because after Stella died, when they came

19

home from the hospital, these clothes still lay in a crumpled heap, right where Stella had dropped them when she got ready for bed. She knows this because for days she carried them around, pressing them to her nose for the last hints of Stella's little-girl scent.

Dylan had left that morning while they were still getting ready for school. He always left early, kissing them both on the top of their heads. Stella would yell, "Don't go, Daddy!" and pout, making Mary a little jealous. It was true, she thought, that the parent who did the most caretaking, the driving around and cooking and bathing, didn't get the adoration.

She felt guilty now, of course, that she had no doubt grown short with Stella for dawdling that morning. Stella was a dawdler, easily distracted by the sight of her forgotten rain boots or the sparkles on a picture she'd drawn and hung on the fridge. Even while Mary hurried her, Stella hummed and dawdled happily, grinning up at her mother as she rushed her into the car. "We're going to be late," Mary probably mumbled that morning, because they were usually late. And Stella probably said, "Uh-huh," before she returned to her humming.

Mary stopped for coffee that morning,

and visited with other mothers at the café, and shared funny stories about their amazing children; she went to work, wasting these last precious hours as a mother with reviews and research and other meaningless tasks; Dylan called her — he always did — to tell her when he'd be home that evening, to ask if Stella had anything special going on; then she raced to pick up her daughter at school, sat in the car, and watched her come out, dreamy and tired, her backpack dragging on the ground. And as she watched her, Mary's heart soared; it always did when she saw Stella, her daughter, again.

Unlike the rest of that day, the clarity of their last evening together was so strong that it made Mary double over to remember it. All of it. The late afternoon sun in their kitchen. Stella working on her *Weekly Reader.* Lighting the grill for an early barbecue. Stella drizzling the olive oil on the chicken. Stella scrubbing the dusty outdoor table and chairs, placing the napkins so carefully beside each plate, running into Dylan's arms when he walked into the backyard, grinning, pleased, and said: "A barbecue! In April!" "Yes," Stella had said, "we're eating *outside!*"

That night, Mary placed the portable CD player in the open window and played Stella's favorite CD of dance music, the two of them dancing barefoot: the Macarena, the chicken dance, the limbo, and finally Dylan joined them and all three danced to "Shout," jumping and waving their arms. The sliver of a moon hung above them in the big glorious sky, like a blessing, Mary remembered thinking.

The morning of Stella's funeral, Mary's mother called.

"You have so many people with you," she'd said. "I know you'll understand if I go back this morning. The later flight gets in after midnight, and you have so many people with you."

Mary had frowned, not believing what her mother was telling her. "You're not coming?" she asked. She still wasn't able to say her daughter's name in the same sentence as "funeral" or "died" or "dead."

"You understand, don't you?" her mother had said, and Mary thought she heard pleading in her voice. While her mother explained about the connection in Mexico City, how far apart the gates were, how confusing Customs was there, Mary quietly hung up.

Her mother had disappointed her for her entire life. She was not the mother who went to school plays or parents' nights; she gave praise rarely but never gushed or bragged; she had missed Mary's wedding because of a strike in San Miguel, where she lived, that forced her to miss her flight to the States. "I'll send you a nice gift," she'd said. And she had. The next week a set of Mexican pottery arrived, with half of the plates broken in the journey.

But still, in this most terrible time, Mary had expected her mother to be there in a way she had not been able to so far. When Mary studied the faces in the church, saw the neighbors and colleagues and teachers and relatives and friends, disappointment filled her chest so that she couldn't breathe. She had to sit down and gulp air. Her mother really had not come.

The flower arrangement her mother sent was the biggest of them all. Purple calla lilies, so many that they threatened to swallow the entire room. If Mary had had the energy, she would have thrown it out, that ostentatious apology. Instead, she purposely left it behind.

In the hot sticky summer right after Stella died, Mary's mother called her. She had called once a week, offering advice. Usually Mary didn't speak to her at all.

"What you need," her mother told her, "is to learn to knit."

"Right," Mary said.

Her mother's colonial house in San Miguel de Allende, Mexico, had a bright blue door that led to a courtyard where a fountain gurgled and big pink flowers bloomed. She had stopped drinking when Mary was a senior in high school. Now that Mary thought about it, that was when her mother started knitting. One day, balls of yarn appeared everywhere. Her mother sat and studied patterns at the kitchen table, drinking coffee and chewing peppermint candies.

"Here's what I'm hearing," her mother said. "You can't work, you can't think, you can't read."

While her mother talked, Mary cried. Not the painful sobbing that had consumed her when Stella first died, but the almost constant crying that had replaced it. Her world, which had been so benign, had turned into a minefield. The grocery store held only the summer berries that Stella loved. Elevators only played Stella's favorite song. And everywhere she walked she saw someone she had not seen since the funeral. Their faces changed when they saw her. Mary wanted to run from them and from the berries and the songs and the whole world that

24

had once held her and Stella so safely.

"There's something about knitting," her mother said. "You have to concentrate, but not really. Your hands keep moving and moving and somehow it calms your brain."

"Great, Mom," Mary said. "I'll look into it."

Then she'd climbed back into bed.

When Mary gave birth to Stella, she promised her that very first night that they would be different. Mary was going to be the mother she'd always wished for, and Stella would be free to be Stella, whatever that meant. She had kept her word too. She had spent afternoons making party hats for stuffed animals, letting her own deadlines go unmet. She had let Stella wear stripes with polka dots, orange earmuffs indoors, tutus to the grocery store.

They looked alike, Mary and Stella. The same shade of brown hair with the same red highlights that showed up in bright sunlight or by midsummer. The same mouths, a little too wide and too large for their narrow faces. But it was that mouth that gave them both such a killer smile. It was Mary's father's mouth that they'd both inherited, but in his later life it had turned downward, making him look like one of

25

those sad-faced clowns in bad paintings.

Dylan used to joke that Mary hadn't needed him at all to make Stella. "She's you through and through," he'd say. The only thing Stella had that was all her own were her blue eyes. Both Mary and Dylan had brown eyes, but Stella's were bright blue. Not unlike Mary's mother's eyes, she knew, but hated to admit. Still, the overall effect was that Stella was a miniature version of Mary, right down to the long narrow feet. Mary wore a size ten shoe, and surely Stella would have too.

For fun, they would sometimes both dress in all black and Stella would make them stand in front of the mirror on the back of Mary's closet door and grin together. "You look just like me," Stella would say proudly. And Mary's heart would seem to expand, as if it might burst through her ribs. She had done just as she promised. She was a good mother. Her daughter loved her.

As a child, Mary's life was rigid, structured, and controlled by her mother. Breakfast had all the food groups. Shoes and pocketbooks matched. Hair was pulled into two neat braids, made so tightly that Mary suffered headaches after school until she could free them. Then she would sit and rub her head, wincing.

As she got older, Mary understood that all of her mother's rules, all of the structure she imposed, were an effort to hide her drinking. When she came home from school, Mary sat at the kitchen table to do her homework, in a desperate need to be near her mother. Her mother would make dinner, sipping water as she cooked, *The Joy of Cooking* propped up on a Lucite cookbook stand. Mary found it ironic that this was her mother's cookbook of choice since she seemed to take no joy in cooking or eating.

Still, Mary sat at that kitchen table every afternoon, sometimes asking her mother for help even if she didn't need it, just so that her mother would come close to her. Mary would study her mother's beautiful face then, the smooth skin and perfect turned-up nose, the shiny blond hair, and fall in love with this stranger each time. Her mother's Chanel No. 5 would fill Mary, would make her dizzy.

Sometimes at night, her mother passed out on the sofa, and her father would lift her like Sleeping Beauty into his arms and carry her to bed. "Your mother works so hard," he'd say when he returned. Mary would nod, even though, other than cleaning, she had no idea what her mother did. Then, that night when she was a sophomore in high school, while she was doing the dishes, Mary pressed her own chapped lips to the rosy lipsticked imprint of her mother's on the water glass. She could taste the crayon taste of the lipstick, and then, sipping, the shock of vodka. All of those afternoons, her mother cooking with such concentration, those nights when she passed out on the sofa, her mother had been drunk. The realization did not shock Mary. Instead, it simply explained everything. Everything except why a woman so beautiful would drink so much.

That sad summer, time passed indifferently. Mary would lie in bed and think of what she should be doing — putting on Stella's socks for her, cutting the crust off her sandwiches, gushing over a new art project, hustling her off to ballet class. Instead, she was home not knowing what to do with all of the endless hours in each day.

Mary was a writer for the local alternative newspaper, *Eight Days a Week,* affectionately referred to as *Eight Days.* She reviewed movies and restaurants and books. Every week since Stella had died, her boss Eddie called and offered her a small assignment. "Just one hundred words," he'd say. "One hundred words about anything at all."

Holly, the office manager, came by with gooey cakes she had baked. Mary would glimpse her getting out of her vintage baby blue Bug, with her pale blond hair and big round blue eyes, unfolding her extralong legs and looking teary-eyed at the house, and she would pretend she wasn't home. Holly would ring the doorbell a dozen times or more before giving up and leaving the sugary red velvet cake or the sweet white one with canned pineapple and maraschino cherries and too-sweet coconut on the front steps.

Mary used to go out several times a week, with her husband Dylan or her girlfriends, or even with Stella, to try a new Thai restaurant or see the latest French film. Her hours were crammed with things to do, to see, to think about. Books, for example. She was always reading two or three at a time. One would be open on the coffee table and another by her bed, and a third, poetry or short stories, was tucked in her bag to read while Stella ran with her friends around the neighborhood playground.

And Mary used to have ideas about all of these things. She used to believe firmly that Providence needed a good Mexican restaurant. She could pontificate on this for hours. She worried over the demise of the romantic comedy. She had started to prefer nonfiction to fiction. Why was this? she would wonder out loud frequently.

How had she been so passionate about all of these senseless things? Now her brain could no longer organize material. She didn't understand what she had read or watched or heard. Food tasted like nothing, like air. When she ate, she thought of Stella's *Goodnight Moon* book, and of how Stella would say the words before Mary could read them out loud: *Goodnight mush. Goodnight nothing.* It was as if she could almost hear her daughter's voice, but not quite, and she would strain to find it in the silent house.

She imagined learning Italian. She imagined writing poetry about her grief. She imagined writing a novel, a novel in which a child is heroically saved. But words, the very things that had always rescued her, failed her.

"How's the knitting?" her mother asked her several weeks after suggesting Mary learn.

It was July by then.

"Haven't gotten around to it yet," Mary had mumbled.

"Mary, you need a distraction," her mother said. In the background Mary heard voices speaking in Spanish. Maybe she should learn Spanish instead of Italian.

"Don't tell me what I need," she said. "Okay?"

"Okay," her mother said.

In August, Dylan surprised her with a trip to Italy.

He had gone back to work right away. The fact that he had a law firm and clients who depended on him made Mary envious. Her office at home, once a walk-in closet off the master bedroom, had slowly returned to its former closet self. Sympathy cards, CDs, copies of books and poems and inspirational plaques, all the things friends had sent them, got stacked up in her office. There was a whole box in there of porcelain angels, brown-haired angels that were supposed to represent Stella but looked fake and trivial to Mary. Stella's kindergarten teacher had shown up with a shoe box of Stella's work. Carefully written numbers and words, drawings and workbooks, all of it now in a box in her office.

"I figured," Dylan had said, clutching the plane tickets in his hands like his life depended on them, "if we're going to sit and cry all the time, we might as well sit and cry in Italy. Plus, you said something

31

about learning Italian?"

His eyes were red-rimmed and he had lost weight, enough to show more lines in his face. He had one of those faces that wore lines well, and ever since she'd met him Mary had loved those creases. But now they made him look weary. His own eyes were changeable — brown with flecks of gold and green that could take on more color in certain weather or when he wore particular colors. But lately they had stayed flat brown, the bright green and gold almost gone completely.

She couldn't disappoint him by telling him that even English was hard to manage, that memorizing verb conjugations and vocabulary words would be impossible. The only language she could speak was grief. How could he not know that?

Instead, she said, "I love you." She did. She loved him. But even that didn't feel like anything anymore.

They spent a very peaceful two weeks in a large rented farmhouse, with a cook who came each morning with fresh rolls, who made them fresh espresso and greeted them with a sumptuous dinner when they returned at dusk. The time passed peacefully, though mournfully. The change of scene and change of routine was healing, however, and Mary hoped that they might return with a somewhat changed attitude. But, of course, home only brought back the reality of their loss, their sadness returning powerfully.

That first night, as Mary stood unpacking olive oil and long strands of sun-dried tomatoes, the answering machine messages played into the kitchen.

"My name is Alice. I own Big Alice's Sit and Knit —"

"The what?" Dylan said.

"Ssshhh," Mary said.

"— if you come in early Tuesday morning I can teach you to knit myself. Any Tuesday really. Before eleven. See you then."

"Knitting?" Dylan said. "You can't even sew on a button."

Mary rolled her eyes. "My mother."

The second time Mary showed up at the Sit and Knit, she had her week's work in a shopping bag. After Alice had sent her on her way the week before, Mary had taken to carrying her knitting everywhere. She was reluctant to admit her mother had been right; knitting quieted her brain. As soon as Stella's face appeared in front of her, Mary dropped a stitch or tied a knot. Once she even dropped an entire needle and watched in horror as the chain of stitches fell from it to the floor.

It wasn't that she didn't want to think of Stella. She just didn't want to lose her mind from that thinking. The hospital scenes played over and over, making her want to scream; sometimes she did scream. That was the kind of calming the knitting brought. Yesterday she walked into the supermarket and saw the season's first Seckel pears, tiny and amber. Stella's favorites. Mary used to pack two in her lunch every day in the fall. Seeing them, Mary felt the panic rising in her and she turned and walked out quickly, leaving her basket with the bananas and grated Parmesan behind. In the car, after she had cried good and hard, she picked up her knitting and did one full row right there in the parking lot before she drove home.

Standing on the steps of the knitting shop that second morning, waiting for Alice to open for the day, Mary examined her work. She could tell that what she had worked on all week was a mess. In the middle a huge hole gaped at her, and the neat twenty-two stitches Alice had cast on for her had grown into at least twice that. One needle was clogged with yarn, wound so tight she could hardly fit the other needle into one of the loops.

"That's a mess," Alice said from behind her. Mary noticed she had on the same outfit, but with a different sweater, this one a sage green. It made Mary aware of how she must look to Alice. She had gained weight since Stella died, a good ten pounds, and wore the same black pants every day because they had an elastic waist. And she was still wearing flip-flops despite the fall chill. But the idea of searching for other shoes exhausted her.

She wiggled her naked toes and held out her knitting.

Alice didn't even unlock the door. She just took Mary's knitting and in one firm yank pulled the entire thing apart.

Mary gasped. "In my line of work, you fix things, make them better. You never press the delete button like that."

Alice unlocked the door and held it open for Mary. "It's liberating. You'll see."

"I worked on that all week," Mary said.

Alice dropped the yarn into her hands and smiled. "It's not about finishing, it's about the knitting. The texture. The needles clacking. The way the rows unfold."

Already the bell announcing the arrival of customers was ringing, and women began to fill the store. They all seemed to carry half-finished sweaters and socks and scarves. Mary watched them fondle yarn, feeling its weight, holding it up to the light to better appreciate the gradations of color.

Alice took Mary's arm and gently led her to the same seat where she'd spent most of last Tuesday morning.

"That yarn's a little too tricky, I think," Alice said. She handed Mary a needle with twenty-two new stitches already cast on. "This yarn is fun. It self-stripes so you won't get bored."

Mary hesitated.

"Go ahead," Alice said.

Mary knit two perfect rows.

"Keep doing it, just like that," Alice said. Then she went to help another customer.

Mary sat, knitting, the sounds of the other customers' voices softly buzzing around her. The bell kept tinkling, marking the comings and goings of people. A purple stripe appeared, and then a violet one, and then a deep blue.

She was surprised when she felt someone standing over her.

"You've got it," Alice said. "Now go home and knit."

Mary frowned. "But what if I mess it up that way again?"

"You won't," Alice said.

Mary stood, feeling both elated and terrified.

"Alice?" a woman called from across the room. "How many do I cast on for the eyelash scarf?"

"Fifteen," Alice said. "Remember, fifteen stitches on number fifteen needles."

It's like another language, Mary thought, remembering her idea to learn Italian. The yarn in her hand was soft and lovely. Better than complicated rules of grammar.

"Thank you," Mary said. "I'll come next week, if that's all right."

A customer handed Alice a scarf made of big loopy yarn.

"I dropped a stitch somewhere," the woman said, her fingers burrowing through the thick yarn.

"I'll fix that for you," Alice said.

Mary turned to go. But Alice's hand on her arm stopped her.

"Wednesday nights," Alice said, "I have a knitting circle here. I think you'd like it."

"A knitting circle?" Mary laughed. "But I can't knit yet."

Alice pointed at her morning's work. "What do you call that?"

"I know, but —"

"These are women you should meet. All

levels, they are. Each with something to offer. You'll see."

"I'll think about it," Mary said.

"Seven o'clock," Alice said. "Right here."

"Thank you," Mary said, certain she would never join a knitting circle.

The next tuesday night, when she finished her second skein of yarn and, Mary realized, an entire scarf, she thought about what she would make next. The scarf's stripes moved from that original purple all the way through blues and greens and browns and reds, ending in perfect pink. Excited, Mary wrapped it around her neck and went to show it off to Dylan.

He sat in bed, watching CNN. He was addicted to CNN, Mary decided.

"Ta-da!" she said, twirling for him.

"Look at you," he said, grinning.

She came closer to show off the neat rows.

"Do you wear the needle in it like that?" he asked.

"Until I learn to cast off, I do." She sat beside him, close.

"How will you learn such a thing?" Dylan whispered, stroking her arm.

Mary closed her eyes.

"I joined a knitting circle," she said. "It starts tomorrow night."

Dylan pulled her into his arms. It was dark out, the television their only source of light.

The knitting shop looked different at night. The parking lot was very dark and the store seemed smaller against the sky and trees. Tiny white lights hung in each window, like bright stars. Mary could clearly see the women inside, sitting in a circle, needles in hand. She considered driving away, going home to Dylan, who would be in bed already watching the news, as if he might hear something that would change everything.

Sighing, Mary opened the door, her scarf with the needle dangling wrapped proudly around her neck. If Alice was surprised to see her, she didn't act it.

"Find a spot and sit down," Alice said. "Beth brought some real nice lemon cake."

Mary sat on the worn sofa beside a woman around her own age, with long red hair and dramatic high cheekbones.

"You finished!" Alice said. "Hey, everybody, this is Mary's first project."

The women — there were five, plus Alice and Mary — all stopped knitting to admire her handiwork. They commented on what a natural she was, how even her gauge, the depth of the color, and the length of the scarf. Mary realized that in this world, she could talk about these simple things and keep her grief to herself. She was anonymous here. She was safe.

"What size needles did you use?" the woman across from her asked.

"Elevens," Mary said, pleased with her certainty after so many months of uncertainty.

The woman nodded. "Elevens," she said, and returned her attention to her own knitting.

"That looks complicated," Mary said as the woman maneuvered four small needles like a puppeteer.

"Socks," she said. "The heel is tricky. But otherwise it's just knitting."

"What size are those needles?" Mary asked. "They're so tiny."

"Ones," the woman said, blushing slightly.

"Ones!" Mary said.

"You'll be making those in no time. But first let me show you how to cast off," Alice said to Mary. "Then we'll get you started on something else. Maybe another scarf, but you can learn to purl."

Mary unwound her scarf and handed it to Alice. "No purling yet. I need to bask in my success for a bit."

"I hear you," the woman beside her said. Even though Mary felt uncomfortable among strangers, she liked her immediately.

Alice kneeled next to Mary and demonstrated casting off. "Knit two stitches, just like you know how to do. Then the needle goes in the bottom one and you pull that loop over. See?"

"Pull the stitch out?" Mary shrieked. "After all that hard work keeping them all in?"

"Pull it out," Alice said, laughing.

Mary watched as a neat finished edge began to appear.

"Now you do it and I'll find you some fun yarn," Alice said.

"The way I learned," said a woman in her sixties with a salt-and-pepper bob, "was you start with scarves, you only do scarves. Start with sweaters, you learn how to knit."

She was knitting a sweater with a pattern across the bottom. Mary saw all the colored threads of yarn hanging from it and shuddered. Maybe the woman was right and she would be making scarves for the rest of her life. Maybe she would start a scarf business. Maybe she would never leave her house again except to buy yarn and she would stay inside and knit and knit her scarves.

"Nice job," the red-haired woman said.

It took a moment for Mary to realize that she was talking to her. The scarf, free from the needle, lay in her lap.

"It's like having a baby, isn't it?" someone said, and Mary's heart lurched. Babies and children were the last thing she wanted to discuss.

"Except it's fun," the woman knitting socks said.

Mary didn't look up. Instead she concentrated on her scarf.

"Tonight," Alice said, standing right in front of her, "you're going to learn how to cast on and you're going to make a scarf with this beautiful yarn."

Grateful for the change of subject, for the start of a new project, for the feel of this yarn in her hands, Mary could only nod.

"Tell us who you are first," the red-haired woman said to Mary.

"Mary Baxter," she said.

"Have you ever eaten at Rouge?" Alice asked Mary.

"Of course. It's great."

"Well, she's Rouge."

"But most people call me Scarlet," she said. She patted the woman in the chair next to her. "This is Lulu. And that's Ellen," she added, pointing to the sock woman.

Mary tried to remember, to put the name to something about each person. Scarlet was easy with all that red hair. Lulu, with her short hair dyed platinum above black roots, her cat glasses, and dressed all in black, looked like she'd been dropped here from New York City.

Ellen reminded Mary of someone from another era. The forties, she decided. Her dirty blonde hair fell in long waves down her back. She wore a faded vintage house-dress in a red and white pattern. Bare legs and black Mary Janes. Her face was what Mary's mother would call horsey, and her head seemed too big for her small, thin body. Yet the overall effect worked, all the elements coming together in an interesting combination of sexiness and innocence.

"I'm Harriet," the older woman with the salt-and-pepper hair said, all matter-of-fact and slightly sour.

Harriet the sourpuss, Mary thought.

"And this is Beth," Harriet said almost possessively. "Beth can knit anything. She's amazing. See that little knit bag she's practically finished with? When did you start that, Beth?"

"At lunch," Beth said.

"Today!" Harriet said. "Isn't she something?"

Everyone agreed that Beth was something. But Mary took in her shiny dark hair, styled and wisped and sprayed; her full makeup, the carefully lined eyes and glossy lips; her color-coordinated outfit, the sweater and those shoes the same beige, the creased plaid pants, the amber earrings and matching necklace. Mary took it all in and thought, *She's something all right.*

"Do you remember how to get started?" Alice was asking her.

"Uh . . . no," Mary said.

"First," Alice said, "you cast on."

Mary watched how deftly she moved the yarn, how easily the needles flew in her hands. Clumsily, she followed.

The two hours ended too quickly. That was what Mary thought as she said goodbye to this circle of strangers. Somehow, in the course of the evening, their presence had soothed her. Unlike her friends — her "mommy friends," Dylan called them — whose lives still revolved around their children, these women's lives remained a mystery. All that mattered, sitting there with them, was knitting.

In the dark parking lot, she watched Harriet and Beth get into a car together and drive away. Briefly she wondered what their story was, what had brought the older woman to boast so possessively about Beth, what had brought them here tonight.

The lights in the shop went dark. But Mary still stood there.

"Mary?" Scarlet said from behind her. "Wishing on a star?"

"You know," Mary said, "I don't believe in that anymore."

Scarlet leaned against the car beside Mary's and lit a cigarette. "Fuck," she said. "Neither do I."

They both looked up at the sky. Clouds floated by, blocking the stars, then revealing them.

"You know something else?" Scarlet said. "I don't believe in comets or meteor showers."

"Those are scientific facts," Mary said.

"Do you know how many times I've gotten my tired ass out of bed to go and see Hale-Bopp or the best meteor shower in a zillion years and it's always a disappointment. I sit in a freezing car staring up at the sky waiting for this phenomenon. This once-in-a-lifetime incredible thing. But it never happens."

It does, Mary thought, and Stella's face took shape in the dark sky.

"It does happen," Mary said. "It's just fleeting."

Scarlet took another drag on her cigarette, then put it out under her boot. From the depths of her oversized bag she pulled out a business card. "I'll teach you how to purl," she said. "When you finish that scarf, you'll be ready."

"Great," Mary said. "So I'll call you in what? A million years?"

"You'll finish that thing in a couple of days," Scarlet said. "That's how it is at first," she said, her voice low. "You knit to save your life," she said like someone who knew. She touched Mary's arm lightly, then got into her car. That was when Mary saw Lulu inside, slouched in the passenger seat. "Call me," Scarlet said. "Anytime."

Mary waved goodbye. She got into her own car and waited for Alice to come out. But she didn't. When Mary finally backed away, her headlights illuminated the shop and she could see Alice inside, alone, knitting.

■ ■ ■ ■

PART TWO:
K2, P2

■ ■ ■ ■

Once you are comfortable with the knit stitch, you should move on to the purl stitch. These two stitches are the foundation of knitting. From these two stitches, you can create everything you'll ever want to knit.
— Nancy J. Thomas and Ilana Rabinowitz,
A Passion for Knitting

3
SCARLET

In three days, Mary finished her second scarf. She draped it over a chair at the kitchen table for Dylan to see as soon as he got home. Her fingers followed the stripes of color down the length of the scarf. It would look good with tassels, she decided. If she went back to the knitting circle she would ask Alice how to make tassels, and how to attach them.

The phone rang and Mary let the machine pick up.

Her boss's voice filled the room.

"Hey, Mary, it's me, Eddie," he said. "Just, you know, checking in."

As Eddie talked, Mary set the table for dinner. Two plates, two napkins, two forks, two wineglasses. Even after all these months this simple act made her gut wrench. That third seat — Stella's seat — empty.

"So there's this truck driving around town selling tacos," Eddie was saying. "Or empanadas. Something. And I was thinking, you could maybe find this truck and eat some tacos, or whatever, and write about the experience."

"Shut up, Eddie," Mary said to the answering machine.

"I don't know, Mary," Eddie said, his voice soft. "Maybe it would help a little."

Her mouth filled with a sharp metallic taste and she swallowed hard a few times.

"The thing is," Eddie continued, "I know you're standing right there listening to me and I just wish you would pick up the phone or go and eat some empanadas or something." He waited, as if she might really pick up the phone. "Okay," he said finally. "Call me?"

At the sound of him hanging up, Mary said, "Bye, Eddie."

The faces of the women in the knitting circle floated across her mind. She liked that they were strangers, that her story, her tragedy, was unknown to them. And, she realized, their stories were unknown to her. For all she knew, they each held their own secret; they each knit to . . . what had Scarlet said? To save their lives. To them, she was a knitter, a woman who could make something from a ball of yarn. Her friends would never believe this of her. Once, out of frustration, her friend Jodie had come over and sewn on all of Mary's missing or loose buttons. "Hopeless," Jodie had called her. It had been weeks since Jodie had even called. Like many of her friends, Jodie had run out of ways to offer comfort.

Mary heard Dylan's key in the door and ran to meet him.

"What a welcome," he whispered into her hair.

She held on to him hard. She hated being alone now, and she hated her neediness.

"Smells good," Dylan said.

"Me?" Mary said, flirting. "Or dinner?"

"Both," he said.

"Can you believe it?" she said, walking to the stove. "Eddie wants me to chase some food truck around town."

"And?" Dylan said too hopefully.

"And write about it," Mary snapped. "As if I could write about the importance of a taco," she muttered.

She plucked a strand of spaghetti from the boiling water and bit into it, testing. She tried not to think of Stella standing at her side, her pasta tester, the way she would bite into a strand and wrinkle her nose with seriousness before pronouncing it was almost ready. "Two more hours," she liked to say.

"It might be fun," Dylan said, but she could tell his heart wasn't into having this argument again. It had become a pattern with them, his frustrated urging for her to go back to work, her anger at him for being able to work at all. A few times it had grown into full-blown fighting, with Dylan yelling at her, "You have to try to help yourself!" and Mary accusing him of being callous. More often, though, it was this quiet disagreement, this sarcasm and misunderstanding, the hurt feelings that followed.

Mary sighed and drained the pasta, stirring in the sauce she'd made — onions, crushed tomatoes, pancetta. As she grated cheese over it, Dylan opened a bottle of wine.

"I can't get used to it," Mary said, turning her attention to the salad, drizzling olive oil over the greens and sprinkling sea salt. "The silence."

Dylan stood, head bent, while she struggled to explain how the kitchen, the house, the world felt to her without Stella in it. But finally she shrugged, and finished dressing the salad. Words, her livelihood, her refuge, even at times her salvation, were now the most useless things in the world. Dylan couldn't understand that.

Stella would be singing while Mary finished making dinner. Or she would be showing off her work brought home from kindergarten that day. She would ask for an apple, sliced and peeled, to nibble. She would ask for a cup of water. She would make noise. Guiltily Mary remembered her impatience with these distractions. How could she have grown impatient with Stella?

Mary heard her loud footsteps as she brought the food to the table. The screech of the chair as Dylan pulled it away from the table. Mary's own sigh.

"Your latest creation?" Dylan said, motioning to the scarf.

He was trying to move past the awkwardness. She knew that, but she still smarted from it.

"How'd you make that pattern?" he asked, impressed.

"It self-stripes as you knit."

"My wife, the knitter," he said.

Mary was acutely aware of the sounds of chewing, of forks on plates, of their breathing.

"I wonder about those women," she said after a time, softening. "At the knitting circle."

"What about them?" Dylan said.

"You know, who they are. There's this one woman, Beth. She's so rigid. Hair in place.

53

Clothes pressed. Lipstick. Apparently she does everything perfectly."

Mary didn't mention the few facts she had gleaned about Beth. The four children in matching sweaters who smiled out of a posed studio photograph she'd passed around. *Four children!* Mary had thought, shuddering at that abundance, that good luck.

"I'm certain she has one of those houses, those center-hall colonials with the big square rooms and window treatments." She flushed, embarrassed. "God," Mary said. "Listen to me. I hardly know the woman. I hate her because she has so . . . so much."

"I do it too," Dylan said. "When I see a father walking with his little girl on his shoulders I want to yell at him. How could he have this privilege? This blessing?"

His voice trembled and Mary touched his hand lightly. Who are we becoming? she wondered.

After a moment, she said, "You know that great bakery? Rouge?"

"With the really buttery croissants?" Dylan said. "And those special things? What are they?"

"Cannelles," she said. "The owner's in the knitting circle. Scarlet. She's lovely. Long red hair, like . . . like . . ." She'd show him,

54

Mary thought. She was a writer after all, surely she could come up with a good description. "Like rusty pipes," she said finally.

"Rusty pipes?" Dylan said, grinning. "That sounds very lovely."

Mary slapped his arm playfully. "It is lovely. And she has these cheekbones. Real style. She must have lived somewhere fabulously sophisticated."

Dylan put his hand to her cheek. "You're lovely," he said softly.

Mary let him pull her close. Whenever they kissed, she wanted to cry.

"Holly left us cupcakes," she whispered when their lips parted. "A dozen of them. She colored the frosting toxic orange."

"Later," Dylan said.

They left the half-empty plates on the table and together went upstairs to bed.

Her hands needed to do it. It was as if the movement of the needles coming together and falling apart took away the horrible anxiety that bubbled up in her throughout the day. Just when Mary began to consider the challenge of tassels, her mother called.

"Sometimes I miss the leaves changing," her mother told her. "Those gorgeous colors. The cactus are beautiful in their way, but still."

"I've done it," Mary said reluctantly. "I've learned to knit."

"Ah," her mother said. "So Alice called."

When Mary didn't reply, her mother said, "It's good, isn't it? They say to some women, religious women, each stitch is like a prayer."

Mary had no interest in discussing spirituality with her mother. "How do you make tassels? I've made this scarf and I think tassels would really complete it." Plus, Mary added to herself, I'm about to lose my fucking mind and I think if my hands stay busy it will help and I've even thought about sitting here and knitting scarves until I die.

"Simple," her mother said. "Take some leftover yarn and cut it all the same length and then make bundles of three or four of those. Tie them along the hem in good strong knots."

"How many, though? How close together do I tie them?"

"Be creative, Mary. Do whatever suits you."

Mary frowned, eyeing the hem of her scarf.

"I have Spanish at eleven," her mother said. "Better go."

"Right," Mary said.

One day, a few months after her mother had stopped drinking, Mary came home from school and found her sitting on the sofa rolling yarn into fat balls. By this time, her father had started to recede from the family, as if once her mother stopped drinking he no longer had a role there. When Mary left for college, her parents got divorced, but their separation from each other began before that.

"You're knitting?" Mary said.

"I used to knit socks and hats for the GIs," her mother had explained.

"What GIs?"

"During World War Two. Betty and I would walk down to the church and sit with all the other girls knitting. It was very patriotic."

"So now you're going to sit here and knit all day and send socks to soldiers in Vietnam?"

"Babies," her mother said softly. "I'm knitting hats for the babies in the hospital. The newborns," she said, holding up a tiny powder blue hat.

For the rest of that year, small hats in pastel colors piled up everywhere, on end tables and chairs and countertops. Then they would disappear and her mother began new piles. Eventually she knit striped hats, and white ones flecked with color, and then zigzag patterns.

"She's lost her mind," Mary whispered to her best friend Lisa.

Lisa could only nod and stare at all the tiny hats everywhere.

Mary lost her virginity in her bedroom while her mother sat downstairs knitting hats for babies she did not know. Every afternoon that spring, Mary and her boyfriend Billy had sex on her pink-and-white-striped sheets, Billy turning her every way he could, entering her from every direction, kissing every part of her, while her mother sat, oblivious, and knit those stupid hats.

Sometimes Mary imagined that she could see through the hardwood floor, past the ceiling, into the living room where her mother sat surrounded by yarn. Maybe, Mary thought, her mother was only capable of loving one thing at a time. There had been her father at some point, she supposed. And then the drinking. And now this, knitting. But Mary couldn't help wondering why she had never been her mother's obsession. Nothing Mary had ever done — playing Dorothy in the third-grade production of *The Wizard of Oz,* getting straight A's her entire sophomore year, winning her school's top literary prize — nothing, had ever earned her more than halfhearted praise from her mother. "You'll go far," her mother liked to say. She'd make her toads-in-the-hole for breakfast and call it a celebration.

While her parents watched *The Fugitive,* Mary took Billy upstairs to her room. As she unbuttoned the five buttons on his jeans, he whispered, "I don't know, Mary. They're both downstairs."

She kneeled in front of him, taking him into her mouth. From downstairs, she heard David Janssen searching for the one-armed man. Her mother would be knitting without even glancing down at her stitches. Her father would have *Time* magazine opened in his lap. Billy groaned and Mary yanked her head away. Already her mind was far from here, from the tiny hats and her mother's glazed stare and her father's impenetrable front. She could imagine her future, bright and near.

It took Mary almost the entire next morning to do the tassels, but when she finished she decided to go to Big Alice's and buy more yarn. The idea that these scarves were becoming like those long-ago infant hats her mother made occurred to her. But she was different, she told herself. She would give them as Christmas gifts. Mary earmarked the striped one for Dylan's niece, Ali, who went to college in Vermont and certainly needed scarves. The first one she would keep for herself; Alice had said you should keep the first thing you knit.

Satisfied with her practicality, she entered the store. The smell of wool comforted her, the way the old-book-and-furniture-polish smell of libraries used to. Mary could still remember how the ball scene in *Anna Karenina* had helped calm her after one of her mother's tirades; how Marjorie Morningstar's kiss under the lilacs had let her forget her own broken heart one summer; how Miss Marple used to make her smile.

Now here she stood in a knitting store, and that same sense of safety, of peace, filled her. The store was crowded, but Mary spotted Scarlet's red hair across the room. She had on a green shawl with elaborate embroidery and long fringe wrapped around her, and beneath it she wore a startling fuchsia turtleneck.

Scarlet turned, her arms filled with a dozen or more skeins of fat loopy yarn in shades of beige and rust and white. Her eyes crinkled at the sight of Mary.

"Told you," Scarlet said.

"I admit it," Mary laughed.

Scarlet dropped her yarn on the counter and made her way over to Mary. "You need to learn how to purl and you look like you need a cup of coffee."

"Coffee, yes," Mary said. "But purling still seems . . . unnecessary." Already she was eyeing a variegated yarn in moss green with gold and red and orange pom-poms woven throughout. It made her think of autumn. Hesitantly, she lifted a skein.

"That yarn is fun to work with. It makes a great child's sweater," Scarlet said, pointing to a small sample hanging up.

Mary swallowed hard and managed to shake her head.

"It also makes a great scarf," Scarlet said easily. "But not for purling. Let's pick out some multicolored yarn and get us that coffee. I make a café au lait that, if you close your eyes, will make you think you're in France."

Relieved, Mary followed Scarlet's soft green shawl through the crowded store, toward her next lesson.

Mary sat at the counter that separated Scarlet's living area from the kitchen in her loft in an old jewelry factory. The walls were brick and the ceiling had steel beams across it. Below the wall of windows city traffic inched toward the highway.

Scarlet handed Mary a yellow ceramic bowl of café au lait. "Let's sit on the sofa where the light's better," she said.

Mary's yarn was pink and yellow and blue. A funny tangle of Stella's favorite colors, she realized as she watched Scarlet cast on for her and the colors revealed themselves.

"Knit two stitches," Scarlet said.

She smelled of sugar and the sour tang of yeast. Up close like this, Mary saw pale lines etched at the corners of her mouth and eyes.

"Remember when you purl it's tip to tip," Scarlet said, pulling the loose yarn in front. "The tip of this needle goes here and they form an X, see?"

Scarlet purled two stitches and then turned it over to Mary. "Knit two, purl two," she said. "It's tedious as hell, but when you finish that scarf you'll be an expert purler."

Mary knit two easily, then hesitated.

"Tip to tip," Scarlet said, picking up her own knitting.

When Mary successfully purled two stitches, Scarlet said, "I knew you could do it."

They knit in silence, the clicking of the

wooden needles the only sound except the traffic below. Scarlet's apartment was like a slice of Provence. Everything in soft yellows and blues with splashes of red, the wooden tables rough-hewn and worn, with drips of wax from candles and rings left from wet glasses. Mary imagined exotic men here, good red wine, the smells of a daube simmering on the stove, and pungent cheese and olives on this coffee table.

"How did you end up in Providence owning a bakery?" Mary asked. "You seem like you belong somewhere entirely different."

"Like where?"

Mary blushed. "I don't know. France, maybe."

Scarlet nodded but didn't reply. She had removed the ornate shade from the table lamp to give them more light, and that bright bulb showed something in her face that Mary could not identify. A sadness, perhaps. No, Mary decided. Regret.

After a time Scarlet looked up from her knitting and right at Mary. She was using very large needles and her sweater had already begun to take shape while Mary's scarf still seemed small and new.

"Everyone has a story, don't they?" Scarlet said. "Mine is about bread and the sea and, you're right, about France."

Mary held her breath for a moment, her needles poised. Then Scarlet began to speak, and Mary exhaled, put her needles together with a soft click, and listened.

"I was always good with my hands," Scarlet said. "Even when I was little, I liked to touch things. I used to carry a stuffed dog everywhere with me. Pal, I called him. I rubbed away the fabric on one of his ears. And I rubbed holes into all of my blankets. I loved the feel of fabric in my fingers. It brought me . . . not joy, exactly, but . . . comfort. Yes, comfort."

Scarlet paused, lost in thought.

"The first time I baked bread," she continued, "I knew this was something I could do for the rest of my life."

She took a breath, then continued.

"I was a terrible student. An art major only because I liked textiles and ceramics and it didn't require a lot of reading or tests. Mostly, I smoked pot and had sex with other art majors. The summer after I graduated from college, I needed a plan or my parents were going to make one for me. So, out of the blue, I said that I wanted to live in France. Before I knew it, everything was set. My father knew a professor in Paris, Claude Lévesque, and he arranged an au pair job for me with Claude's family. Claude and his wife Camille had two daughters, Véronique and Bébé."

Mary thought of her own father, an insurance salesman who, other than his clients, seemed to know nobody. He moved through the world alone, circling her mother and Mary, a shadowy, quiet man.

Scarlet said, "They sent me pictures in a big envelope that one of the children had decorated with a border of flowers drawn in pen and ink. I wondered where I could get my pot in Paris and what I would do with the children and if they spoke any English. Their faces in the photographs seemed blank and uninteresting. The mother looked severe. But the father, Claude, looked like Gérard Depardieu, a big hulking guy with a bulbous nose and unkempt blond hair. Sexy and French.

"I left for Paris right after Christmas. When the plane was landing I looked out the window at the gray overcast city still lit up and something settled in me. I knew somehow that this was really where I belonged and that I would never leave.

"I know it sounds like a schoolgirl's fantasy, but when I met Claude I knew that I would be with him somehow, that we would be connected forever. The wife, Camille, was not stern like in her photograph. She was actually quite pretty. A petite woman with that style that Parisian women have. I remember her coat was tangerine, and thinking how odd that would look in Cambridge among all the ugly L.L. Bean down coats everyone wore there. Her blond hair pulled back in that perfect knot, and her eyes always lined in black, and her skinny legs in their black stockings beneath that coat. She was aloof, and she smoked too much, but she wasn't stern.

"The children were fine and we took to each other right away. I taught them how to knit, and we made blankets for their dolls and little hats for their stuffed animals. I would walk them to school and then go to French lessons for two hours and then run errands for Camille. I was alone in the apartment, a cramped two-story place in the twelfth arrondissement filled with really ugly antiques, until two o'clock, when I went to pick up the girls at school.

"At first I stayed in my room and watched television. But before long I began to wander the streets. I had a pass for the Métro and I would ride it all over and then get out and walk around, into cheese shops and pâtisseries and vintage clothing stores. One day I ran into Claude in the Latin

Quarter. He was sitting having a carafe of wine at a café and he motioned for me to join him. We spoke to each other in English, which felt very foreign to me, and exotic. Claude spoke fluent English. Camille did not speak any English, and the children studied it in school but spoke it badly.

"We began to meet on Tuesdays, which was his free afternoon. Together we explored the city, speaking English like it was our own secret language. Then I would go and pick up the children, and once the weather turned warm we would go to the park and ride the carousel. At home I helped make dinner and ate with the family and helped to clean up and give the children their baths and then I went to my room. Claude ignored me during this part of the day. Our few hours together on Tuesdays seemed like a dream, unconnected to anything else that happened.

"This continued for two years. The schedule like that and the Tuesday meetings. Over time I lost my baby fat and I began to dress like the women I saw on the streets. I grew my hair long. I stopped taking my French lessons because I was fluent really. So my free time was plentiful. I befriended a baker named Denis. His family owned one of the oldest bakeries in the city, and I would go there for my favorite baguette to nibble while I strolled.

"Soon Denis and I became lovers. He was a distracted young man, careless with everything except bread. But we would go dancing and to his small flat above the bakery and I felt very romantic, not in love with Denis, but romantic. Perhaps in love with the city and this simple life I led there. Sex with a handsome Frenchman! Fresh baguettes and wine in bed! His hands always had flour in the creases and I would trace them, pretending I could see into the future.

"One night I said, 'Teach me to make that bread I love.'

"So we went downstairs and he showed me. Watching a man knead dough and create bread from just flour and water and yeast is the sexiest thing imaginable. Because he had to be at the bakery at four a.m. to begin baking the bread, he always brought me back to Claude and Camille's around three. But this morning I stayed and made the bread with him. It was as if my hands had finally learned what they were meant to do. I could feel the change as I worked the dough. How it grew less sticky. How it took new forms and properties. When I got home it was almost six and I was giddy. I would be a baker. I was meant to be a baker.

"I had forgotten that Camille and the girls had gone to meet Camille's parents for a weekend in Brittany, on the coast. So when I quietly entered the apartment and found Claude sitting there, obviously awake all night, I thought something terrible had happened.

"I even forgot to speak English. I began to tell him, in French, about my discovery, how I had to find a baker to apprentice with. My hands tingled from the feel of the dough in them.

" 'Rouge,' he said — privately, that's what he always called me; he didn't think Scarlet suited me. This name, he told me, it's too ridiculous — 'I thought something terrible had happened to you. I thought you had been killed or hurt.'

"His English sounded, oddly, harsh.

" *Je suis désolée,'* I said.

"He covered his face in his hands and began to laugh. 'I think you've been savagely murdered and all the while you've been baking bread.'

"I didn't see what was funny. But I forced a smile. I caught a glimpse of myself in the oversized mirror and saw that I was covered with flour.

"As if he read my mind, Claude said, 'You have flour everywhere.'

69

"And he got up and walked over to me and began to brush the flour from my sweater and my hair and my arms. That was when it began, the thing I knew would happen. I have wondered many times over the years how I knew with such certainty that this man and I were to be linked forever. And I have never been able to find an answer. I was so young when I arrived in Paris. And unsure of so many things. Yet this one thing I knew absolutely.

"That weekend, with Camille and the girls away, we made love in that particular way that new lovers have, as if nothing exists outside each other.

"This was long ago now. Twenty-two years. What I remember is Claude making us an omelette and how we ate it in my bed, cold. I remember how thoughts of running away with Claude began to fill my mind. I remember how on Sunday afternoon he held my face in his hands and said, 'You know you must leave here, Rouge. We cannot be like this with Camille and the girls.'

"He didn't mean, of course, that I had to leave right then. But that is what I did. I packed my suitcase, the same one that I had arrived with two years earlier, and I left that apartment with Claude's fingerprints and kisses all over me. It was raining, a warm rain that diffused the lights of the city. Like the blurry colors of a Monet painting. Like tears. I went to the only place I knew to go: the bakery.

"Denis took me in. I told him I had fallen in love with someone, that I needed a place to stay for a while. He said something like, *'C'est dommage,'* nothing more than that. I slept on his sofa and helped to bake the bread. And I began to meet Claude in his office in the afternoon, where, on a scratchy Persian rug, we would make love to the sound of a typewriter pounding in the office next door and students rushing down the hall, arguing or worrying or laughing.

"I went on this way, in a happy blur, for a month or so. Summer came and I learned to bake croissants and pain au chocolat, the intricacies of butter and dough, the delicate balance of sweet and sour. I did not ask about Camille, though I did inquire about the children, who I missed sorely. Especially the little one, Bébé. By this time she was eight, but small like her mother, with that fine hair that tangled easily and skin so fair that the pale blue veins shone just beneath. She carried a doll, Madame Chienne, everywhere with her. A rag doll that was loved away in spots, like my own dog Pal. Véronique was more polite, but less imaginative, and though I got on well with her, it was Bébé whom I adored. Claude brought me pictures that she'd drawn, and read me little stories she wrote. And I suppose in my fantasy of Claude running away with me to a place with golden sunshine, Bébé came too.

"Denis wanted me to go to a small village near Marseille to apprentice with an old man who Denis himself had worked with. This man, called Frère Michel by everyone, was famous all over France for his cannelles, the small sweet cakes made by nuns in the fourteenth century with vanilla bean and rum and egg yolks. They are made in special fluted tulip-shaped molds, and Frère Michel still used the wooden ones his own grandmother had used.

"I thought, I must go and take Claude with me. The only image I had of the south of France was one I had invented from van Gogh paintings and travel posters that hung in a travel agency window near the bakery. I could imagine walking through fields of towering sunflowers with Claude, or wandering the Roman ruins together. I could imagine the two of us plunging into the blue sea naked, then drying in the hot sun on pink rocks. But I could not see myself without him.

"So I let Denis talk about Frère Michel and cannelles, nodding as if I was considering the offer, until the day I realized that I was most certainly pregnant. On this particular morning, I awoke sweaty and suffocating in the hot apartment, and I felt a flutter, like a butterfly had burst from its cocoon and set off in flight. I put my hand to my stomach and my butterfly fluttered against it."

Instinctively, Mary paused in her knitting and placed one hand on her own belly, as if she could feel that familiar fluttering, the first sign of a baby there. She remembered lying in bed with Dylan and gasping slightly, taking his hand and pressing it to her stomach.

She nodded at Scarlet before she picked up her knitting needles once again.

"My first impulse was to go immediately to Claude. At this time of the morning he would be teaching, and I got up quickly to dress and meet him at his classroom with the news. The happy news. On the bus to the university I made a plan in which we went together to the south, and we lived in that small town near Marseille, and I baked cannelles and madeleines, and Claude wrote the book he always talked about writing, and there in the plan was a little girl, not unlike Bébé. And a small house near the sea. And almond trees, and olive trees, and wild fennel.

"But as I raced up the stairs to the building where he taught, something struck me and sent a shiver through me even on such a relentlessly hot day. I remembered clearly when I'd had my last period, and it was back in June on an evening when Denis and I were still lovers. I sat hard on the steps, feeling the heat of the sunbaked stone through my thin dress, forcing myself to think. But I knew that had been my last period, and that two weeks later I had slept with both Denis and then, in that first weekend together, Claude.

"That flutter rose in me again, this time filling my throat with bile. Around me, students rushed, carrying armloads of books, speaking French and German and Spanish. I could smell their sweat and their cigarettes, and again I tasted vomit.

"I don't know how long I sat there before a cool hand touched my bare arm. I looked up into Claude's face. He was wearing his glasses, those funny rimless half-glasses, and his blond hair was matted across his forehead.

" 'Rouge,' he said softly, 'did I forget that we were going to meet?'

"I shook my head.

" 'You look so pale,' he said, and touched my cheeks with the backs of both his hands. 'Are you feverish?'

"I shook my head again. 'It's just so hot,' I said.

"He helped me to my feet and held my elbow firmly for support. 'Let's get you some water, yes?'

"I let him lead me to his office. I had never been there in the morning, and I thought the Persian rug looked faded and worn in this light, that the color of the walls seemed dingy. I drank down the water he brought me without stopping, and then I immediately threw it up. Once I began vomiting I couldn't stop. Claude grabbed the wastebasket and held it under my chin.

"A secretary appeared in the open doorway, wearing a concerned face. 'Professor?' she asked.

" 'This young girl is ill from the heat,' Claude said. 'She'll be fine.'

" 'You have class now,' the secretary said. 'Shall I take her?'

" 'Call maintenance,' Claude said, 'to clean up here.'

"The secretary hesitated a moment before leaving.

" 'I was in the neighborhood,' I said. 'Silly

of me. No breakfast. I just wanted to see your face.'

"Claude grinned at me. 'Go and eat some eggs and a big café au lait in a cool café and you will be your old self again in no time.'

"I stared at him, puzzled.

" 'And we will meet here as usual at two o'clock,' he said, straightening his shirt and tie, gathering his books and briefcase.

" *'Au revoir,'* he said.

"I nodded because that was all I could manage. This was the first time we had been together and Claude had spoken to me entirely in French.

"I almost didn't go back that afternoon. But I could not stay away. In the hours in between seeing him, I took his advice and sat in a cool café and ate eggs and toast, and I thought about this baby. I would never know for sure if it belonged to Denis or Claude. For some women, perhaps, that would not matter. They could convince themselves that the father was of course the man they loved.

"But for me, I only wanted this baby if it was Claude's. Denis meant nothing to me. What if I had the baby and it was like Denis, distracted and lazy? Then I would know that it wasn't Claude's and I would have to live a charade with Claude. No, this little one would never be born.

"By the time I arrived back at Claude's office, the secretary away at her lunch, the outer office empty, I had decided not to tell Claude anything. I would get the name of a doctor and get this done quickly, pretending that it never happened. It seemed so simple that when Claude came in I threw myself at him, tearing at his tie and the buttons on his shirt, wanting only to fill myself with him.

"He laughed softly. 'You are revived,' he whispered in English.

"Of course, these things are never so simple, are they? That very evening I told Denis about my situation. Not the details of it, just that I was pregnant and needed an abortion. He studied my face, as if he could find there some evidence of his own involvement in this predicament. But I remained unreadable.

" 'I can arrange this,' he said finally.

"He took longer than I had hoped and it was several weeks later before he handed me a name and address on a slip of paper right before we began to make the morning's baguettes. I took it and thanked him, but he waved away my gratitude with his hands.

" 'Let's not talk about this again,' he said.

"I was happy to oblige.

"That week, Claude and his family were away in Spain. How perfect, I thought. I had begun to read everything as a sign about who the father was. Claude's absence during the abortion made it clear that Denis was the father. But on the very day it was to be done, as I combed my hair in preparation to leave, the phone rang and it was Claude — a sign that the baby must be his. My heart beat fast as I listened to him speak into a pay phone in a café at the beach.

" 'Rouge,' he said, 'I am miserable without you. I will never be away from you like this again. I'll figure out a way for us to be together. Do you believe me?'

" 'Yes,' I said.

" 'I love you,' Claude was saying, over and over again.

"He did not stop until I said it to him.

" 'I love you too, Claude,' I said, the words burning my throat.

"When it was done, I was made empty. The weight stayed on me. My hips and waist were thick, my breasts larger. But beneath that, was stone. Or worse, nothing at all. As soon as I woke from the anesthesia, I knew in my heart that it had been Claude's child after all. The nurse gave me something to calm me, but I couldn't stop crying.

"This new me, empty, overweight, unhappy, tried to continue life as it had been before. Denis and I baked bread in the early morning. I met Claude in the afternoons, and could hardly appreciate the changes in him. The declarations of love, the promises of a future together. One day he pinched my waist, and teased me that I was growing too fat and too happy.

" 'You look the way you did when I first saw you,' he said when I pulled away from him. He made me turn back to face him. 'That day I knew,' he said, serious now. 'I knew you were going to change my life.'

" 'I knew too,' I said.

"Soon afterwards, after the weather had turned crisp and cool, Denis once again asked me about Frère Michel. 'He will take you on,' he said. 'But I wouldn't waste time if I were you. He's very old. He won't be around forever.'

"I looked into Denis's face. He had flour across one cheek, and flecks of sticky dough on his apron.

" 'I'll go,' I said. 'I'm ready.'

"Can you believe it when I tell you that I went a week later and I never told Claude? I saw him those last afternoons. I listened to his ideas for us to have a life together. He would pay for an apartment for me to live, and it would be ours. He would go to America to teach and I would come with him; he had done it before, why not again? Perhaps, he sighed, he would leave Camille, get a divorce, marry me.

"I said nothing. I let him make love to me as if it was not the last time. Then I went directly to pick up my bag at Denis's apartment, and from there to the train heading south. On that train I thought about nothing. Not what I was doing. Not what I had done. During the nights before I left, I wondered how Claude and I would be linked forever. Was it through this baby who would never be born? Or was it through our love? Did love's energy continue even after the lovers separated? These thoughts kept me awake. But once I was on the train south, my mind stopped.

"On a whim, I had stopped at a yarn store near Denis's apartment and bought a skein of light blue mohair and a pair of bamboo knitting needles. As the industrial cities passed my window, and cypress trees appeared beside barren fields of wheat and flowers, I knit. My hands seemed to knit away the noise that had kept me awake, to erase the questions for which there were no answers.

"My story could have ended here. In many ways, I wish it had. I arrived in the village, a village so small it is not on any map, and made my way to Frère Michel's. People from all over France came to his bakery for his cannelles. They had perfect contrasting textures — the crunchy exterior, the almost-custard interior. The shop was filled with villagers, city people from Marseille, tourists holding guidebooks, vacationers. And Frère Michel, wrinkled, toothless, bent like a question mark. He yelled at people to be quiet, to make a better line. He threw out the ones who complained or pushed. He was a hateful man who baked heavenly pastries.

"I had my own house, a shed, really. One room with a bed and a table with one short leg and two chairs. When spring came I made a garden in the back and grew oregano and lavender, tomatoes and beans. My skin turned brown from the sun. I lost the pregnancy fat. All of it seemed long ago. I ordered more of that blue mohair yarn from the store in Paris and I kept adding on, knitting a blanket that I could eventually wrap myself in many times over.

"At work, Frère Michel screamed at me. I was an idiot. Too stingy with butter, unable to gauge when it was the proper time to take the dough for the cannelles from the refrigerator. His yelling did not bother me. He was teaching me something, after all. Cannelles are very tricky to bake. The sugar must be molten enough to form the shell, but if it's too hot it will burn. Over time I learned that one day wasn't enough for the dough, and four was too many. I learned to brush the old molds more generously and to whisk more firmly. I could tell by instinct when to remove the batter from the heat, or when it was too humid to bake them that day. The tourists liked to practice their English with me, despite Frère Michel's grumblings.

"Then one day, in the dead of summer, Claude walked into the crowded shop. He was thinner, his face creased with worry. A big man, he seemed to fill the shop when he entered.

" 'Did you think I wouldn't find you?' he said quietly.

"I untied my apron and walked around the counter, through the crowd. 'Let's go outside,' I said, not wanting a scene.

"Frère Michel yelled at me to come back, but I took Claude's hand and walked with him down the crooked village street, through the field to my little house.

" 'I hate you,' he said once we were inside.

"And then we were kissing each other, and it began again in a new way. He had left Camille, believing my disappearance came from a lack of trust in his promises. He had his own apartment near the university. He wanted to marry me as soon as the divorce was final, after Christmas.

"I felt I was ready to say yes. I could put what had happened behind me. We would have other children together. I would open a small shop and make cannelles and madeleines the way they did in the south. Our life together unfolded so clearly that I became gripped with happiness.

"Just like that, my simple life changed. Every weekend Claude came south from Paris and we began to make plans together. I wrote my parents that I was engaged. We would have a real wedding, we decided. My family would come from America. Frère Michel would bake our cake. Giddy with our new life, Claude decided that when he came the next time, he would bring the girls. Véronique was mad at him, he explained. But Bébé was excited and missed me. He rented a cottage on the sea and I would join them there in a week.

"I couldn't stop speaking of our future to the regulars who came in each morning. The old women pinched my cheeks and made jokes about how rosy sex made them. Frère Michel grumbled that I was stupider than ever now that I had fallen in love.

"That Friday I took the local train to the village where Claude and the children waited for me. It was early September and the southern light had already begun to change. I arrived under a purple sky to find an eager Bébé and a sullen Véronique at the station, and Claude holding a bundle of lavender for me. I felt like a bride already, carrying the stalks of small fragrant flowers and walking hand in hand with Claude.

"Bébé chattered about her new puppy and the storybook she was writing and how she had thoughtlessly left Madame Chienne back in Paris. 'Nothing feels right without Madame Chienne,' she said sadly. 'Do you think it's bad luck to not have her with me?'

" 'Of course not,' I assured her. 'Madame Chienne does not like the sea.'

"Véronique said almost nothing. I decided to let her be angry instead of coaxing good cheer from her.

"In the morning, we hiked the mile or so to the beach. The hike was arduous — the path was rocky and the sun was hot. When we finally arrived, we put our blankets under the shelter of a cove of rocks, and prepared for a swim. Almost immediately,

Claude realized that we had forgotten to bring the lunch he'd so carefully prepared; he wanted everything to be perfect and he'd gone into town early for fresh bread and to choose good meats and fruit at the outdoor market there.

" 'We'll go back to the house for lunch,' I said. 'It's no big deal.'

" 'No, no,' Claude insisted, 'we must have a picnic here, and swim to that sandbar, and stay until late.'

"He stood and put on his funny Indiana Jones hat. Like all Frenchmen, he wore a tiny Speedo bathing suit and his stomach hung over it slightly.

" 'You look funny and beautiful,' I told him.

"He explained to the girls that he would be back with lunch and then he kissed me hard on the lips. I heard Véronique mutter as she pulled away from him.

" 'She'll have to get used to it,' he told me. He kissed each girl on top of her head and began the hike back.

" 'Papa!' Bébé called after him. 'I'll collect sea glass for you!'

" 'Wonderful!'

"The three of us swam for a long time in the cool water. We could see our legs and toes flapping about beneath it, and hundreds of small fish swimming around us. Even Véronique enjoyed our time in the water. Then, feeling lazy, I stretched out on one of the hot rocks and closed my eyes.

"I woke to find Claude kneeling beside me with the backpack of food at my feet.

" 'Rouge?' he said. 'Where are the girls?'

"I sat up slowly. 'I don't know,' I said, scanning the beach. 'Isn't that Véronique down there?' I pointed.

" 'Yes,' he said, relieved.

"He opened the backpack and spread the cloth, and the food, and took out a bottle of white wine. I watched as Véronique made her way back to us.

" 'Funny,' I said, standing. 'I don't see Bébé.'

"Claude got to his feet and yelled to Véronique. 'Where is your sister?'

" 'I can't understand you,' she yelled back. 'Speak French!'

"Claude began to run toward her, and I followed close behind.

" *'Ta soeur!'* he yelled.

" 'She was there, looking for sea glass,' Véronique said.

"We looked at where she pointed. A small cove now filled with water from the tide.

" 'Bébé!' Claude called, racing down the beach.

"Was it a premonition of tragedy that I had that first time I saw Claude and knew that we would be linked forever? I can't say. But the little one, Bébé, was gone and I was to blame.

"They found her washed up on another beach the next morning. We don't know what happened because it happened as I slept."

"Oh," Mary said, and it sounded more like a moan than a word. Her heart seized in on itself as she thought of this other lost child, and she said, again, "Oh."

"We never discussed what happened next," Scarlet said. "I simply came back to the States, alone. He blames me, of course. Why shouldn't he? I'm guilty. I didn't watch his daughter and she died. I can never make that right. The guilt used to keep me up at night. It used to drive me crazy. I would try to rewrite that day, that morning. In this version, I would make myself stay awake. We would build sand castles, Bébé and I, with elaborate turrets and moats filled with seawater. And Claude would come back to the beach with our lunch, and we would eat it together, all four of us. And we would swim in the ocean and grow brown under the hot sun. And we would fill our bucket with shells and sea glass. And we would live happily ever after.

"But, of course, then morning would come and I would be left with the real story and the awful true ending."

The day had turned to dusk. Outside Scarlet's wall of windows the sky was slashed with violet and lavender. Mary had dropped a stitch early on, and a run of emptiness climbed up the center, cutting through the happy wool like a scar.

"I know about your daughter," Scarlet said. "I remember reading it in the paper. Meningitis, right?'

"Yes."

"We have this in common," she said softly.

There was a small silence. Then Mary said, "Her name was Stella."

Neither of them was knitting anymore.

"I'll show you," Mary said, her voice shaky.

She opened the bag at her feet and from it took the picture of Stella she carried everywhere with her. It wasn't the most recent photo, or even the most beautiful. It was just the one that looked the most like Stella, her head cocked, smiling broadly, her eyes bright beneath her tangled hair.

Scarlet's breath caught.

"Yes," she said finally. "Lovely."

They sat side by side, and watched the sky grow dark.

4
THE KNITTING CIRCLE

For several weeks Mary did not go to the knitting circle. A kind of inertia took hold of her, and even though when Wednesday night neared, she thought of going, she could not get herself there. She admired Scarlet, who, after losing Bébé, after losing everything, had managed to make something of her life again. Rouge — and how that name took on such significance now, Mary realized — was always crowded. Why, Mary had written a rave review of it when it first opened, marveling at the butteriness of the croissants, the intensity of the hot chocolate. She wanted to find inspiration in Scarlet's story, but her still-new grief kept her paralyzed.

Alone in the late afternoons, Mary tried not to think about how six short months ago she would be picking up Stella at school, watching her run down the front steps with her impossibly oversized backpack, her collection of key chains jingling. She would be swooping her daughter into her waiting arms. Trying not to think of these things, Mary picked up her needles and knit. Scarves unfolded in her lap — fat ones; textured ones; eyelash scarves made of thin strands of yarns knitted together — one glittery and multicolored and one soft and fluttery.

On warm autumn days like these, she and Stella would go to the playground on the corner. Or they would walk to the small library up the street and fall into the plump cushions in the children's section and read. Mary remembered these things as evening approached. She remembered them, and she knit.

On one of these afternoons the phone rang and Mary answered it. Often she didn't. She let the machine pick up and listened as friends checked in on her, offering cups of tea, afternoon movies, martinis. But on this afternoon she answered because outside her window she could clearly see her neighbor Louise, and Louise's three children, placing their just-made jack-o'-lanterns on their front stoop. The excited giggles from those kids made Mary want to run across the street and smash those goofy carved pumpkins. Even worse: Halloween was two days away.

"It's Scarlet," the voice on the other end of the phone said. "I thought you might want me to pick you up tonight."

"Knitting," Mary said.

"Six o'clock?"

Beautiful-colored leaves floated down from the tree in Mary's yard. She watched them lift, hover, fall.

"Sometimes," Scarlet said, "you need to get out of the house. Out of your brain."

Mary thought of that day at Scarlet's, of Scarlet's story about Claude and Bébé.

"Okay," Mary said. "See you at six."

Dragging a comb through her tangled hair, Mary imagined sharing her own story with Scarlet. She would tell her about Dylan, and how they had found each other late in their lives; how Stella had been their one chance to make a family. Perhaps she could tell Scarlet what kind of father Dylan had been, how he liked taking Stella grocery shopping, just the two of them. He would bring a lemon to her nose and have her inhale its scent. He taught her how to tell when a melon was ripe, how to choose an avocado, how to order meat from the butcher. After Stella died, Mary took over the grocery shopping, wandering the aisles alone. The sight of a father there with his little girl safely strapped into the cart, nibbling on blueberries or crackers broke her heart. Somehow Mary believed that maybe Scarlet would understand what she and Dylan had lost.

When she thought of her, of Scarlet, she saw her in the south of France, happy. That happiness had lasted only a moment, Mary knew. It seemed to her she'd had Stella for only a moment.

Staring at the stranger in the mirror, Mary sighed. Her face was rounder, her hair duller, her eyes flat. It was another person who used to like what she saw when she looked in a mirror, who playfully added mascara to her lashes and sparkly blush to her cheeks. Mary dug around in her cosmetics bag until she found the hot pink tube of mascara inside. But it had caked from lack of use, and she couldn't find her blush at all. Who was she kidding? she thought. She looked bad, she felt bad, and she was not ready to talk about any of this to anyone. She had paid a grief counselor a hundred dollars a week for almost two months and all Mary did was sit and cry, which was what she did at home for free.

Mary scrawled a note to Dylan, *Gone knittin',* and left it on the kitchen table. At ten after six, Scarlet pulled up in front of Mary's house. A new friend, Mary thought as she carefully locked the front door. Just that day Jodie had finally called and said, "I don't know what to say. Should I ask how you are? Should I mention Stella or not? God, Mary, I am so sorry to let you down." And Mary had said, "No, no, I'm fine. Really." The lie had burned in her throat for the rest of the afternoon.

Eddie had called and Mary had lied to him too. "You know," she'd said, "I'm doing so much better. Really I am. Maybe I'm ready to come back to work." "Uh-huh," Eddie had said, knowing better.

As she approached Scarlet's car, she saw that someone else was already in the front seat beside Scarlet.

"You remember Lulu?" Scarlet said after Mary slid into the backseat.

"Of course," Mary said, trying to hide her disappointment.

Lulu's platinum blonde hair was newly razor cut in uneven chunks, shiny from some expensive hair care product like wax or mud that kept it looking slightly dirty. She had on black again: a leather motorcycle jacket, turtleneck, skinny pants, and boots.

Mary settled back into the seat, wishing she hadn't come.

"Lulu's loft is right beneath mine," Scarlet said. "She's a glass sculptor."

"Really?" Mary said.

"You moved here from where?" Lulu said. Her voice sounded like she'd been smoking and drinking whiskey her entire life.

"San Francisco," Mary said.

"Have you noticed," Lulu said, turning slightly, "that everyone in this city is from somewhere else?"

Despite herself, Mary relaxed. Lulu wasn't so bad. It was Mary herself who couldn't relate to anyone.

"A glass sculptor," Mary said. "That seems so . . . I don't know, to work with such a fragile material seems impossible."

"The beauty of glass," Lulu said almost dreamily, "is that it's remained unchanged for hundreds of years."

"She trained in Venice," Scarlet said.

"Maybe you'll show me your things sometime," Mary said.

"Maybe," Lulu said unconvincingly, looking straight ahead.

"Wait!" Beth said. "I brought pictures."

She pulled a set of glossy photographs from a large envelope. Four children — two boys standing behind two girls — smiled stiffly out from them, all wearing matching red and green sweaters. Did she get her kids' picture taken every fucking week? Mary thought.

"Have you ever seen such perfect children?" Harriet said softly.

Yes, Mary thought. *Yes, I have.*

Mary hated the way Harriet looked at Beth, as if she were the only person who'd ever had children. She watched Harriet watching Beth's proud face. No, Mary decided, she looks at her as if she might disappear.

Scarlet glanced at the picture politely, then passed it on to Lulu. "Nice," Scarlet said without much conviction.

"What a brood!" Lulu said.

Beth laughed. "I always wanted a lot of children."

"She graduated magna cum laude, you know," Harriet said.

Beth shrugged off the boasting. "In early childhood education. It wasn't too challenging. It was just what I loved."

"She loves kids," Harriet said, her voice so tender that Beth flushed with embarrassment. "Of course, I worry about her," Harriet added. "She does too much."

Mary rolled her eyes and lost track of what she was doing.

"Did I just knit?" she said. "Or purl?"

Scarlet leaned over to help and locked her eyes with Mary's. She wants to take that picture and tear it to shreds too, Mary thought.

"The knit stitches look like little Vs," Scarlet said. "See? And the purls look like bumps."

"Like pearls," Harriet said.

"So I just purled?" Mary said.

Scarlet grinned. "No, you just knit."

Mary settled back and concentrated. *Purl two. Knit two.* Beth's voice swirled around her. *Purl two. Knit two.*

"Chris is my comedian. And Nate is my athlete. He plays three sports . . ."

Purl two. Knit two. Purl two.

". . . Caroline is the scholar. She always has her nose in a book. I don't know where she got that . . ."

Knit two. Purl two.

". . . And what can I say? Stella's my baby. We named her after my grandmother, you know, and believe me, she's the only Stella in her nursery school."

Mary stared at the yarn in her hands and gulped. It looked unfamiliar suddenly, and she wasn't even sure what she should be doing with it.

"If I could only keep her four forever," Beth said with a sigh.

Scarlet kneeled in front of Mary. "Do you need help?" she said softly.

"I, I don't know what I'm doing here," Mary said.

"You just purled two stitches," Scarlet said, her voice calm and even. "Now you're going to knit two stitches. Then purl two." She didn't move until Mary finally knit two stitches. "Now knit two," Scarlet said softly. "Now purl two. Now knit."

"Come with us for martinis," Scarlet said as they drove back to Providence.

Exhausted, Mary said, "Maybe another time. I didn't even tell my husband I was going out."

"See?" Lulu said. "Husbands are a grand liability, Scarlet. They keep you away from martinis." Lulu pointed out the window. "Look!"

The moon hung full and orange in the sky ahead.

"Blue moon," Lulu crooned.

"Looks red to me," Scarlet said.

"No, no," Lulu laughed. "A blue moon is the second full moon in the same month."

"Lulu knows more fun facts than anybody I know," Scarlet said.

"Correction. More *useless* facts," Lulu said, her gaze focused out the window.

Two hundred and twenty-eight thousand children and young adults die every year. Sixty thousand children a year under the age of six die. Two thousand children a year die from bacterial meningitis. The children who live often lose limbs or hearing or eyesight.

"You know," Mary said, her voice quivering, "a martini sounds like a great idea."

The bar was downtown, on a block of deserted buildings, tucked away without a sign or awning. Inside, it was crowded and smoky and the three women had to stand crushed close together at the bar.

Two oversized martinis later, a small table opened and Lulu pushed her way to claim it. Mary was starting to like Lulu. She reminded Mary of her old self, the one who had something to say about everything.

Sitting with a fresh round of drinks in front of them, Mary said to Lulu, "I can't believe you ever left the city. It seems like a perfect fit for you."

Lulu fished an olive out of her drink and popped it in her mouth. She ordered her martinis dirty, extra olives and their juice.

Mary frowned, wondering what she had said wrong.

"Beth can be a bit much," Scarlet said,

breaking the awkward silence. "The matching sweaters. The pictures."

"Always with the fucking pictures," Lulu said.

Mary's stomach tumbled, remembering Beth's voice. *What can I say? Stella's my baby . . .*

"Mary?" Scarlet was saying, her hand resting tenderly on Mary's arm. "Are you all right?"

"I should get home," Mary managed.

"Sadie, Sadie, married lady," Lulu said.

Later, standing in her bedroom doorway, dizzy and melancholy, Mary studied her husband's sleeping face. It had become topographical from grief. Even in sleep he wore his sadness plainly. CNN blared from the television, talk of wars and distant tragedies. Mary walked over to the television and turned it off, sending the room into darkness except for the blue moon that lit up the sky.

■ ■ ■ ■

PART THREE:
KNIT TWO TOGETHER
(K2TOG)

■ ■ ■ ■

Patterns are more specific about decreasing than increasing. Decreases done in certain ways slant the stitches to the right or left. For many patterns this is an important element; for others it doesn't matter at all that much.
— Nancy J. Thomas and Ilana Rabinowitz,
A Passion for Knitting

5
LULU

On halloween night, Mary stayed in bed and watched TV. Even as the doorbell rang and children's voices chirped, "Trick or treat!" to Dylan, Mary stared at the television.

Downstairs, Dylan marveled at miniature Spider-Men and Harry Potters. He claimed each witch the scariest, each princess the loveliest. Mary did not think of the way that Stella always chose a winged creature for her Halloween costume: butterfly, bumblebee, fairy. She did not think of how meager that list was, how it should have grown over the years, adding bats and ladybugs, raptors and dragonflies.

Eventually Dylan came upstairs.

"What a crowd!" he said. "We never have such a crowd."

"Usually we're among them," Mary said without looking at him. "We're trick-or-treaters."

He stood in front of the television, holding a pastry box tied with string.

"Someone got mixed up and gave *us* candy instead of the other way around?" she said, taking it from him.

She pulled the string from the box and opened it. Inside, nestled in a tight row, sat three cannelles.

"Scarlet brought them?" Mary said.

"I found them on the doorstep. No note."

Dylan sat beside her on the bed.

"What a terrible night," he said.

Mary handed him one of the pastries and took one for herself, letting its perfect sweetness fill her mouth.

"It might have been better if we'd done it together," he said, not looking at her. "If we'd both been down there."

Mary shook her head. "I told you I couldn't," she said. "You could have hidden up here with me." She tried not to sound defensive.

But Dylan said, "I guess I can't hide from everything like you can," and she heard that too-familiar edge in his voice.

"I'm sorry," Mary told him, though she wasn't certain what she was sorry about: sorry that Stella had died and she couldn't handle it? Sorry she couldn't be more like him in the face of this?

"I'll fight you for the third one," Dylan

said, changing the subject, letting their frustration lie there between them.

"One holiday down, and an infinite number to go," Dylan said, licking crumbs from his fingers.

"And my mother's threatening to come for Thanksgiving," Mary said, her hands shaping the string into the Eiffel Tower.

Too early one morning her mother had called. "I've been invited to eat with Saul and his family," she'd said, "but if you want me there, there I'll be."

"Saul?" Mary had said, cranky. She hated starting the day with a phone call from her mother. "Who's Saul?"

"I've only mentioned him a few hundred times," her mother said. "A neighbor. A friend. His children, all three of them, come down from Houston for Thanksgiving. With their spouses. And their children."

"Lucky Saul," Mary said.

"Eight grandchildren. He'll have a full house, that's for sure. I said I'd make my sweet potatoes. The ones I do so beautifully? The casserole? And of course help with the turkey."

"It sounds like you should stay there then," Mary said. Her first year without Stella, and didn't all the books and groups and advice about grief warn that all the firsts were the worst? Couldn't her mother figure that out when everyone else seemed to know it?

"That's what I thought," her mother was saying. "You and Dylan should get away. Go to Havana. That's the place to forget everything."

"What if I don't want to forget?" Mary said, closing her eyes against her mother's voice, against the sun that was beginning to show its bright face in her bedroom window, against the whole world beyond her bed.

"I understand," her mother said. "But running away for a bit won't erase anything. It will just take the edge off a little. I remember that trip your father and I took —" she began.

But Mary didn't care about some long-ago vacation, or about her mother's philosophies on loss.

"Mom, you don't know anything about it," Mary interrupted.

"This was a long time ago," her mother continued. "Before you were born. We went to Key West. And we walked on those little streets with all the palm trees —"

Her mother sighed, then spoke again.

"Cuba. Havana, Cuba," she said. "I hear it's time to go to Cuba."

"Thanks," Mary said. "That's really great

advice."

A few minutes after she'd hung up, the phone rang again.

"You can't take your knitting on the airplane."

"Mom?" Mary said.

"In case you go to Cuba. They don't allow you to bring the needles on board anymore."

"I'm not going to Cuba, Mom," Mary said.

"Mrs. Earle said that they let you bring circular needles. But you're not working on those yet, are you?"

"It doesn't matter," Mary said. "I'm not flying anywhere."

Lying in her bed Halloween night, Mary imagined flying somewhere. She thought of Stella last Halloween, a perfect fairy, all sparkles and tulle. And then she thought of herself, so earthbound, so stuck.

When her mother called again, Mary was lying on her bed, staring at the ceiling, willing herself to take off, to actually burst through the roof and into the sky.

"I've been thinking about Thanksgiving," her mother said. "I don't want to make it worse for you. It's going to be bad. I know that. And for the life of me I know that I can't make it any better. Stay with your husband. I'll barge in on Saul and his family. Next year will be a whole other story."

"That sounds great," Mary said. "Have fun."

She hung up the phone and stared hard at the ceiling, as if she could by sheer force break a hole in it and see all the way up to the sky.

On thanksgiving morning they drove to Dylan's sister's house in Connecticut. The night before there was enough of a snowfall to leave a perfect dusting on the yards and trees of Sara's neighborhood. The houses, set back from the street, emitted warm yellow light from inside, and lovely puffs of smoke from the chimneys. A few had already strung small white Christmas lights around their doors and windows, and these twinkled in the gray afternoon.

"It looks like a movie set," Mary said, hating it here.

"Yeah," Dylan muttered, "a horror movie."

She thought of Beth from knitting. This was where she would live. She and her four matching children, her *Stella.*

They pulled into the driveway behind Sara's Volvo wagon. One like it sat in every driveway here. Sara had an annoying habit of referring to her things by brand — the Volvo, the Saab. Her purse was the Kate Spade; her shoes were the Pradas, the Adidas, the Uggs.

Sara stood on the front steps, dressed head to toe in camel, ready to pounce on them.

"Hey, you two," she said. "Can you believe it? Snow on Thanksgiving? I had to pull my Uggs out of the attic."

She hugged them both in turn, firmly, the kind of hug Mary had come to learn was meant to express sympathy.

Fires roared in each fireplace of each room they walked through. So perfect was each fire that Mary concluded they must be gas, not real wood ones. But then a log crackled and sent blue sparks against the screen. Maybe the fires were the only real things here.

In one of the living rooms — Sara actually had three rooms that could be living rooms, all with carefully arranged sofas and love seats and overstuffed chairs, and small tables with magazines neatly lined up, or large books about amusement parks and Winslow Homer — stood Sara's husband, Tim, and their two teenage sons, Timmy and Daniel, along with another family, who looked like carbon copies of them. Except

Liz and Dave also had an unhappy-looking daughter, Sylvie, who stood alone sullenly eating miniature quiches.

"Ali's with her roommate," Sara told Mary conspiratorially. She said everything conspiratorially. "In Virgin Gorda. Poor thing, right?"

"Wow," Mary said stupidly, which was how she said everything, she realized. "Virgin Gorda."

"Get these two a Tanqueray and tonic," Sara told Dave, after introductions.

"You bet," Dave said in his overeager voice. He sold something Mary could never remember. Pharmaceuticals?

The boys all stared at their loafers, so Mary went to stand beside Sylvie.

"What grade are you in now?" Mary asked, finding comfort in the superfluous gesture. "Eighth?"

"Sixth," Sylvie said between mini quiches. "I did junior kindergarten so I'm like a year older than everyone else." She moved on to a platter of dates wrapped in bacon.

"Do you know about this?" Liz asked Mary. "It's a wonderful way to build self-confidence and self-image. They do a year between kindergarten and first grade, working on social skills and reinforcing basic learning skills. Then they get into first grade and they are at the top of their class. Honestly, it's the best idea ever."

Mary nodded politely and gulped at her gin and tonic. Here was where she should feel smug at how self-confident Stella was. And smart. A kid who knew her own mind. A kid who sailed through kindergarten, printing her letters perfectly, writing her numbers just so, and coloring maps of South America and China in bright colors.

Tears stung Mary's eyes and she turned, pretending to admire a painting that hung over the fireplace.

Mary turned from the painting and sighed. Sylvie was standing with the boys now. When Mary moved toward them, they all stopped talking.

"Your daughter died," Sylvie said matter-of-factly.

Her brother Davey elbowed her in the ribs.

"Yes," Mary said.

"How?" Sylvie asked, her lips shiny from grease.

"Meningitis," Mary said. She hated the word, the way it sounded in the stillness.

"Brad Pitt had meningitis and he didn't die."

"There are different kinds," Mary said. "Stella had a bad kind. The worst kind."

Sylvie narrowed her eyes. "In school, in

science, they said that antibiotics can treat anything."

"Sylvie," Davey hissed.

"They did!"

"Not this," Mary said. She remembered how a nurse had told her that some children lived but were blind or deaf or paralyzed. Ravaged, she had said. The disease ravaged them.

Sylvie nodded solemnly, considering.

The boys squirmed uncomfortably.

"That's so sad," Sylvie said softly.

"Yes," Mary said.

When Sara appeared a few minutes later to call them to dinner, Sylvie took Mary's hand in her own soft sweaty one and walked with her to the dining room.

The following monday morning, the phone rang early. Mary was absently swishing water in the coffeepot.

"So you made it!" a voice said.

Mary frowned and didn't answer.

"Through Thanksgiving," the woman continued.

Mary hesitated. "Well," she said.

"What a dope I am," the woman said. "I expect everyone to recognize my voice immediately. It's Lulu. From knitting."

"Lulu," Mary said, surprised.

"I was thinking about you," Lulu continued. "The holidays suck. And I know Christmas is lurking. I always go away for Christmas. Are you going away?"

"I don't think so," Mary said.

"You should! Somewhere warm. That's what I do. I get on a plane and head south. Palm trees. Rum. Turquoise water."

"That sounds pretty good," Mary said. She glanced out the window at yet another gray day. The wind whistled menacingly. They were in for a bad winter; everyone said so. "My mother suggested Cuba."

"Cuba? That's, like, illegal, isn't it?"

"Not according to my mother," Mary said.

"I'm sitting here instead of at my glass studio and I'm getting ready to knit hats. That's what I'm making everyone for Christmas this year. Hats. And I thought you should come over and knit hats too."

"Hats sound so complicated," she said.

Lulu laughed. "So easy! In five hours you can make five hats. Christmas shopping done and you can spend your days reading travel brochures and booking your airline tickets to Havana."

"I was going to sit here and watch bad morning television, but your offer sounds pretty tempting," Mary said.

"Downstairs from Scarlet," Lulu said. "I'll

see you in fifteen minutes."

Every place that Scarlet's loft was soft and warm — furniture, colors, lighting — Lulu's was hard. A mishmash of flea market bargains and sidewalk finds, everything Lulu owned had a story.

"This table was sitting on Prince Street. Just sitting there! I picked it up, hailed a taxi, and took it home." She tapped the turquoise-and-yellow-speckled top affectionately. "Vintage thirties," she added.

Lulu plopped on the red velvet couch. "I love my junk," she said, patting the worn cushion beside her.

Mary sat down, adjusting herself to find a comfortable spot.

"The coffee table's nice," she said. Mission style with a gleaming dark wood surface.

"That was my ex-husband's," Lulu said.

The thing about Lulu, with her spiky hair and skinny body and quirky clothes and furniture, was that Mary forgot that in fact Lulu was probably in her late thirties. Something about her — her fragility, maybe — made her seem much younger.

"I didn't know you were married," Mary said.

"Nine years." Lulu smiled wanly and

began to cast on to a pair of circular needles. "A lifetime ago."

She grew quiet for a moment.

"You can make whole sweaters on these things," Lulu said finally. "Except sweaters are boring. Hats are fast and hypnotic. Good therapy."

"I need that," Mary said softly.

Lulu didn't look up. "I know," she said. "So do I."

"I reinvented myself, you know," Lulu said a little while later. "I used to be Louise Peterson, child of suburban Chicago, mall aficionado, private school snob."

Mary laughed. "This story is not true," she said. On the circular needles, the hat took shape quickly. Its brim rolling perfectly as the stitches added up.

"I have pictures to prove it," Lulu said. She went to a bright blue chest of drawers that had once been painted red and another time green; both colors showed through here and there. The drawer stuck and Lulu gave it a hard tug. Once it opened, she dug around a bit before producing a shoe box decoupaged with pictures of Manhattan that had been cut from magazines.

Sitting cross-legged on the couch beside Mary, Lulu opened the box and held up a picture of four teenage girls, all with Dorothy Hamill haircuts and identical blue and green plaid uniforms — kilt, kneesocks, polo shirt.

"I don't even know which one is me for certain," Lulu said. "Looking like everyone else was the key to my youth."

"Meet Louise Peterson," Lulu said. "Age sixteen." She pointed to the next picture. "The prom," she said. "The date," she continued, tapping on the tuxedoed boy. "Lost my virginity that night. We all did. We made a pact to get it over with. After all, we had been with these boys since forever. We had plans to keep dating them through college — University of Michigan, all of us — and marry them and live happily ever after.

"Our lives were so set, so predictable," she said, studying the third picture. It was her senior picture, cut from a yearbook. "I pretended, you know. I wore the Izod shirts and the Fair Isle sweaters and I walked around the mall for hours and hours trying on earrings and lip gloss. Then I'd go home and cut out these pictures of New York City from magazines.

"Eighteen years old, my acceptance to the University of Michigan sitting on my desk in my pink and white bedroom, my spot as the fourth girl in a suite with my friends in the freshman dorm secured, I got into my little Ford Pinto and drove east. Neatly folded in my drawers back home were all my snowflake sweaters with their matching turtleneck shirts, my tightly wound spools of hair ribbons in every color, one entire drawer of alligator shirts.

"I arrived with my belongings in one American Tourister soft red suitcase and one thousand dollars — my life savings from a summer job at the ice cream parlor in my local strip mall. I parked the Pinto on St. Marks Place, stepped into the heat and stench of a late August New York City afternoon, and I knew I would never leave.

"That's when I became Lulu."

Lulu paused to pick up her knitting needles. The yarn she was using was soft aqua mohair. Small pieces of fluff floated in the air as her needles flew.

"I knew I would never leave," she said again. "I managed to get this place, a railroad flat with a tub in the kitchen on the third floor, across the street from a crack house. I loved that place. For fun, I spray-painted the floors. Kind of like my hair, I kept changing the colors.

"Manuel, my bodega guy, the guy who guarded the crack house, even the crazy guy who walked seven dogs on leashes made of clothesline knew my name. All those years growing up back in Illinois, no one really knew me, you know? I used to get a Slurpee on the way home from school every day at the same 7-Eleven and the same girl used to sell it to me and she never once recognized me."

Lulu added brown yarn and stripes began to appear. Aqua. Brown. Aqua. Brown. She was a fast knitter. Her hands seemed to fly as she knit.

"I bought a bike from a guy in Tompkins Square Park. An old red bike. And I put streamers on the handlebars and I rode that bike everywhere. It got stolen about a million times but I always found it again. One time I chased this guy all the way to Broadway to get that bike back.

"I waitressed at every restaurant in the Village at one time or another. I fell in love a lot. With a guy in a bad band. With a bartender where I worked. I liked long lean men. Leather jackets were good too, but not required. I learned to knit. Men all over New York City were wearing my scarves.

"After one of these big disastrous relationships, I was riding my bike down Second Avenue and I saw this flyer about a glassblowing class. So I signed up.

"The teacher was this guy named Michael Angelo. He was from Italy and just my type.

Tall and thin with these amazing hands. Huge hands. With long fingers. He had a studio on Prince Street, in this totally empty building. I fell totally in love with him. But what I really fell in love with was glass. What heat did to it. The shapes it could take.

"I became obsessed with him and with glass. I would go to the library and sit at the old wooden table and read about glass. My teacher made money by selling these leopard- or zebra-striped glasses to fancy stores in SoHo. Eventually he taught me how to do it and I made leopard and zebra glasses every Saturday, all day.

"He became the guy whose main purpose was to break my heart. He lied, he cheated on me, he kept me waiting. Then one day, out of the blue, he asked me if I wanted to go to Italy with him for the summer. To Venice. The glass mecca, right? I pretended to think about it for about a week. By the time I told him I'd go, I'd already sublet my apartment and quit my job. Hell, I'd already packed my bag.

"That summer. Definitely in the top five best summers ever. Food. Sex. Glass. That was it. The whole summer. And then we got back to New York and right back to the old pattern. The fights. The other women. So I decided, fuck Michael Angelo. I would

119

waitress my ass off and save enough money to go back to Venice and study on my own. I worked two waitress jobs and I took Italian classes and I painted my floor and I got a cat. Cats are good. People don't realize how loyal cats are."

As if on cue, a fat orange cat jumped down from the windowsill, stretched languorously, and draped himself over the arm of the couch beside Lulu.

"This is Katmandu. That first cat was Cat Stevens. I loved that cat."

She held up her aqua-and-brown-striped hat. "Time to decrease," she said. "On a pattern it'll say K2tog. Knit two together." She inserted her needle into two stitches and knit them.

She was quiet while she finished the hat. When it was done, she put it on her head, cast on forty more stitches, in orange this time, and began to knit again.

"Three years," Lulu said. "That's how long it took me to earn enough money to go to Venice. And all this time I'm pouring my heart out to this cute bartender at one of my jobs. At the NoHo Star, on Bleecker. After work we'd stay at the closed restaurant and drink and talk. Three years this went on. Every now and then we'd grab a bite to eat, but basically our entire friendship existed sitting at that bar at four in the morning drinking the bits of wine left in other people's bottles, and talking.

"Then right before I left for Venice, he said, 'Maybe when you come back you'll marry me.' And I laughed and said, 'Okay, sure.' And he said, 'Good.' So that's what I did. I went to Venice for a year and studied glass. And I had these little flings. But I thought about him a lot. Practically every night for three years I had talked to him and I really missed him. I sent him a lot of postcards. Every week I'd write a whole story on the back, whatever story I wished I could tell him.

"When I got back to New York, I went straight to the bar with my bags and everything and there he was, right where I left him. 'I'm back,' I said. He smiled. 'I can see that.' 'Do you still want to get married?' I said. He said, 'Absolutely.' Three days later, City Hall, we're pronounced husband and wife."

Lulu sighed, but her eyes did not stray from her knitting. In fact, she focused even harder, narrowing her dark-lined eyes and bending forward slightly.

"Smitty. That's what he was called. Like every other Smith in the world, I guess. But he wasn't like anyone else. He was this big open heart. We moved into a loft on Bond Street, a real mess. A work in progress, we called it. Plaster everywhere. Sawdust. We'd spend an afternoon on Bowery, where all the restaurant supply stores are, looking for stuff. Appliances and things. Then we'd come home with like the best espresso maker ever. An industrial size thing that took us months to learn how to use. Meanwhile, we're cooking on a hot plate because we've dumped all our money into that instead of a stove. God, we had fun."

She let her yarn drop gently into her lap and looked out the window.

Mary touched Lulu's arm lightly. "Did something happen to him?" she asked.

Lulu shook her head. "Something happened to me," she said.

Mary waited.

"Did I tell you about the dogs?" Lulu asked suddenly. She picked up her needles and began again. "He had two. A chocolate Lab and a bichon. Mutt and Jeff. He had rescued them both from the pound. Mutt, the Lab, had scars all over his body. Like he'd been crucified. And Jeff had bald spots everywhere. His hair simply didn't grow in places. Ugly, scruffy, marvelous dogs. Both of them.

"I used to get up early and walk them over

to Washington Square Park, to the dog run there. You know how the city is really early in the morning? Kind of empty. And so beautiful. The sun just coming up shines on the buildings in a different way. It positively illuminates them. On the way back, I'd pick up a *Times* and I'd have the paper in my hand, and I'd be going down Bond Street, and the sun would hit our building just so, like a blessing. And I would think that I was the luckiest person in the world. The happiest, luckiest person in the world.

"I'd step over all the Chinese take-out menus inside our dingy foyer and get in the creaky freight elevator that always smelled like Indian food, and step out on the third floor and pull the heavy elevator door open and then I would stop. I could smell the espresso that Smitty was making. I could smell us, our smells. They smelled so beautiful.

"This one morning I decided to walk east instead of west. Why did I do that? I have gone over and over that in my mind and I still don't know. Was I bored with my little routine? Did I need something over in the East Village? I just stepped out the front door with both dogs on their leashes, and instead of turning left, I turned right. I remember thinking that I would go over to

Tompkins Square Park for a change. Near my old apartment.

"But this is important for you to understand. I was completely happy with my life. I liked filling out forms that asked if I was married, and checking off *Yes* and writing my husband's name down as next of kin. I wore the fattest gold wedding band you've ever seen, and I brandished it whenever I could.

"And by this time I rented a teeny studio on Elizabeth Street and I was making my own glass there."

Lulu paused in her story. "Do you know about Venetian glass?" she asked, but before Mary could answer, Lulu continued. "People think of it as the elegant shapes from the sixteenth century, but typically it's made in more unusual shapes that combine a lot of different styles." She pointed to a lamp beside the table. "Like this. See spouts and handles? And these blobs? They're called prunts." Gently, she ran her fingers over the base of the lamp. "They're just decorative, but I always use them."

The room grew quiet until Lulu spoke again. "Smitty made documentary films. And he got a grant to make a film about Virgin sightings around the city. Like in Queens in this phone booth a weird stain appeared on the glass and people thought it looked like the Virgin Mary and they would line up to pray to this phone booth.

"We would go together on the subway to all of these places. This woman in Washington Heights made tortillas and everyone saw the Virgin's face in them. Things like that. He'd talk to people and film them holding their children. Sick children and deformed children. They would rub them against the phone booth or press the tortillas to their cheeks.

"This was what our life was like. Crazy and wonderful. Eight years together and we still sat up all night talking to each other. Smitty wanted a baby. He was starting to talk me into it. He created this next life, you know. Smitty, Lulu, Baby. He liked common names. Jane, he'd say. But I would spin fanciful names. Iris, goddess of the rainbow. Indigo? I'd say.

"When I was alone in the loft I would try to imagine it. A baby crawling across the floor. A baby in our bed. At first I couldn't see it, but slowly it began to make sense. We'd been married eight years. We should have a baby. And it would be the most special baby ever born.

"That morning when I left the apartment and for no reason turned right instead of left, I had been off the pill for two months. Maybe that's what I was thinking. In my memory I wasn't thinking anything at all. I simply stepped outside and turned right.

"It was dark still. February. Cold. We'd had a big snowstorm a few days earlier and you know how snow gets in the city after a few days. Dirty. Black. Chunked with ice. I walked slowly east. I remember wishing I had worn a hat. It was so cold.

"I walked up Avenue A. No one was out. Too cold. Too dark still. After a few blocks a drunk walked right into me. He bowed, took off this funny stocking hat that he had on, and apologized. Bowing all the way down the block. God, I thought, I love this city.

"There were people in the park. I remember that. A small group, maybe four or five, huddled together. To keep warm, I guessed. I didn't pay them any mind and they didn't seem to notice me at all. I sat on a bench and let the dogs off their leashes to run. I wished I'd brought something to read. I remember looking across the street at the bodega on the corner and thinking about getting a newspaper. Out of the corner of my eye I saw that group. They were kids. Kids without hats, like me. They had hoods pulled up over their heads. I remember that. But this was all in an instant. I stood to go

126

buy a paper, the group seemed to split up. The dogs were chasing a plastic bag caught in the wind.

"That's it. That's the last second of my life."

Lulu looked directly at Mary.

For the first time, Mary noticed the scars on Lulu's face. Long and thin, they snaked down her jaw to her neck. More were partially hidden by her spiky bangs. Mary's hand impulsively shot to her mouth.

"They raped me right there and left me for dead. Everyone told me it's a good thing I don't remember any of it," Lulu said. "You know what's strange? The one boy, the ringleader, he took Jeff, the little bichon. He took him home. When they arrested him, there was Jeff, in a little dog bed with toys and rawhide bones."

The Tompkins Square Dog Walker, Mary thought. The story had been all over the news, even in San Francisco. First, the discovery of the body. Then the search for identification. Then the reports on her condition, every day for months. No one — not doctors, not her husband, no one — expected her to live. Then one day, the announcement that she was going to make it. Months passed and the story grew smaller. Tompkins Square Dog Walker released to rehab center.

Then the story made headlines again, the arrests of those boys, the grim details of the attack. At their arraignment, the boys had looked smug. They had been out all night, they said. They were bored.

"It's like it happened to someone I don't know," Lulu said. "I had twenty-seven operations. To repair my jaw. To fix my skull. My nose. Dental surgery. Plastic surgery."

Now emotion ravaged her face. Her eyes were shiny with tears; her cheeks and eyebrows grew furrowed; and a small muscle under her left eye twitched rhythmically.

"In the hospital, I used to imagine that when I walked back into my life, it would still fit. I would close my eyes and picture myself in our apartment, the way it used to be. I could almost feel Smitty's leg draped over mine, the softness of our sheets and the smell of the laundry detergent our cleaner used. Or the spitting sound of that espresso maker. Or the way the light came in at different times of day, how it spread itself on the table first, so that when we sat there and ate breakfast we were always warm.

"But the loft was gone. We had to sell it to pay for the surgeries. Even that stupid oversized espresso maker was gone. Smitty rented a studio apartment in Chelsea. He bought real furniture — a chair with a sofa. This coffee table." She nudged it gently with her foot. "And he built a loft bed with a desk underneath it, all very orderly and neat. He had this little round table, the kind you see in an ice cream parlor.

"That's where he took me. We drove in a friend's borrowed station wagon from the rehab place in New Jersey to this strange apartment. The building had a little foyer that smelled like disinfectant, and an elevator that opened and shut on its own. I still had trouble walking then. I was using a walker, and so I had time to take it all in. The mailbox with the name *Smith* on it. The speckled floor. Then the elevator took us up to the fourth floor, and when we stepped out, Smitty scooped me up in his arms, wrestled some keys out of his pocket, opened this door with the number 4F on it, and said, 'Welcome home, Lulu.'

"Home to a place I'd never seen, with nothing of ours in it. I know how heartbroken he was when he sold our things, when Cat Stevens died, when he left the neighborhood we had both loved so much for the one that felt, as he said, neutral. He was so tender, my husband. He helped bathe me. He clipped my toenails and dyed my hair. At night he held me while I slept. Without drugs there would be no sleep. Because of the pain. Because of my fear that I would remember something if I fell asleep. So I took a handful of pills, washed them down with vodka, and just before I fell asleep, I would hear the sound of a plastic bag caught in the wind."

"I remember it," Mary said. "From the papers. On the news."

Lulu nodded. "I was a very important story. My survival. Inspiring." She shuddered.

"I couldn't stay," Lulu said. "You can understand that, can't you? Lulu Smith was killed in Tompkins Square Park that morning."

Mary nodded.

"An old friend from that first glassblowing class was teaching at RISD. She got me an adjunct thing. Introduction to Glass. I became this person." Lulu gestured to herself, her hands taking in her whole scarred self. "Lulu Peterson. I teach a class every semester. I make my own glass. I knit. That's what I am. I'm afraid of things. The dark. The sound of wind. Footsteps in a hallway. Leaves rustling in trees. Voices I can't identify. Being out there alone."

Mary understood. After Stella died, the

grocery store, the gas station, even her own backyard held danger.

"I don't go out to eat or anything unless Scarlet takes me," Lulu was saying. "And when we get back she unlocks my door and steps inside and turns on the lights and walks around checking the apartment. Sometimes she spends the night because I cannot be convinced that no one is waiting to hurt me."

"I never let my daughter eat a hamburger," Mary said. "I was so worried about E. coli. I remembered all the stories, from fast-food restaurants, and outdoor barbecues. Children dying. Then this bacteria enters her body and kills her."

"Oh, Mary," Lulu said, her voice cracking. "All I can do is this for you." She inched closer to Mary and examined the hat. "Look at what you've made."

Mary nodded, the tears hot in her eyes.

"I'll teach you patterns too," Lulu said, her own eyes wet with tears. "Snowflakes. Horses. Ducks. You have to concentrate so hard when you do them that you have no room for anything else."

"Snowflakes," Mary said. "That would be good."

"When I first got here, I asked my friend at RISD where I could get yarn. She told me to call Big Alice. I told her my story. I told her everything. Next thing I know, I've joined the knitting circle. Ellen was there then. Alice. Roger. You know Roger? A few people who've moved away. Or moved on. When the knitting circle ended, Alice drove me all the way back home. One of those nights, I was getting out of her truck with this big bag of yarn when I met Scarlet. She lived in the building too, and eventually I got her to join the circle too."

Lulu paused.

"You know rosary beads?" she said. "Knitting is like that. One stitch is like a prayer, just like each bead is a prayer. It's perfect for contemplation."

"Or escape," Mary said.

Lulu smiled sadly. "We can't escape, can we? But we can knit."

6

THE KNITTING CIRCLE

Mary used to drop Stella off at school and then drive to the Coffee Exchange. She always saw someone there she knew. Another mother from Stella's school. Stella's ballet teacher. One of their babysitters. Soon she would be table-hopping, getting coffee refills, her newspaper unread. Sometimes she would see a group of women, all with children who played with or took a class with or went to school with Stella. Then they would sit for too long and talk about their amazing children.

Since Stella died, Mary avoided the Coffee Exchange, where all those women still sat — that's how she imagined it, all of them right where she'd left them the morning before Stella got sick.

But this morning, Mary awoke and decided that she would go for coffee. Not to the Coffee Exchange; she would never go back there. But across town to Rouge,

133

where the café au lait tasted the way it did in France and the croissants were rich with butter. Where, Mary thought, she might see Scarlet.

It was a cold day. The pewter sky held the promise of snow. But inside Rouge was warm, from the ovens and the heat that hissed from old radiators and from all the people crowded at the small tables.

"Aren't you Mary?"

Mary twisted her neck to see who was talking. Squeezed into the table right behind her sat a vaguely familiar woman. Her long dirty blonde hair was pushed off her face by a scrap of faded floral fabric. A half-eaten croissant on the white plate before her, ignored for the complicated handiwork the woman held in her hands.

"I'm in the knitting circle," the woman said in a soft southern accent. "Ellen."

"Size one needles, right?" Mary said, remembering her now.

"Socks!" Ellen said, brightening. "I like them because you have to keep changing what you're doing. Stockinette, then several inches of garter, then it's time to turn the heel, which is absolutely crazy to do, and then more garter until you have to do the toe and the Kitchener stitch. Plus people love them. They're so warm and beautiful."

She blushed, and shrugged.

"I don't think socks are for me," Mary said.

"I spend so much time waiting that they keep me busy, you know?" Ellen said, still red-cheeked.

"What do you do?" Mary asked.

"I teach music. Part-time, at the music school. I can't do a full-time position." She glanced away again. Then looked up and smiled, gathering her things as she rose to leave. "See how neatly they fold up," she said. She collapsed the four thin needles and stuck them and her yarn into a Ziploc bag.

"Off to teach now?" Mary asked.

Ellen shook her head. "I'm cheating. I've had a dreadful few days and I'm sneaking off to the movies."

Mary surprised herself by blurting, "Maybe we could go together sometime."

Ellen looked surprised. "My schedule is tight," she said awkwardly. "But I'll see you Wednesday night, right?"

"Of course," Mary said. "I'm sorry."

But Ellen was already pushing her way through the crowded café, her head bent, her bag held close to her chest.

Mary watched her as she walked across the parking lot to her car. From where she stood, it looked as if Ellen was crying. It must have been the glare from the bright winter sunlight on the tall window.

Wednesday night brought an icy snow and high winds. Dylan lit a fire in the living room fireplace and put the McGarrigle Sisters on the CD player.

"Remember that trip to Nova Scotia?" he said, pouring himself a glass of merlot and settling onto the sofa.

"That church hall," Dylan was saying, "and the strawberry shortcake? The fiddle music?"

"I got pregnant that night," Mary said.

That trip, driving together all the way to Nova Scotia and beyond, to Prince Edward Island and the small red house on top of a red cliff overlooking a rocky beach. Two weeks of sun and vistas of the Atlantic Ocean. It had seemed impossible that England lay on the other side. That anything did. For Mary and Dylan those two weeks were spent driving, buying homemade pies on the roadside and eating them with their fingers; sex in the morning, sleeping late, groggy sweet breakfasts; digging for clams in the afternoon; evening meals of briny chowders cooked in big pots; then evening stargazing or dancing to fiddle music in the church basements; then more sex, sun-burned and beery, the falling together.

"Don't go with the knitting ladies," Dylan said. "Stay here with me."

Six o'clock and already dark outside. The wind rattled the old windows; the icy snow pinged against the glass. Scarlet had the flu and was staying home in bed. Lulu wouldn't go without Scarlet. But Mary needed yarn. She had used all she'd bought knitting scarves and hats. She needed the rhythm of the needles catching stitches. Needed the sound of one needle clicking against the other. Needed the way it felt like prayer, how her mind could grow calm as she counted: *k1, p1.*

"I'll be back early," she said. "The weather's so awful."

She saw the disappointment in Dylan's face, but still she put on her down coat and one of the scarves she'd made and the hat that matched it, and then she kissed her husband lightly on the lips.

"Don't go to sleep," she said softly. "Wait up for me."

She said it like a promise. Dylan pulled her close and kissed her for real. A surge of passion shot through Mary and she realized that Dylan did not kiss her very much anymore. Dylan had already turned away from her. He had opened a book, one of the histories he had taken to reading these past months, stories of warriors and victors.

As she walked outside from the warm house, the sidewalk was slippery and for a moment Mary considered turning around. But then she thought of all the days ahead, the lonely hours stretching before her in that house. She should be making sugar cookies, letting Stella cut them into stars and bells and sprinkling red and green sugar on top. She should be hiding presents in her office closet, bags of paints and bottles of sparkly nail polish and colorful hair ornaments and boxes of beads and all the things that would make Stella happy on Christmas morning.

But here she was, on a cold December night, driving away from home instead of placing her collection of Nativities around the house, and hanging lights and Christmas stockings. Inside the car, she turned the heat on full blast. Its stale smell filled the car but Mary did not get warm. She shivered all the way to Big Alice's.

Usually, Mary was one of the first to arrive at the knitting circle, especially when she drove in with Lulu and Scarlet. She liked the settling in, the way they each gravitated toward the same seat every time, Lulu in the center of the lumpy sofa, Scarlet in the green rocking chair. Mary always sat beside Alice so she could ask for help if she needed it or simply to breathe in her clean citrus scent. Alice was the freshest-looking person Mary had ever known, as if she'd just emerged from a good hot bath.

But tonight, with the hard rain turning to snow as she neared the coast, turning the roads slippery, Mary didn't pull into Big Alice's parking lot until almost quarter after seven. There weren't many cars there, the weather too nasty even for these diehard knitters. The same white lights that always twinkled in the bushes shone in Mary's headlights. She appreciated that Alice did not put up any Christmas decorations. Even in the store, the only sign of the holiday drawing close was that even more yarn than usual lined the shelves and baskets.

Mary walked up the path to the door, relaxing finally when she felt its heft in her hands and heard the small sigh it gave as it opened. Stepping inside, she saw only three heads bent over piles and piles of white yarn. Alice's own silver hair. Ellen's soft blond ripples. And the shiny pink of a man's scalp. The three of them had pulled their chairs into a tight circle in the center of the small room.

"Out on a night like this?" she said. Big Alice finally looked up.

Mary thought of the warm fire burning back home, the wine, Dylan's hopeful face.

"I didn't want to" — she stopped herself before she said the truth: *I didn't want to be home* — "to miss a night."

She felt foolish standing there without even a project in her hands. She had completed enough hats and scarves for ten Christmases, and thought tonight she might try something new, something impossibly hard that would keep her concentrating on it until Christmas had passed altogether.

"This is Roger," Alice said. "You know Ellen, of course. Although you might not recognize her knitting something besides socks."

Ellen's cheeks flushed. "We're trying to help Roger finish this blanket."

Hesitantly, Mary drew a chair into their circle. She could see now that the yarn wasn't just white, it was different shades of white, from ivory to champagne, vanilla to eggshell. The colors ran in long curving stripes, each stripe several inches thick.

"It's beautiful," Mary said.

Roger was back at work, his long bamboo needles shaping a pinkish white stripe.

"Roger and Michael were regulars here,"

Alice explained. "Every Wednesday for, what? Five years?"

"Seven," Roger said.

"Seven years," Alice repeated, as if this even surprised her a bit. "And could those boys knit! The sweaters they made! I still remember the beautiful cables Michael could knit. Nothing like Michael's cables."

"Why did you stop coming?" Mary asked. "Did you move away?"

Roger looked at her, and she saw that his pale blue eyes welled with tears. "No," he said, "no. We live just down the road."

"They have this eighteenth-century farmhouse," Alice continued, "that they completely renovated. Everything perfect."

Roger glanced at her.

"Everything perfect," Alice said firmly. "And every year they gave a New Year's Eve party that you couldn't believe. Roger is the chef, and Michael is the baker. He always made a bûche de Noël. If I close my eyes, I can still taste it."

"No more parties these days," Roger said, sighing.

Alice reached into her knitting basket, which seemed to hold an endless number of supplies, and pulled out a pair of knitting needles, squinting at them before she handed them to Mary. "Get to work," she instructed. "Cast on in this yarn. The color's called snow. Isn't that appropriate?"

Mary took the yarn and the needles even as she demurred. "I couldn't work on something this lovely. I'm not a very good knitter at all."

"It's a straight knit," Alice said. "I'll tell you when to decrease."

Ellen nudged Mary gently with her knee. "It needs to get done tonight," she said softly. "You can only help."

One of the things Mary always had trouble figuring out was how much of a tail she needed to cast on and not run out. She guessed wrong and had to undo all the cast-on stitches. Then wrong again. Once more her mind drifted back home. By now Dylan might be asleep, despite his promise to wait up. Despite that strong kiss he'd left her with. The other night, he'd blurted, "Maybe we should try and have another baby." Before Mary could answer, he'd said, "Forgive me. I could never do that. Never." "I'm too old anyway," Mary had said, even though she didn't know if that was true or not. Every week she read in *People* magazine — the only thing she ever read — about actresses in their late forties having babies, twins and then even another baby after that. The thought had crossed her mind. But she'd dismissed it as foolish, as desperate.

"Two inches a stitch and you can't go wrong," Roger said.

"Thanks," she said.

They sat knitting as the snow fell outside and the small white lights twinkled in the bushes. From time to time Alice spoke, remembering a cake Michael had made for her birthday one year, or the lilac bush they planted in her yard. "French lilacs," she said. "So lovely."

Dylan did wait up for her, even though it was almost midnight before she slipped into bed beside him.

"I thought you'd be early," he said.

She repeated what Ellen had whispered to her while Roger and Alice folded the beautiful white blanket and carefully wrapped it in shiny red paper.

"A man was there making a present for his dying lover. He won't live until Christmas, so he sat at Big Alice's all day and into the night making this extraordinarily beautiful blanket to give him tomorrow."

Dylan took her hand in his.

"I wanted to tell him that someday he would be walking down the street and realize that time had finally passed and that he was all right. It's what people keep telling me will happen. But I'm not sure it's true."

"Honestly," Dylan said, "I wonder where this will all lead."

Mary tugged her hand away. "Where what will lead?" she said.

"Without Stella, it's hard to remember who we are."

She considered this. "Or who we should be now."

Mary waited for him to say more, but he didn't.

Then she told him what Ellen had said in the snowy parking lot.

"Tomorrow," Mary said, "I learn how to make socks."

■ ■ ■ ■

PART FOUR:
SOCKS

■ ■ ■ ■

The history of the humble sock is a long
and interesting one. . . .
— Nancy Bush,
*Folk Socks: The History and Techniques of
Handknitted Footwear*

7
ELLEN

On city streets or navigating subway systems, Mary could find anything. The Paris Métro, the London Underground, the canal-crossed alleys of Amsterdam. But Providence, this city where she still felt like a visitor, remained a mystery.

The sky was a flinty gray, cloudless and flat. The familiar landmarks — historic streets, the run-down buildings of the downtown area, the jumble of highways with their endless construction — vanished as she headed toward the Armory District. Here, bodegas sat at corners, boarded-up buildings overshadowed newly renovated Victorian houses painted happy shades of purple and yellow and green, and the fortress-like Armory, empty and eerie, dominated.

Mary glanced at Ellen's address, scrawled on the back of the receipt from the yarn and tiny number one needles she'd bought to make the socks. The yarn miraculously created a complicated pattern of stripes and zigzags no matter how loosely it was knit. "You'll be amazed," Ellen had promised in her soft, nervous voice.

The streets were empty. Mary hesitated in front of a pale pink house with bright blue trim. Across the street was a park, also deserted except for a young black teenager, his head covered with a white piece of cloth tied kerchief-style and the hood of his sweatshirt. He paced. The wind blew hard, sending small gusts of dirt and random litter into brief spirals. Mary thought of Lulu's story, and shivered.

Ellen, with her vintage dresses and sweet face and Ziploc bags of yarn and half-knit socks, did not fit into this landscape. Although Mary seldom came to this part of the city, she knew that it attracted young hipsters boasting tattoos and piercings, or newly married couples with small down payments investing in the hope that the neighborhood would come around. Holly lived here somewhere, Mary remembered. And yesterday Eddie had called to tell her about a new breakfast place nearby. "You could go and try it out," he'd said hopefully. But despite a few trendy stores that sold Swedish housewares and funky jewelry, more people moved out than in, overrun by drug dealers and muggings.

This was it. Number 74. The boy in the park squinted at Mary as she climbed from her car and locked it, then checked to be sure it was indeed locked. Her mind drifted, as it often did, to San Francisco, to the view of bright blue sky and the nearby bay that used to greet her every morning as she left her apartment in North Beach. The streets smelled of baking bread, strong coffee, salt air. Thinking of this made her nose twitch against the bracing cold and strong odor of garbage.

Up the stairs to the front door, and just as Ellen had described, Mary found three doorbells, none of them marked. "Ring the middle one and wait for me to buzz you in," she'd said.

Mary pressed the buzzer, and waited. It was 10 a.m., exactly the time she'd been told to come. Even with getting lost and circling the park twice before finding the house, she'd managed to arrive on time. She marched in place to keep warm. She rang the buzzer again. The windows in the bottom apartment were decorated with press-on snowflakes, already peeling.

When the buzzer finally did ring, she grabbed the doorknob and quickly yanked the door open. Inside, the smells of gas and cabbage. A dark hallway with scuffed parquet floors. The stairs were covered in cheap dark green carpet. An open door awaited her at the top and she moved toward it, the way she moved toward everything these days, slowly, as if walking through gauze.

"Hello," Mary called. Then, when she got no answer, "Hello?"

"Back here!"

Mary stepped inside, into a living room filled with musical instruments. A cello, a fiddle, two banjos. Other stringed things Mary didn't recognize. She had to step over them to move in the direction of the voice that had called to her. More instruments lined the wall that ended at the kitchen, a small ugly room with ancient appliances in avocado green and a strange collection of plastic hoses, measuring cups, and bottled water. Through the kitchen and down a dark hall with closed doors, and then finally, at the end, a smattering of light, an open door.

"I made it, Ellen," Mary said.

But when she walked into the room at the end of the hall she found not Ellen, but a young girl in a hospital bed and a boy in a chair beside her.

"Oh," Mary said, stepping back.

The girl smiled. She was fourteen or

fifteen, with long pale blond hair, sunken cheeks flushed red, and two thin tubes snaking into her nose. Mary recognized the gurgle of an oxygen tank, the smell of sickness, and she stepped back even farther.

"I'm Bridget," the girl said. "You're looking for my mom?" She rolled her eyes. "She always does this. She forgets to tell me someone might show up. I mean, I could have put twinkly lights on my oxygen or something."

"She was going to help me make socks," Mary said, struck dumb to find herself in the very place she most hated to be — around a sick child. Ellen hadn't mentioned a daughter, she was certain of that. Certainly not a sick daughter. She held up her bag. Knitting needles lay in the girl's lap, and a long train of sparkly yarn.

"Socks," Bridget said, rolling her eyes again. "They're impossible, you know. I'm making the world's longest scarf." She held it up for Mary to see.

"Pretty," Mary said, wanting to flee.

"Have you ever heard of Sadako?"

Mary shook her head no.

"Really? She's this amazing girl who survived Hiroshima. You know, the A bomb? Only to be struck with this horrible deadly cancer. I guess a lot of survivors got it. From

151

the radiation. So her friend decided that if she made a thousand cranes out of origami, Sadako would live, despite all odds. So all of her friends, and then all these Japanese schoolchildren, and eventually the whole world started making origami cranes. But they didn't reach a thousand and she died. I can't do origami so I'm knitting this scarf until it's a thousand feet long." She lay back, out of breath, and closed her eyes. "Jeb, how many miles are a thousand feet?" she said without opening them.

"I don't think it's *any* miles. I think a mile is like *five* thousand feet," the boy said. His hair was dark and curly; beneath it his eyes shone green above a narrow face.

"Drat," Bridget said. "It would be nice to knit a mile-long scarf."

"Could you tell your mother I came?" Mary said.

"She had to go to the drugstore and stuff," Jeb explained quietly. "Sometimes things get a little worse. You know."

Mary found herself watching Bridget's shallow breath, the small up-and-down of her chest, the way she'd sat and watched Stella, willing her to keep breathing. She had grown short of breath herself that long hospital night in her frantic attempts to keep her daughter alive.

"That's all right," Mary said, wanting to go but unable to shift her gaze from Bridget.

"So I'll tell her that who came by?" Jeb was asking.

Mary inhaled deeply. Exhaled. Finally turned away. "Mary," she said.

It was enough to send her into her bed. Ellen had a daughter and that daughter was very sick. Mary didn't want a friend with a sick daughter. She didn't want to know a young girl who was going to die.

"But maybe she's recovering from something," Dylan had said.

His optimism made her angry.

In the morning he would leave for work and she would pretend to get up. She would even get dressed, like she had somewhere to go. She would sit at the kitchen table eating toast, feigning interest in the newspaper. She would comment on a headline, or read a piece of a review to him. Sometimes he quizzed her cautiously. "So you're going to hang out with that woman from knitting?" he'd say. Or, "So you might call Eddie today?" And Mary would nod and pretend that anything was possible. When Dylan bent to kiss her goodbye, Mary smiled up at him as if she were going to have a good day.

From the window, she watched him drive

away, a man in a suit going to his office. A man who didn't have a clue that his wife was getting worse. A man, she thought, who could still go into an office every day and defend clients and write briefs and go to court and even have friendly cocktails with his partners after work. She watched Holly pull up and leave Christmas cookies on the front step and Eddie slide an invitation to the office Christmas party through her mail slot.

Across the street, the neighbors had put electric candles in all the windows and they glowed bright all day. They had put a big fat wreath on their door. Not just a basic wreath, but a complicated one made of greenery and small blue berries and gold ribbon. And the house next door had the biggest Christmas tree anyone had ever seen, an obscene tree, really, with tinsel and garland and colored blinking lights.

She couldn't even knit. Instead, she put on the television and watched chefs on the Food Network make impossibly complicated meals. One made pudding out of mortadella. One made marshmallows from scratch. Mary hated these chefs, with their efficiency and creativity. They demonstrated how to core a pineapple, peel a mango, split a vanilla bean and remove its seeds.

When the phone rang, she listened as people left her messages. "Let me take you Christmas shopping," Jodie shouted into the answering machine. "Scratch that. It's a stupid idea. I'm sorry." Eddie called several times, reminding her to come to the Christmas party. "I left an invitation," he said. Scarlet asked her to come to knitting; that was how Mary knew it was Wednesday and that she'd been in bed for almost a week.

The next time the phone rang, Mary answered it. If it was Eddie, she would accept an assignment. If it was Scarlet or Lulu, she would agree to go to the knitting circle. The phone seemed, suddenly, important. A lifeline. A way out of bed, at least.

But it was her mother.

"Do you know what day today is?" her mother was saying.

"Wednesday," Mary said.

"No," her mother said. "Well, yes. But I mean the date. It's Pearl Harbor Day," her mother continued without waiting for an answer.

"Pearl Harbor *Day?*" Mary said.

"You know something, Mary? You mince words. You're too particular. It's not Pearl Harbor *Day,* like an official holiday or something. It's the anniversary. Don't you even turn on the TV?"

Mary's eyes drifted to her television screen where a chef was making a salsa out of strange ingredients like peaches and ancho chiles.

"All morning it's been Pearl Harbor this and Pearl Harbor that. Personally, I'm sick of it. Enough already."

"Thank you for that, Mom. Now, if you don't mind, I'm in the middle of something —"

"I hope this isn't what your life is, Mary," her mother said. "Not doing anything at all day after day. Not staying connected to the world or people or —"

"My daughter died, Mom, and I don't give a shit about what day it is."

"I know," her mother said.

"You don't know, okay? So stop trying to help me. Please. Stop."

"Listen, honey, I could come up there for Christmas," her mother said.

The chef was putting the salsa on lamb chops of all things.

"Don't do that," Mary said. "I don't have the . . ." The what? she wondered. Stamina? Energy? Patience? ". . . the holiday spirit," she said finally.

"On the Weather Channel the whole Northeast is one big blue cold front coming in from somewhere freezing. You and Dylan can go somewhere warm and get away from all the cold weather and the commercialism of the holiday. My friend down here, Kay? You've heard me speak of her?"

"I've got to go," Mary interrupted. "I'm making this really complicated dinner. Lamb chops with a peach and ancho chile salsa. You have no idea."

Her mother was quiet for so long that Mary thought perhaps her mother had hung up on her. But then she said, "I know, Mary-la. I know."

When she was very young, her mother would whisper this name to her. Mary-la, her mother had said, her first small offering of comfort since Stella had died.

Mary woke to a chef telling a woman why her coq au vin never turned out right. He was going to help her. "This," he told her, "is Food 911." If only there was Grief 911, Mary thought. A number to call where a handsome energetic man would come to your house and explain everything you'd been doing wrong. Then he would fix your grief, your broken heart.

Wait. Someone *had* come. Mary squinted her swollen eyes to find Dylan standing at her side, his overcoat covered with a light dusting of snow.

"Uh-oh," Mary said.

"You don't get up at all?" he said, his face crumpled with worry.

She pointed to the TV. "That man makes house calls," she said. "He fixes cooking disasters."

Gently, Dylan took the remote from her and clicked off the television.

"Eddie called me at the office."

Mary licked her lips, shrugged.

Dylan reached into his pocket and pulled out two airline tickets.

"Oh, dear," Mary said. "Did my mother call you too?"

"No, I thought of this all on my own." Dylan sat beside her on the bed. "I asked myself where was a place that made you happy and right away I thought: San Francisco. When I met you, you told me you could never live anywhere else."

"And here I am," Mary said. "Happy as a clam."

"I need to feel happy again," Dylan said. "I can't go on feeling like this."

Mary shrugged, wanting to give him that happiness, but unable to do it.

"We leave on Friday. Stay through New Year's."

Mary allowed this fullness in her chest to rise. "Thank you," she said.

"When we come back, this fucking year will be over," Dylan said.

Mary closed her eyes, let him cradle her in his arms, and tried to see it: the view from that hill. Blue sky. Sparkling bay.

Before they left, Dylan talked Mary into going with him to a grief group. Dylan had gone alone a few times, and come home red-eyed and exhausted, full of sad stories of loss. Children who fell out of windows, died without explanation, grew into adulthood only to die of heart attacks or cancer or an accident at work.

"How is this supposed to make me feel better?" she'd said.

But now, the promise of escape in a few days, of a New Year ahead, and her husband's growing frustration with her, made Mary agree to go.

Oddly, the group met in the very hospital where Stella had died. Driving into the parking lot, Mary did not see the glow of the streetlights or the security guard watching the cars. Instead, she saw herself, sitting beside her daughter, telling her, foolishly, that she would be all right.

"I can't go in there," Mary told Dylan. "Who has a grief group in a hospital?"

"Once you get inside it'll be fine," he said.

Wasn't that what she had believed just eight months ago when she lifted Stella into her arms and walked through those automatic doors for help? Then, thirty-six hours later, she'd walked out empty-handed, and nothing had been fine since.

Still, she let Dylan lead her through those very doors. Mary glimpsed a child on her mother's lap, head resting against her chest; a boy crying; a toddler screaming; a woman with an infant in her arms.

"This way," Dylan said, guiding her by the elbow in the opposite direction.

The elevator door opened and there was a folding table covered in pamphlets and officious-looking women bustling around with sign-in sheets, name tags, and smiles.

Soon, she was signed in and name-tagged and handed pamphlets. *Getting Through the Holidays. The Worst Loss of All. A Broken Heart Still Beats.*

"Some of us," one of the women said, "write the name of our child on our name tag." She pointed to her own. *Frannie,* it said. Then, beneath it, *Sabrina.*

Mary did not want to write Stella's name on this name tag. But the woman seemed to be waiting for her to do just that.

"Thank you," Mary mumbled, and walked away.

Frannie, as it turned out, ran the meeting. She smiled and welcomed everyone, and then explained that they were going to go around the circle and each say their child's name and age and how they died.

"I'm leaving," Mary whispered to Dylan.

"Ssshhh," he said, and squeezed her hand.

An Asian woman was crying and telling a complicated story in broken English. Then an older man started talking about the daughter he'd cared for with Lou Gehrig's disease and he too started crying. Frannie nodded and passed boxes of Kleenex. Crying parents talked about mistakes they'd made: missing the signs of drug abuse, not checking if a car seat was buckled in properly, leaving their child alone for just five minutes.

And then without warning everyone was looking at her. She couldn't speak.

"Our daughter Stella," Dylan was saying, "was five years old."

Mary pushed her chair back with a loud squeak. "I'm sorry," she said, though she wasn't sure what exactly she was sorry for. With her head bent to avoid all of those eyes on her, Mary quickly left the room.

The hospital walls, with their brightly colored tiled murals made by children — Marika, age 4, and Sally, age 7 — seemed to mock her loss. When she finally made it to the car, she was crying so hard she couldn't even unlock the door. The pamphlets in her hand looked childlike. *Don't Make Changes for One Year. Don't Push Yourself. Don't Take Long Trips as a Way to Heal; You Always Have to Come Home Again.*

The hard awful truth was that they needed their daughter back. Escape was just the thing for them. Four months after Stella died in this very building, she and Dylan were on an airplane to Italy where, jet-lagged, she had finally slept. In Italy, she did not see Stella's fingerprints on everything. It was as if she'd come to a pure place, with ridiculously tall sunflowers reaching upward and the safe refuge of plane trees overhead like a mother's arms, enveloping her.

"Mary? It's Ellen," the voice on the other end of the phone said. "From knitting?"

Mary frowned. She did not want to speak to Ellen. She wanted Ellen and Ellen's sick daughter to disappear.

"This is a bad time," Mary said. "We're getting ready to go away for the holidays and I'm kind of crazy."

She was, in fact, packing.

"I just wanted to apologize for the other

day. You came all that way and —"

"No, no," Mary said. "No problem. But I've really got to go —"

"I thought I'd see you at knitting on Wednesday but when you didn't come I figured I'd just call and apologize and set up another date."

Mary thought of Ellen's daughter, knitting a thousand-foot-long scarf to ward off death. "I'll tell you what," she said, "I'll give you a call when we get back."

"Okay," Ellen said.

She sounded like she might keep talking, so Mary said, "Great! Bye!" and hung up. Her heart was pounding. There was no way she was going to call Ellen. No way.

For those ten days in San Francisco, Mary pretended to be happy even though she felt like she'd left something important behind. The ache hummed through her body. At night she'd wake up, startled and confused, the hotel room disorienting her, and she'd think: Where's Stella? And then she'd remember and sit up, awake, missing her daughter, that humming reverberating deep, deep inside her.

Dylan urged her to call her old friends, but instead Mary avoided them. Some of them had come out to Stella's funeral, and the blur of their tearstained faces, their stunned looks, made Mary never want to see them again. The ones who hadn't come, she couldn't think of what she would say to them. She wasn't angry that they didn't fly across the country. Instead, she felt like she'd lost them too somehow. Was she expected to talk about what had happened? Was she expected to act a certain way?

Back in Providence, a few weeks after Stella died, Mary had been putting gas in her car at the corner station when a mother from Stella's school pulled up at the pump beside her.

"Mary?" the woman said. She had seemed surprised that Mary was standing there, getting gas for her car.

"Hello, Jill," Mary had said.

But Jill could do nothing but stare, as if she was taking inventory. Shoes. Pants. Shirt. Face. Hair. What was she looking for? Mary felt that she too was expected to disappear, along with Stella. But her car still needed gas. She still needed things out in the world.

"I think about you every day," Jill finally said.

"Thank you," Mary said.

"If Laci had died, I wouldn't even be able to stand up."

"Yes you would."

"No. I don't know how you can do it."

This happened over and over. Women in the supermarket, in the post office, staring at her as if she should not be alive herself. And Mary expected that her old friends here would be the same. Except April. April had flown out for the funeral and stayed, holding Mary's hand, answering her phone, even somehow making her laugh. She'd come back a few months later and done the same, sorting unpaid bills, forging Mary's name on checks, and writing thank-you notes.

On New Year's Eve they accepted April's invitation to dinner at her house. "Just the four of us," April had promised. What Mary had not thought about was that April had a daughter now, a three-year-old named Cassie. When Mary and Dylan walked into April's apartment on Dolores Street, the first thing, the only thing, Mary saw was Cassie.

Since Stella had died, Mary had broken down over the distant sight of a little girl with hair the same color as Stella's. She'd had to leave the supermarket more than once simply because a little girl sitting in the grocery cart had smiled at her a certain way. But what really slayed her was a little girl's hands. The dimpled knuckles, the pink fingernails. How could she spend an evening here and not see Cassie's hands?

April bustled into the room, dressed in a black sparkly minidress with a turquoise boa, her arms outstretched for hugs.

"We've got champagne and gorgeous hors d'oeuvres and tenderloin for dinner. I've spent a fortune."

Mary managed a smile, and it was as if April knew.

"And I've found a babysitter on New Year's Eve," she said, putting her hand on Mary's arm. "The last one in the entire Bay Area, I'm sure."

Mary found her way into that hug.

Staring out the airplane window as they headed east, toward home, Mary thought of a new year without Stella. Sighing, she pulled down the shade on the window, blocking out the endless clouds. Dylan snored lightly beside her. A new year, Mary said to herself. She took the airsick bag from the seat pocket and wrote those three small words on it. Then she made a list. Go back to work. Read a book. Learn to knit socks. She crossed this last one off, then wrote it again, adding: Maybe. Dylan stirred, readjusted himself, then began to snore again.

Mary picked up the knitting in her lap, and continued.

The first day back home, she woke up and took a shower and pulled on her Betsey Johnson miniskirt with the big pink buttons and her snow boots and her baggy black winter coat with the hot pink scarf and hat she'd knit. She walked to the Coffee Exchange and got a large latte to go. She walked the ten blocks to the office, navigating unevenly shoveled sidewalks and mounds of snow and patches of ice to get to the old jewelry factory that housed the newspaper. She walked in and everything, even eight months later, was exactly the same.

Mary stood just inside the door and took it all in. Holly was working at the computer, the phone headset attached, her black Buddy Holly glasses already slipped to the tip of her nose. Steam from some organic tea rose from a cup at her elbow, sending the smell of dirt and grass and something spicy into the overheated front office.

Behind the glass doors, Mary saw Eddie pacing in his office, his Kramer hair bouncing as he moved, his stomach straining against a worn argyle sweater. He was pacing in front of Jessica, one of the feature writers, who always missed deadlines, refused to rewrite, and swore like crazy. Jessica turned men on with her dirty language and tall, too-skinny body. She kept her hair cut close to her head, and wore frighteningly oversized jewelry. Jessica was from Texas, and after she told one of her stories about how ballsy she was, she always said, "Don't y'all mess with Texas!"

There was the mural of an old-fashioned newsroom with comic book characters that one of Eddie's ex-girlfriends had painted.

Holly glanced up at her. "Whoa," she said. "Look what the cat dragged in." Holly always spoke at a slower speed than the rest of the world, and hearing her voice made Mary smile.

Mary walked past Holly and over to Eddie's office. Tapping on the door to get his attention, Mary wiggled her fingers at him when he finally stopped pacing long enough to see her there.

Eddie grinned and motioned her inside.

His office, with its familiar smells of ink and carbon paper and Wite-Out — Eddie still preferred a typewriter to a computer — made Mary feel like she had come home. She put down her latte and went to give Eddie a hug. He hugged her back, his sweater scratchy against her cheek.

"Enough frivolity," Eddie said. "I'm putting you right to work." He handed her assignment sheets. "A new Indian restaurant in Downcity that's open only for lunch. A show opening at the RISD Museum on the male nude. And what about this French-American School? Who goes there anyway?"

"French-Americans?" Mary said.

"Ha-ha," Eddie said. "Now get to work."

Jessica, looking bored with Eddie and Mary and life, stood slowly. "I'll be at City Hall," she said, "if anybody needs me."

Mary followed her out of Eddie's office and then walked into her own. Everything was different and everything was the same. Someone had taken down all the pictures of Stella and brought them to Mary months ago, leaving the walls blank. Her desk was empty, with a thin layer of dust where her notes and press releases and memos used to crowd each other. Even her screen saver of Stella blowing bubbles had been replaced with a new one of tropical fish, endlessly swimming.

Mary turned on the radio to the all-news station, a habit that drove everyone in the office crazy. How can you write or think while all these people are talking? Holly used to say. She preferred Cold Play or the White Stripes pouring from her iPod; Eddie played Dean Martin and Bing Crosby records on a beat-up phonograph; Jessica liked country. The writers created their own world in their tiny office. Even now, Mary could hear the babble of different music beyond her own office.

She closed the door, sat at her desk, and read the details of her assignment sheet. Soon, she was making notes, making phone calls, making appointments. At lunch in the Indian restaurant, she shared samosas and nan with the owner. Before she knew it, Holly was at her office door, saying good-bye.

"I'm going to my yoga class," Holly said. After Stella died, she had taken Mary to one of these classes. It was held in a hot room to help you sweat out impurities. But it had only made Mary nauseated. "Want to lock up?" Holly was saying.

"I'm the last one?" Mary said, surprised.

Holly nodded. "Welcome back."

When Mary finally did lock up and walk into the dark evening, clutching a bag of saag paneer and chicken tikka leftovers, she had to lean against the brick building and try to catch her breath. By the time she got home and reheated the food and poured herself a glass of wine, she had calmed down again. The phone rang just as Dylan's car pulled into the driveway.

"Mary? It's Ellen. It's a new year, right?" Ellen said. "Time to knit some socks?"

And because she was trying to have a normal day, and the French-American School was over in Ellen's neighborhood and Mary had an appointment to go there the next day, and because her husband was walking in and looking at her with such relief, and the saag paneer was green and fragrant, Mary said, "Yes."

"Sometimes," Ellen said, "my daughter tries to go to school. She has a portable oxygen tank and a wheelchair and her boyfriend Jeb takes her around all day. It exhausts her. But she wants to try."

Mary swallowed hard. She was sitting on the lumpy moss green sofa knitting what would eventually be the band of a sock. *K1, p1,* on size one needles. Impossible. And she would never make it if Ellen kept talking about her daughter and oxygen and illness. She willed her to stop, to just talk about this most simple act of knitting.

Ellen had moved all the musical instruments to make room for the two of them, but the dip of the sofa made her sit too close. Mary could smell the strawberry of Ellen's shampoo.

"I have to let her try," Ellen said.

"Uh-huh," Mary said, concentrating on her knitting. Such tiny needles. *K1, p1.*

"It's her heart," Ellen said, after a few minutes of welcome silence.

Mary shifted uncomfortably, glancing at Ellen's long open face, her deceptively happy eyes. Should she mention Stella?

Ellen met her gaze. "Sometimes we go along for a bit and I can almost forget she's so sick. Then she takes a turn for the worse and all hell breaks loose. Like that day you were here."

In spite of herself, Mary asked, "What's wrong with her heart?"

Ellen touched Mary's arm lightly. "Now just knit for six inches. Pretty soon you'll start to see the pattern emerge." Ellen paused. "Stories are kind of like knitting, aren't they? Everything intertwined. Everything connected." She took a deep breath. "It's complicated," she said.

Ellen was young, Mary realized. It was this pain that made her seem older.

Ellen sipped her herbal tea, staring into the glass as if it held her future. Or maybe her past, Mary thought, peeking at her. As soon as she looked at Ellen, though, she dropped all of the stitches from one of the tiny needles.

"Shit," Mary said.

Gently, Ellen took it from Mary, and carefully placed all twenty-one stitches back on the needle.

"This relaxes you?" Mary said. "Knitting on toothpicks?"

"You just knit," Ellen said. "You'll see."

"What's with all the instruments?" Mary said.

"I was a folksinger," Ellen said, blushing. "I've played these instruments since I was a little girl. I grew up in Appalachia. The mountains in North Carolina. My mother taught me the guitar and the banjo. My grandmother taught me how to fiddle. My father and my uncles and my granddaddy traveled around and sang at weddings and funerals. The Brighton Boys. That's what they were called." She hesitated as if maybe Mary might have heard of them.

Mary shrugged apologetically.

"Anyways," she continued, "my mother and her mother and all of us sang down in Asheville sometimes, and once we went all the way to Chattanooga to perform. I was just a little bitty thing. And shy as a coon in the daylight."

Mary looked up again, laughing. "A coon?"

"You'd better keep your eye on your

173

stitches," Ellen said, taking Mary's knitting from her again. She held it up to show her that she'd dropped a needle's worth again.

"Anyways," Ellen continued after she'd picked up the stitches and returned them once more to Mary, "I couldn't hardly talk to anyone without turning red as a July tomato, but hand me a fiddle or a guitar and let me sing and I was a different person. It was like the music spoke for me. And these were all traditional songs, you know. We didn't have a stereo or anything and our radio only got but the one station.

"I was the only one of my parents' children that lived. Three boys all died as wee babies. And one sister lived a month or two. I used to walk up the hill and look at their tiny stones. Boy Brighton. Boy Brighton. Boy Brighton. Then Margaret Brighton, Our Little Angel. No one knew why they all died like that. Mama said they just turned blue real slow and died." Ellen's voice caught. "Of course now I guess I figured it out." She took a breath before she continued.

"Anyways," she said finally, "my grandma used to sew me up the prettiest dresses. Big full skirts and the tops all hand-smocked. And I had shiny black patent leather shoes and white ankle socks with a big old ruffle around the tops. They would wash my hair with eggs to make it shine, and I always wore a great big bow in it, to match my dress. This was when I was only so high, and off we'd go to this place and that and I'd pick up my fiddle and open my mouth and steal the show. But if anyone tried to talk to me, I would throw up. No exaggeration. I would throw up if I had to talk to people. That's strange and I know it and it makes the irony of my life now even more profound since I have to talk to doctors on a daily basis.

"Anyways, I didn't really go to school. There wasn't one nearby. My grandma taught me to sew and to knit with my fingers. She taught me how to kill a chicken, how to clean it, and how to fry it just right. I can take the bitterness out of collard greens and I can tell which mushrooms will kill a man and which'll taste good in rabbit stew. My granddaddy taught me how to hunt and how to fish and how to grow tomatoes as big as a fist. It was Mama who sat with me before supper and showed me the letters and the numbers, and how to read the Bible. But my daddy gave me the gift of music. He could play anything — spoons, jars without tops, washboards, he could even coax a song from certain leaves.

"Pretty soon, it was the Brighton Boys and Little Ellen. And then it wasn't too long before it was Little Ellen and the Brighton Boys. My daddy used to pick me up by the waist so I could see the flyers in the store windows. I would trace my name with my finger and feel a tingle there while I did. 'Don't you forget, though, girl,' Daddy'd say, 'a voice like an angel is both a blessing and a curse.' I only saw it as a blessing, though. It made people listen. It made people smile. Why, it even made people jump out of their chairs and dance. What's the curse in that?

"Well, that curse came in the name of Aidan O'Malley, an Irish boy with a tenor voice that could send chills up your spine from its outright purity and beauty. He came to one of our concerts down in Asheville. By this time, even though I was still called Little Ellen, I had grown up. I was sixteen years old and those ruffled socks and hand-smocked dresses had been handed down to little cousins a long time ago. I still wore country clothes, dresses handmade from thin cotton and big old men's shoes that worked just fine out in the mountains but I guess looked pretty funny even down in Asheville, the biggest city I'd ever seen.

"We sang in this cellar club called the

Potato Cellar because that's what it had been once. It was tiny and smelled like dirt and the people could pack in all sweaty and full of beer and we'd have a good old-fashioned hootenanny down there. I would be a liar if I said I never noticed Aidan till he noticed me. Because I did. I saw his big old blue eyes and this wild mane of black hair and I thought, God keep me from that devil. When we'd show up to sing, first thing I'd do is find him in the crowd. If he didn't come, I'd feel all wrong in my stomach. But if he did, I'd sing right to him. Not looking at him. No! I could never do that. But from my heart to his." Ellen blushed deeply. "I know how foolish that sounds. But I was just a foolish girl then.

"Anyways, one day we go to play at a big outside festival with dozens of singers from all over Appalachia, and there are hundreds of people there, and it's July and hot as a dog with the brightest sun you've ever seen. We're scheduled to go up late in the day, so I was left to wander by myself. But I was not someone who would go up to PeePaw Lewis, one of the greatest fiddlers ever, and introduce myself and talk awhile, or sit down at a table of ladies and ask them how they baked such a good blackberry pie. What I did was fill a plate with ham and biscuits and beans and potato salad and walk way far from everybody, down by a small creek in the woods. I took off my shoes and sat on a rock with my feet dangling in that warm creek water and I daydreamed about songs and maybe even about Aidan O'Malley. Then, all of a sudden like, I happened to see Aidan sitting on another rock a ways away. My heart started going crazy. I couldn't believe my good luck. Or maybe my misfortune."

"But surely he had followed you there," Mary said.

Ellen looked at her, surprised. "Why would you ever in a million years think that?"

Mary laughed. "Maybe I've had all the romantic notions drained out of me. It just makes sense that he would have seen you go off and that he would follow you there."

"You got five inches there," Ellen said, "so pay attention to what you're doing. One more inch and then you've got to turn the heel."

"That's the way I was around that man. I couldn't think straight. I couldn't tell which end was up and which was down. He made me dizzy and he made me dumb."

Mary turned her attention back to the sock. A pattern had appeared, a seemingly complicated pattern that reminded her of an old Fair Isle sweater she'd had as a girl. "Look what I've done," she said.

Ellen grinned at her. Something about Ellen made Mary feel safe.

"So what happened with this Aidan character?" Mary said.

"That is such an enormous question that I'm not even sure how to answer it. What happened that day? Well, I can start there. I saw him and he came right on over. 'You're Little Ellen,' he said, and of course all I could do was nod like a bullfrog. 'You sing like an angel,' he said, 'yes, you do.' Turns out he was a singer himself. Straight from Ireland too. He knew all the traditional songs, and before I knew it we were laying on that sweet green grass by the creek singing together with that hot sun beating down on us. My goodness, when I talk about it I can smell that creek, a little sulfury, and the rich earth that is Appalachian earth. All of a sudden I realized that time had been passing and I needed to get back. So I jumped up and found my shoes, all flustered, like I'd been doing something wrong instead of just laying there singing away the afternoon. Aidan, he jumped up too, but he was all calm. He pointed his finger at me and he said, 'Little Ellen, I am going to marry you

179

someday and keep that voice of yours all to myself. You wait and see.' "

"He kept his word, didn't he?" Mary said. "He's your husband, isn't he?"

Ellen frowned, good and deep, and chewed her lip. "It's time to turn that heel," she said.

"Isn't he?" Mary asked again.

"No, he is not. Never was neither."

Mary waited, but Ellen didn't say anything more.

"Okay," Mary said. "Time to turn the heel."

Ellen turned the sock to the purl side. "Purl eleven stitches. Purl two together. Purl one. Turn the sock around."

It sounded like poetry, the way Ellen said these words.

"He took me away from there. That's the first thing I can never forgive him for," Ellen said softly. "Appalachia runs in my blood. If you've never seen the mist over the Appalachian Mountains come evening, then you've never seen anything at all."

"Then why did you leave?" Mary asked.

"He started courting me. Bringing me small bouquets of wildflowers, and sitting on my porch strumming and singing and whispering to me with that Irish brogue. He was from the town of Galway. He would go on and on about the Atlantic Ocean. How big and stormy it was. How magnificent. He would go on and on about the little islands across from Galway. He would speak to me in Irish and it was like he was putting a spell on me. When he was away from me, all I could do was think about him. And when he was with me, I couldn't think at all. A very unhealthy situation."

She glanced at Mary's sock. "Now slip one stitch. Then knit five. Good. Knit two together through the back loop. Why, look at you! You're a pro at this. Knit one and turn it around again."

Ellen instructed her through the next two rows. "Now you just keep on repeating all that until you've used up all the stitches on either side of that old gap and there are just twelve stitches on that needle."

"This is going to turn into the heel of a sock?" Mary asked.

"You bet," Ellen said.

"So?" Mary prodded. "What happened?"

"So finally my mama takes me aside one day and she tells me to take that boy down into the woods and to make love to him until I got him out of my system."

"Your mother said that?"

"My mama was a practical woman. She knew a person couldn't live so full of love. I took a big old bath with lavender in it and brushed my hair until it was all shiny and when Aidan came up our path I ran to meet him. 'Let's go pick some blackberries,' I said. We walked and picked these perfect blackberries. All fat and purple.

"Mama said don't come back until I was clearheaded. But I never did get my head cleared. Once I started, I only got more full of him. If I couldn't think straight before, why, he made me go brain-dead. We stayed away that afternoon and that night and the next morning. Until Aidan said, 'I'm taking you back to Galway with me. With your voice and all the people I know there, we'll get rich and famous in no time.'

"So we stumbled back up to Mama and I said, 'I'm going away with him.' Well, she dragged me inside and said, 'Don't be stupid, girl. What you two have been doing gets done every day by men and women and goats and cats and every one of God's creatures. That isn't love. You don't run off with a boy just because you like doing that with him.'

"She tried to talk sense into me. But I wouldn't listen. I packed my things and took my fiddle and walked down that path with Aidan O'Malley into my future.

"If I close my eyes, I can see that old

house, and hear the creak of the rocking chair on the front porch, and smell my Appalachian Mountains. But that day I just left it all behind. I had just turned seventeen years old that summer. A child, like my very own Bridget is now.

"Before I knew it I was living in a flat in Galway, Ireland, with no heat or hot water and my fingers were so cold it was hard to fiddle. Plus we were so broke we were living on cabbage and potatoes and day-old bread. Aidan took to yelling at me if I complained or if I cried, so I tried to be quiet about it. Then you know how it goes. When you believe things can't get any worse, they go on and get worse. So when I was late one month, I talked myself into believing it was from not eating so good. A girl needs nutrition to keep herself regular. But when I missed a second time, and I found certain smells, like those potatoes and salty air and even Aidan himself, made me feel all queasy like, I couldn't deny it any longer.

"When I told Aidan, he said, 'I thought you were taking care of things.'

"I didn't have any idea how a girl took care of things like that.

"Then he said, 'I got you booked at clubs all over the county, and the next one too. We need the money.'

"I guess I had already figured out we weren't getting rich no matter how many jobs he booked. But I still hoped he'd marry me. Especially with a baby coming. He never said a word about it, though, like that wasn't why I had come across that ocean with him.

"Back home, Old Lady Hera way up in the hills had a way of getting rid of babies. You drank something and the baby just slid right out of you, nice and easy. I had heard it didn't even look like a baby, just a glob of blood. But I didn't know who could do such a thing in Galway. That's the second thing he did that I could never forgive. He made me think, ever so briefly, about getting rid of my daughter. I tell you, that man was the devil.

"He took to dropping me at whatever rooming house was putting us up in that village, and he'd go to the pub and find some girl and go home with her. Some girl who didn't have swollen ankles or a stomach out to here. My skin got all splotchy too, and that's when I knew I was having a daughter because a girl takes her mother's beauty. She needs to.

"One day, we were in some village somewhere. The rain had finally stopped and it almost looked pretty, all the thatched-roof houses and green hills in the distance. Aidan was acting kindly that day, even though he could hardly stand to look at me anymore, what with my big belly and my splotchy face and my hair all lank. But we went and got fish and chips and sat on this stone wall to eat them. There were purple flowers all pretty against the green, and for the first time in a long while I almost felt happy. Aidan even kissed me, like he used to. I was thinking he might coax me into those fields, and I would kiss him until he remembered how much he loved me. Next thing I knew, there's water everywhere.

"Aidan jumped off the wall and said, 'Holy Christ, your water broke.'

" 'It's too soon,' I said. 'My baby's not coming until September.'

" 'He's coming now,' Aidan said.

"I felt so bad for him, all wild-eyed with panic, that I didn't even tell him that the baby was a she, not a he. No sooner did I have that thought than the first pain came and doubled me over.

" 'Holy Christ,' Aidan kept saying. 'We are in the middle of fucking nowhere. Holy Christ.'

"He led me back into the village, stopping every time another pain took me. I had only gone in the ocean one time, but that's what

I kept thinking about, how the waves grabbed hold of me and took me into shore.

"Finally we got to the pub, and it seemed like everyone figured out what was going on as soon as we walked in. An old red-faced lady took me away from Aidan and led me to a back room where there was a narrow bed with the freshest-smelling, whitest sheets I had ever seen.

"Eighteen hours in that room, and the baby just not coming. The pain like a hot iron inside me. Aidan kept saying, 'Holy Christ, Holy Christ, Holy Christ.' He kept saying, 'Somebody's got to help her.' Then that red-faced lady said, 'I got no choice,' and she put her foot up on the end of the bed to brace herself, and she stuck her hand up me and she yanked my baby out. I think for maybe a minute or two I passed out from the pain. But then there was a lot of commotion and I heard the worst words I had ever heard. The red-faced woman said: 'This baby is blue, may God help her.' And right away I thought of home and that row of small stones. Baby Boy Brighton. Baby Boy Brighton. Baby Boy Brighton. Margaret Brighton, Our Little Angel. I thought of my mama saying that those babies were just blue, and they died."

"Ellen," Mary said. Gently, she laid her

knitting on her lap so that she could reach over and place a hand on Ellen's arm. "My God," Mary said.

"You know what it's like for a mother to want to save her child's life?" Ellen said.

Mary wanted to tell Ellen she did know what that was like, that she had once believed a mother's love could save her child. Wasn't that what a mother was meant to do? To protect her child? Now she knew the guilt that came from letting your baby down. But all of those thoughts caught in her throat.

"Somehow she did make it through the night," Ellen said, as if she still marveled at that. "When morning came and she was there, breathing big deep breaths, still tinged blue, Aidan wrapped me in a blanket and carried us, one at a time, to the car. The village women had brought the baby clothes, tiny white things, hand-stitched and soft.

" 'What should we call her?' I asked him as we raced toward Shannon.

" 'We shouldn't call her anything at all,' he said. He kept his eyes on the road ahead. 'It will make it harder when we lose her.'

" 'I'm not going to lose her,' I said.

"After we got to the hospital, and they took her from me, a doctor came in and asked us, 'Any heart disease in your

187

families?'

" 'Course not,' Aidan said.

" 'My mother,' I said. 'She had four babies like this. One lived a month or two. But the others —'

"Turned out the only people who would consider surgery on such a small baby were in Boston, at Children's Hospital.

" 'Then we'll take her there,' I said.

Aidan looked at me without shame and said, 'She's not one to save, Ellen. Even if she makes it to Boston and lives through this surgery, she'll die anyway.'

" 'Is that true?' I asked the doctor.

" 'I've never heard of a case where the child lived past ten.'

"I thought about ten years. A decade. Already I saw Aidan disappearing from my life, growing smaller and smaller right before my eyes.

" 'I'm taking my baby to Boston,' I said. 'I'm saving her life.' Of course, I didn't know it then, but I was saving my own life too. Because if I had let her stay there, and die, I would have stayed, and died too.

"Aidan let us go. He watched me with Bridget in my arms get on that Aer Lingus plane to Boston and he stayed behind.

"Bridget had that operation, and another one when she was three, and another one

188

when she was seven. And now we're waiting for a new heart for her. Without it, she can't live. At night, when I hear sirens, I pray for a match. God forgive me, but I do."

"And Aidan?" Mary managed to ask.

"He calls from time to time. 'It's my dad,' Bridget says, 'calling to see if I've kicked the bucket yet.' I used to send him pictures, and little drawings she'd made, but over time I've come to see he doesn't deserve them. I live here because I can't go home to Appalachia. Too far from a hospital. And even the closest one, in Asheville, couldn't help her. We tried to live in Boston, but the city was too big and I felt nervous there. So we came here. I teach music and I wait for my daughter's new heart."

Mary's hands had stopped knitting, and Ellen covered them with her own as if she too knew Mary's pain.

"Look," Ellen said, "you've turned the heel."

Mary did look, and there was a perfectly shaped heel.

The door opened noisily, and Jeb appeared backwards, pulling Bridget sitting in her wheelchair inside. The girl was pale, and her oxygen pumped loudly.

Ellen jumped to her feet. "Was it a good day?"

"A good day," Bridget managed to gasp.

"I'll put her to bed," Jeb said. "She's tired."

When the room was empty again, and just Ellen and Mary were together, Mary said, "God help me, my own daughter died, Ellen. I couldn't save her and she died. My prayers weren't any good."

"A mother's prayers are always good, Mary," Ellen said. Then, under her breath she whispered, "God bless that child."

8
THE KNITTING CIRCLE

"It's a waste of time, in my opinion," Harriet said. She shook her head, disgusted. "Knitting socks," she muttered.

It was a small group at the knitting circle tonight, below zero temperatures keeping everyone except Ellen, Harriet, and Mary at home.

"I'm staying under every blanket I own," Lulu had told Mary earlier. "You might not see me again until the spring thaw."

"Hot chocolate, warm bread and honey, and all those back issues of *Gourmet* magazine I haven't had time to read," Scarlet had said.

When Mary showed up she learned that Beth too had stayed at home — under the weather, Harriet had explained. Alice had turned the heat on high, and the radiator hissed and sprayed and gurgled as it worked overtime. Ellen arrived with a big thermos of hot milky tea to share.

"Why, I have some shortbread too," Alice had said, and brought out neat wedges of buttery shortbread on a white china plate rimmed with pink roses.

Mary glanced down at the almost-finished sock in her hand. "I don't know," she said. "I think it's kind of amazing."

"*Knitting* is amazing," Harriet said. "Basically you're making knots to create fabric. That's amazing. But to then spend hours making something that is not even going to be seen is plain ridiculous."

"My socks are seen," Ellen said, stretching her legs out in front of her to show off her crazy-patterned socks.

"Frivolous," Harriet said with great finality. She turned her attention back to the sweater she was knitting.

"I can make a dozen pair of socks in the time it takes you to make one of those complicated sweaters," Ellen said.

Harriet didn't look up. "That's what I like about knitting. Its complexities. I like to figure out how to make a pattern appear properly. I don't want to buy yarn that figures it out for me." She glanced over her half-glasses at Ellen. "Have you ever even tried to make a sweater?"

"Of course I have," Ellen said. Even though her cheeks were flushed a bright red, she didn't back down. "I made two Aran sweaters."

"I give up," Mary said. "What's an Aran sweater?"

Alice smiled. She was making a throw blanket in shades of purple, and it draped elegantly over her lap as she knit. "They say the Aran Island women each designed her family's unique pattern so that if her husband or son drowned in a storm, his body could be identified when it washed up on shore."

"Rubbish!" Harriet said.

"You don't believe that one?" Alice said, adding a deep plum yarn to the blanket.

"They're traditional Celtic designs," Harriet said.

"Cable stitch," Ellen said to Mary. "You know, they're called fisherman's sweaters. Cream-colored."

"Difficult to execute," Harriet said. "How much help did Alice have to give you on those?"

"Not me," Alice said. "I've known this girl five years and I've only seen her knit socks."

Ellen blushed. "Not true. I've done hats and even mittens."

"So how did you manage the Aran sweaters?" Harriet asked.

"I was there. On Inisheer, and I took a

workshop," Ellen said, focusing on turning the heel of a sock.

"Did you live in Ireland?" Alice said, laying her needles in her lap. "I never knew."

"Oh," Ellen said nervously. "A lifetime ago."

Mary recognized that. The question you don't want to answer. The territory where you don't want to tread. How many children do you have? That was one of her own.

Quickly, Mary changed the subject.

"Maybe I'm ready to knit a sweater," she said. "This cold weather makes me want to try."

Alice picked up a skein of lilac yarn and began knitting it into her blanket. "It's all just knit or purl. Two simple stitches."

"Maybe I'll knit you a sweater for your birthday," Mary told Dylan.

They had just made love, and she was resting her head on his stomach looking up the long length of his body at him.

"Have you gotten that good?" he said. "I mean sweaters have sleeves and collars and necks."

"Hey!" she said. "I've turned a heel."

"Congratulations," Dylan said. "To celebrate, I'm taking you to a party. Bob's wife is throwing him a fortieth birthday party and all the lawyers are going. With their wives," he added.

She opened her mouth to protest, but before she could speak, a gentle snore came from Dylan. Sighing, Mary disentangled herself from his arms and went out into the kitchen. She poured herself a glass of wine, and made a list of all the things she was afraid might happen:

PEOPLE WON'T KNOW AND THEY'LL ASK ME HOW STELLA IS. PEOPLE WILL KNOW AND THEY'LL ASK HOW I'M DOING.
THIS COUPLE WILL HAVE CHILDREN, LOTS OF THEM, AND ALL OF THEM FIVE-YEAR-OLD GIRLS WITH MEGA-WATT SMILES.
I WILL START TO CRY FOR NO GOOD REASON.
I WILL START TO CRY FOR A GOOD REASON.
I WILL NOT HAVE FUN.
I WILL HAVE FUN.

Mary imagined this last part coming true. Then carefully crossed it off the list.

Dylan couldn't remember if the party was dressy or casual. He couldn't remember if it was dinner or just cocktails. He couldn't remember if it started at six or seven.

"You don't want to go either," Mary said.

"It's Bob!" Dylan said too enthusiastically. "It's going to be a terrific party."

"Right," Mary said, pulling on black panty hose. She wondered if little black dresses had somehow fallen out of fashion. If she'd be overdressed or underdressed. She tried to make herself care about how she looked. But when she looked at herself in the mirror, even with foundation smoothing her skin and bronzer giving her a glow, she still saw the saddest woman in the world.

Dylan slowly drove up and down Paterson Street, staring into each house, searching for a party.

"Are you sure it's tonight?" Mary asked, hoping he would suddenly remember it had been last night and they could go home.

She sighed and looked out the window in the opposite direction, toward the park. The street was lined with big old houses on one side and a playground on the other. She was glad it was dark so the swings and slides and jungle gyms seemed like vague shadowy figures. After school on warm days, she and Stella would come here and meet other mothers with their children. Mary would sit over there with the other women while their kids ran, playing and happy.

Stella used to take off her shoes and socks and run through the grass barefoot. There was always one mother who had to supervise the kids, telling someone to be gentle, someone to wait her turn, offering to push another one on a swing. That was the mother who always remembered to bring snacks, pulling goldfish crackers or pretzels from her Mary Poppins bag, enough for everyone. Mary remembered how that woman had looked at her in distaste. "Barefoot?" she'd said. "Don't you know there are germs everywhere?" Even recalling her words made Mary's stomach tighten. Germs like ringworm or colds. Germs like meningitis.

Later, as they drove away, Stella would gaze at the houses across the street from the park and say, "Wouldn't it be great to live right there?" Her feet would be sandy and her face would be dirty and she'd smell of little-girl sweat and goldfish crackers. Now Mary worried: Had she inhaled enough of her daughter's scent to last her the rest of her life?

"Aha!" Dylan said. "There's Alex and Vicky going into that yellow house! Right night. Right time. Right party."

He parked beside the playground, and Mary glanced in as she got out of the car. Thankfully, it was too dark to see anything. She took a deep breath and followed Dylan across the street and up the porch steps. A plaque on the house said it had been built in 1919, a Queen Anne with a beautiful sloping roof.

Dylan knocked and the door opened, sending happy party sounds into the cold night air.

"Dylan! Mary! I'm so glad you came!"

Dylan put his hand on the small of Mary's back and nudged her forward so that she was looking right at that mother, the one who brought snacks and swung Stella on the swing and warned her of germs lurking everywhere.

"Hon, you remember Bob's wife, Laurie," he said.

Laurie gave Mary that look that said, You poor poor thing.

There. One of the worst things on her list had happened.

Mary forced a smile, hoping there was no Hot Tahiti on her teeth.

"What a beautiful house," she said, stepping inside. Her voice grew shrill in her efforts to make everything just fine. "It must be great to live right across the street from the park."

Every time a waiter passed with a fresh tray of chardonnay, Mary took a new glass. She was pleasantly drunk, drunk enough to make real conversation about the cold weather, the new lunch-only Indian restaurant, the restoration of someone's historic house. She flitted from small cluster to small cluster and added a sentence or two to each discussion.

Was this what parties had always been like? A slight buzz from wine? Banal conversation? Too many scallops wrapped in bacon? She thought of all the hours she'd wasted away from Stella doing this, while Stella played Twister with a teenage babysitter.

"Yes, I ate there last week and the saag paneer was the best I've ever had."

She scanned the room for Dylan, and when she finally found him, she joined his cluster — Alex and Vicky and a woman Mary didn't know, peering out behind glasses and wearing a lipstick that clashed with her skin tone.

"Alex and Vicky are doing all the work themselves on the house they bought," he said.

"Wow," Mary said, swiping another glass

of chardonnay.

"What year did you say it was built?" Dylan was saying.

"Seventeen ninety-two," Vicky said. Smugly, Mary thought. She'd never liked Vicky. She was too tall and sharp and wore clothes that took up space — sweeping shawls and dresses with too much fabric and jewelry that jangled loudly.

"We cheated," Mary said, "and bought one already renovated."

"Oh," Vicky said. Patronizing, Mary thought. But Dylan was looking at Vicky in a way that made Mary uncomfortable. As if all that clothing and hard work were admirable.

She wanted a new cluster. But when she looked around, there were fewer clusters. The party, blessedly, was breaking up.

Now Vicky was talking about Tuscany, as if no one else in the world had ever been there. Dylan kept asking questions, and the mousy woman told a pointless story about living in Florence for a year when she was in college. Finally Dylan remembered that Mary was still standing there and he said, "Shall we?"

Then she was thanking Laurie and Bob and the kind waiter who had kept her supplied with chardonnay all night. She wished she'd brought some money. She would give it all to him. Her stomach lurched slightly from eating too much bacon, but then she was out on the porch, gulping cold air, still saying thank you right until the door closed behind them.

She wanted to say something mean to her husband about flirting with that snob Vicky. Had he always flirted like this at parties and she'd had too much fun to notice? Another couple from the party, a couple Mary didn't recognize, were laughing and reliving something someone had said. They kept repeating the same phrase over and over and then laughing, really hard. They were parked right behind Mary and Dylan, and while Mary waited for Dylan to unlock her door, she watched that other happy couple get into a canary yellow Mini Cooper.

"Great car!" Dylan said.

The woman, all honey blond hair and a big smile, leaned out the car window as it began to pull away.

"I know!" she said. "We're lucky! No kids!"

Then the car zoomed past them and disappeared around the elbow of the road. Mary watched them go, those lucky childless people.

■ ■ ■ ■

Mary could not think of how to write these small two-hundred-and-fifty-word pieces Eddie wanted her to write. She'd eaten lunch at the Indian restaurant, twice. She'd sat in on classes at the French-American School and watched inner-city teenagers asking for directions to "la Gare du Nord" and ordering *"bifteck avec petits pois et pommes de terre."* She'd tried to make sense of these things.

It was far too cold to walk around the city, even with all the layers she was wearing. All she could do was sit and stare at the blank computer screen with the file name *Indian Lunch,* mocking her.

"Got a minute?" Eddie said from her doorway. He was holding a pile of books.

Quickly, she exited the file. "Well," she said, feigning busyness, "one minute."

Eddie had on that argyle sweater again and it was starting to smell of wet wool. He pulled up a chair and sat backwards on it, draping himself over the orange vinyl back; it was a school cafeteria castoff.

"So," he said, drumming his fingers on the chair, always a bad sign. "Jessica wants reviews."

"Reviews of what?" Mary said, misunderstanding. Then, "What? You mean she wants to *write* reviews?"

Eddie shrugged, which meant yes.

"*I'm* the reviewer," Mary said. "Hers aren't even any good. I've read them. She called David Mamet a feminist. Come on, Eddie."

"The thing is, Jessica —"

"She covers City Hall. Hard news. Politics. It suits her charming personality." Mary narrowed her eyes. "Jessica really wants it?"

Eddie shrugged, which meant yes.

Mary sighed. "Can I ditch the French-American School piece then? Do just books and restaurants?"

Eddie handed her the pile of books. "This is a month's worth."

"Good," she said.

Eddie slapped the back of the chair and got up to leave.

Mary watched his back as he walked away. The only problem was, she actually had to read these things now.

Before she left work to pick up Scarlet and Lulu to go to knitting on Wednesday, Mary tore off the top page of her new-word-a-day calendar and saw that March was winding down. Too soon it would be April and then it would be one year since Stella died.

Someone had sent her a note right afterward and all it had said was, *April truly is the cruelest month then.*

Sighing, Mary turned off all the lights and locked up, something she did almost every night, not because she was working so hard, but because it was so hard to get any work done. She locked the door that led out and walked to her car, the sensible station wagon. A mother's car. Maybe she would sell it and get her own canary yellow Mini Cooper, and ride around, laughing into the wind. "I can have this teeny tiny minicar because I have no kids," she'd tell women who drove station wagons and minivans and SUVs for hauling children. All those fucking lucky women.

■ ■ ■ ■

PART FIVE:
A GOOD KNITTER

■ ■ ■ ■

Really, all you need to become a good knitter are wool, needles, hands, and a slightly below-average intelligence. Of course, superior intelligence, such as yours and mine, is an advantage.
— Elizabeth Zimmermann,
Knitter's Almanac

9
HARRIET

In March, Mary and Stella had found the tips of purple crocuses in the garden and a blanket of myrtle and then chives began to grow with abandon. They'd made skinny bouquets of myrtle and chives and placed them around the house in bud vases. They had planned a surprise birthday dinner for Dylan: plain pasta with butter and freshly grated parmesan cheese, Stella's favorite. To Stella, surely that was everyone's favorite dinner. Naïvely, they had moved through March and April like those stupid crocuses — showy and blinded by the sunshine, bursting forth into disaster.

Last year, spring had been unusually warm. Hot, really, with temperatures in the eighties. They'd worn shorts and sundresses and flip-flops. Stella wore her hair in a ponytail, her neck glistening with sweat. But this year it rained. It rained and rained, the air bone-chillingly cold. The crocuses stayed hidden. The trees remained bare. It was as if the world was mourning Stella too, Mary thought.

Mary made herself go to the office every day. Her rain boots slogged through small floods at each curb, the hood of her slicker dripping rain onto her glasses. She'd say hello to Holly, then slip into her office and try to read. It took Mary three times as long to read even one page. She was aware of her slowness, of her brain struggling to make sense of each sentence. She high-lighted sections in bright pink, and turned down the corners of pages, hoping that somehow she would write something coher-ent. This made her laugh — she used to strive for intelligent, even brilliant. Now she would be satisfied with a review that at least made sense.

In the middle of all this — March, rain, the calendar ticking off days toward the first anniversary of the worst day of her life, Ed-die came in and ordered her out to lunch.

"A new restaurant," he said, folding money into her hands. "Take your husband. Have a martini." He added more bills. "Hell," he said, "have two."

She closed the book she was reading and took her slicker from the hook behind her door.

"I suppose there's a catch?" she said.

"Oh, sure," Eddie said. Despite the cold weather, he'd started wearing his spring wardrobe, a series of faded T-shirts from long-ago rock concerts. "I'll need a restaurant review. Soon," he added.

"No one wears Ramones T-shirts," Mary muttered. Her waterproof boots were damp inside.

Eddie said, "I'm piling on work to help you."

"I know," she said. "Someday I'll be grateful."

"Don't come back after lunch," he said, walking out beside her. "Go home and read."

Mary would knit a sweater for Dylan's birthday.

"An easy one," she had told Alice.

Alice looked through a pile of patterns, shaking her head.

"Aha!" she said finally. "Even you can do this one."

But apparently she couldn't, because it was clear to Mary already that she had messed it up. Worse, Alice was away.

"How will I fix all the mistakes I'm going to make?" Mary had asked her.

"Call Beth. Or better, Harriet. She can

knit a sweater with her eyes closed."

Reluctantly, Mary dialed Harriet's number.

"Well," Harriet said, "if Alice said to call me, I suppose you can come by. But only for a minute."

Mary's stomach ached by the time she got to Harriet's house in Barrington, a twenty-minute drive from Providence, through a clogged Main Street and twenty-five-mile-an-hour curving roads. But she'd done something wrong and she couldn't figure out what. No one had warned her that knitting a sweater, unlike scarves and hats, required reading a complicated pattern, or any pattern at all.

She pulled into the driveway and tried to calm herself. The house was a rambling ranch-style, built in the early sixties. Mary glanced around. The whole neighborhood was from the same era. It was like stepping back in time. The two-car garage, the bluestone front walk, the black shutters on each window. Then a frowning Harriet answered the doorbell, and showed her into a gold wall-to-wall-carpeted living room with off-white furniture.

"Let me see it," Harriet said, holding out her hand. "That's the garter stitch!" she said, disgusted. "You were supposed to do stockinette."

Mary frowned. "I thought I did."

"It's not rocket science," Harriet said. "It's knitting."

Mary chastised herself for going to Harriet's at all. If she'd looked at it long enough, surely she would have figured out what she'd done wrong all by herself.

"You knit your purls and purled your knits," Harriet said in disgust. She picked up the six inches of ribbing Mary had spent all afternoon doing, and unraveled it.

"Stockinette. Knit a row. Purl a row," Harriet said. She handed the yarn and needles back to Mary. "Not rocket science," she said again.

The bunched-up yarn and needles felt awkward in Mary's hand, and without warning, she started to cry.

"What's this?" Harriet said, taking a step away from Mary. "It's only knitting."

"My daughter," she said. She gulped again. "My little girl," she began, and then she gulped some more. "I lost her," she said, "and the strangest things set me off."

Somewhere, a clock ticked loudly.

"I just want to be able to do this. To make this sweater for my husband's birthday."

"You can do that," Harriet said.

"I can't even do fifteen inches of stockinette stitch without messing up."

"That's ridiculous," Harriet said. She gathered the yarn from the floor and expertly wound it into a ball. "Get up now," she said, offering her hands to Mary. "Come on. Up," she said when Mary hesitated.

Her hands were soft and cool. Lotioned hands. Pampered hands.

"Knit one row. Purl one row," she said.

"Got it," Mary said.

She heard the door close firmly behind her as she walked down the hedge-lined path to the car.

Eddie appeared in her office doorway.

"Do we just knit in here?" he said. "Or do we actually write?"

Almost relieved, Mary tossed her knitting onto her desk. "It would be easier to learn Italian," she said.

"Easier than knitting?" Eddie said. "Now you've got me worried."

"You try it," she muttered.

Eddie loomed in front of her in his The Who T-shirt. "How about that review of Funky Duck?"

"Is that due already?" she said, feigning surprise. Inside she grimaced. She hadn't even been to Funky Duck yet, a take-out duck restaurant on the West Side.

Eddie frowned. "Jessica said it's great."

"I hear you," Mary said.

"Have you ever noticed," Eddie said as he left her office, "that people say that when they aren't really listening?"

She should get up right now and drive to Funky Duck. She should order take-out duck, whatever that was, and she should eat it and take notes about it. Her eyes drifted toward the pattern for the sweater.

"Can you try a little?" Dylan had said to her the night before when he came home and found her watching *Survivor.*

"This is me trying," she'd told him.

He stood there a moment before getting back in his car and driving away. When he came back hours later, smelling of cigarette smoke and beer, she'd whispered, "I'll try to try? How's that?"

"Take-out duck for dinner," Mary said, offering Dylan the greasy bag with the strange red line drawing of a cleaver chasing a frightened duck on it.

"It's almost eight o'clock," he said.

"I got sidetracked," she said.

He raised his eyebrows, waiting.

"I was knitting and there was this instruction, slip stitches to holder, and I couldn't figure it out. Honestly, knitters should be breaking codes for army intelligence."

Mary considered telling him how Harriet had told her, "A stitch holder, for Christ's sake! A thing that holds stitches! A plastic thing! Whoever told you you could knit anyway?"

But Dylan's face had that look on it, that look of disgust and disappointment. Grumpy, she took the bag from him and began to lay the pieces of duck out on a platter.

"Now you know how I feel when you come home late without calling," she muttered. Which, she reminded herself, was happening more and more lately.

"Hey," he said, holding his arms up as if in surrender, "I'm working."

"So am I," she said, the sight of the shiny grease on the duck turning her stomach.

"Sorry," Dylan said in a tone that let her know he was not sorry at all. "It sounded like you were knitting."

Mary pushed her plate away. "I'm going to bed," she said.

"Wait!" Dylan said.

Mary turned. Maybe they would make up, until next time.

"Some lady dropped this off for you." He put a peach-colored plastic thing down in front of her. "Your stitch holder."

"Harriet," Mary said softly. "What a strange duck she is."

Despite himself, Dylan laughed, his face glistening with grease. Mary laughed too; the fight was over.

"This is the greasiest duck I've ever had," Dylan said.

Mary smiled. "Jessica loves it," she said. She dug around in her bag until she found her notebook. *Greasiest duck ever,* she wrote.

Eddie was waiting for her when she got to work. It was the first day of spring and right on schedule the sun came out, flowers bloomed, buds appeared on the tips of trees. I will not think about how I took Stella outside every March 21 and we used to say together: *Spring has sprung, the grass has riz, I wonder where the flowers is.* S tog, Mary thought. *S tog.* Say together.

"You hated Funky Duck," Eddie said, opening her office door and following her in.

"Yup," she said. Her throat felt like she had swallowed a tennis ball. Inside that tennis ball, she knew, were endless tears.

"Good," Eddie said gently.

He flashed her a peace sign — or maybe it was victory? — and left.

When Mary and Stella had walked outside last March 21 and S tog, Stella only had three short weeks to live. Mary closed her eyes against the image of Stella pointing to the dogwood tree. "Look, Mama!" she'd announced. "It's about to burst!"

Anniversary: The date on which an event occurred in some previous year (or the celebration of it).

Birthday, jubilee, wedding anniversary, centennial, bicentennial, tricentennial, millennium.

All happy words, Mary thought. Surely jubilee and jubilant were from the same root word. She scrolled word definitions and dictionaries online when she should have been writing a book review. But she could not find anything that explained what this anniversary meant to her. The opposite of jubilant. A day she wanted to forget, not to mark.

Then Eddie was peering over her shoulder.

"Have you ever heard of knocking?" Mary said.

He placed his hands on her shoulders. She could smell him, cigarette smoke and mothballs.

"You don't need to do that today," he said.

"I'm in my office trying to decide, is it better to say something or to shut up? Is it better for you to be here, or at home? I don't know."

"I don't know either," Mary said.

"Where's Dylan?"

"Work," she said.

"Maybe we could take a drive?" Eddie said. "Maybe a drive on a beautiful day is good?"

Mary shook her head. "It only makes me wonder how the fucking sun can still shine. You know?"

He squeezed her shoulders and then stepped away. "I'm thinking about her today," he said. "I want you to know that. How she used to like to spin in my chair. And stamp the date all over her arms. I used to like when you brought her in. I would be back there, in my office, and I'd hear those little-girl footsteps and I'd grin. I would."

Mary turned to face him. "Thank you," she said.

At home, things were waiting on her doorstep. Plants, full and pink and ostentatious. Cards. Notes. It would be worse if no one remembered Stella. Mary understood that, and she was grateful for these offerings. But each petal, each word, broke her heart again

217

and again.

Inside, the answering machine was blinking. She didn't know if she could bear hearing all those messages. She heard the sound of Dylan's key. She splashed cold water on her face and ran her fingers through her hair. But when he walked into the kitchen and she saw his face, stricken, she was crying again, and so was he.

"I just want her back," he said. "I just want Stella."

"Let's hide," Mary said, wrapping her arms around him.

"There's nowhere to hide," he said, his voice full of resignation. "I've tried all day."

The phone jangled. Dylan's voice told the caller they weren't available, then Mary's mother's voice filled the kitchen.

"I am thinking about you today," she said. "I am far away, but I am holding the three of you close."

Mary heard a catch in her voice before she said, quickly, "Bye."

Like a perfect 1950s wife, Harriet greeted her in a smart green shirtdress, belted to show her still-small waist. The gold bracelet. Low-heeled shoes. She must get her hair cut every week, Mary thought. It never seemed to grow, always staying just at chin length.

"Let's go where we can spread out," Harriet said.

She led Mary down a hallway — moss green wall-to-wall carpeting — into a large family room. Down two steps and onto the gray stone floor. Overstuffed dark red leather couches and chairs. Even the coffee table was leather, with big brass nails holding the leather down at the corners. Mary caught sight of a pool beyond the sliding glass doors, an arbor of wisteria, a patio with lots of glass furniture and a grill, also oversized.

"We had some parties out there," Harriet said, following Mary's gaze. "Long ago."

Mary began to take out the pieces of the sweater, laying them on the coffee table. "Are these okay here?" she asked.

"It's *leather*," Harriet said. "You can't hurt it. Cows are outside in all sorts of weather, aren't they?"

Harriet had a way of making her feel small. Or young. Or both. At least she would leave here with a sweater.

Harriet adjusted the blinds until she was satisfied with the amount of light they let in.

"My husband and I bought it in Barcelona," Harriet said, running her hands over the soft leather top of the coffee table. "Had it sent here. Our friends thought we were mad. 'Can't you find a suitable coffee table here?' they all said. But George said, 'No.' It had to be this one."

She stood at the corner of the sofa and gently touched the side table there, a round hammered-brass top.

"This we carried onto the plane from Morocco. The stewardess said, 'I'm not sure I can find a home for that,' and George said, 'Dear, we have a home for it. We just need a place to store it until we get it there.'"

"Are you widowed?" Mary asked, immediately regretting her boldness.

"No," Harriet said. "Divorced." She smoothed her dress and went to sit beside Mary. "Let's see what you need to do here."

"I'm sorry," Mary said. "I didn't mean to pry."

"There's nothing to pry into," Harriet said matter-of-factly. "I was married for twenty-five years and I've been divorced for fifteen. Do you read biographies?"

"I used to," Mary said. "I'm not reading much these days."

Harriet frowned at her in disapproval.

"I told you," Mary said defensively. "I lost my daughter. I can barely get up in the morning."

"I lost my son a few years ago," Harriet said evenly.

Harriet had lost a child? That was why she had this tough veneer. "You know then," Mary said cautiously. "You know how it ruins a person."

"Yes," Harriet said. "I know."

She got up again and walked across the room to the bookshelves. Mary watched her carefully select some framed photographs from the shelves. Her heels echoed as she walked back across the stone floor toward Mary. Almost tenderly she sat again, the pictures on her lap.

"My boys," Harriet said, pointing to the picture on top, a black-and-white studio photograph of two little boys in sailor suits. "Danny and David."

"Cute," Mary said.

Harriet placed that one on the coffee table, standing upright facing them. "Danny's graduation picture," she said. "He went to Williams College. Very bright, Danny was."

"It sounds like you had a nice life," Mary said. "Barcelona. Morocco."

"We did," Harriet said. "I grew up right here in Barrington. On Rumstick Point. My father was a doctor, a surgeon. And my sisters and I never wanted for anything."

There was a tone of boastfulness as Harriet described her family's affiliation with all of the upper-crust institutions in Rhode Island. They meant little to Mary, but she oohed and aahed appropriately, and her enthusiasm softened Harriet a bit.

"When I married George it was one of the happiest days of my life. Even now, with all that's happened, when I look back on that day I smile. It was November. All my girlfriends were June brides, but I wanted to wear a satin dress and to have my maids in green velvet. My dress had one hundred perfect buttons running down the back. It took my sister Viv an hour to button all of them. I was almost late for my own wedding! And I held calla lilies. White ones. I still adore calla lilies. You can't grow them here, you know. I've tried. And I've been told that if I can't grow something, then it simply cannot be grown.

"Viv tried growing peonies for years. Finally, I went to her house and I planted some. Why, she is positively overrun with peonies now. So trust me when I say that one cannot grow calla lilies in this climate. George and I saw them in Sorrento, growing everywhere, in the most gorgeous colors — purples and fuchsia and every wild color you can imagine."

Harriet got up and went to adjust the blinds to accommodate the shifting sunlight.

Mary glanced down at the photos she hadn't yet shown her. On top was a wedding picture. Mary recognized Danny, his hair trimmed now, grinning in his tuxedo beside a blonde wife in a white column of a wedding dress.

"Liza," Harriet said. "I never much cared for her," she continued. "I know we're not supposed to speak poorly of the dead, but she was not for Danny. When they met he had been working in advertising. For J. Walter Thompson. And she was a broker. Wall Street. Big money. She didn't come from anything, so the money really impressed her. I mean, she went to the University of Delaware, for Christ's sake. Pretty, though."

Mary agreed. Long golden hair and eyes so blue that even in a picture crowded with people they showed themselves.

"He looks so happy, doesn't he?" Harriet said. "I've regretted that I didn't like Liza and that I let him know that. I regret so much. How I didn't visit that summer like I was supposed to. They were renting a house in Sag Harbor, and they asked me for the weekend. The Labor Day weekend. But it was too complicated to get there alone. I would have to drive, in all that traffic. Then

David was going to be there with his friend, as he calls him." She glanced at Mary, then averted her eyes.

She took a breath. "The long drive. David being there. Oh, and Liza's parents. What a pair. Instead I went to a lovely barbecue at my niece's. You know, she does everything so beautifully. Tastefully. Liza always had to be over the top.

"Late on that Monday night, about ten o'clock, I was sitting right where you are now, knitting, and I heard a rapping on the sliding doors and who was standing there but David and his friend. 'I couldn't drive by without stopping in to say hello to my dear old mom,' David said. I invited them in, and served them something cold to drink. Finally, David said, 'Danny would kill me if I told you, but he's really disappointed you didn't come this weekend.' I tried to explain about the long drive and the traffic, but he wasn't listening. He said, 'They're pregnant! And they wanted to tell you themselves. Act surprised. They're going to come this weekend,' he said, 'to tell you the news.'

"After they left, I couldn't sleep. I thought about George. We fell in love. We got married. We had these two boys. This house. Every two years a new black Cadillac. Every year a lovely vacation. For our twenty-fifth wedding anniversary, the silver anniversary, we renewed our vows right in the backyard. It was November, but they erected a big white tent. Heated. Our whole family was here, toasting us. The silver we got that night! George gave me a silver bracelet inlaid with all of our birthstones, mine and his and Danny's and David's. Two rubies, a sapphire, and a diamond. So beautiful together like that. The perfect happy family. Everyone said so.

"Two weeks later, George comes into this very room. I was sitting in that chair over there, knitting a sweater for Danny, for Christmas. George pulls up the ottoman, and sits right in front of me, and tells me, very calmly, 'Harriet, would you get naked right now and run through the backyard?' It was three o'clock in the afternoon! I said, 'George, what about the neighbors? What about the fact that it's December?' And he stood up, and he said, 'I'm going to do it, Harriet.' He undressed, right there, by the bookshelves, undressed right down to nothing. Naked! Then he went to the sliding doors, and I jumped up and told him to get back inside. But he walked out. And he faced the house and he yelled, 'Look at me, Harriet!' It was so cold that I could see the puffs of air coming from his mouth. I was horrified. Then he came and stood at the door, letting all the heat out, and he said, 'Harriet, come outside with me.' I said, 'I absolutely will not.' He walked back in, slid the door shut, gathered his clothes — didn't put them on, mind you. Simply gathered them up, and said, 'That is exactly why I cannot stay married to you for one minute longer.' "

Harriet shook her head, took a deep breath before continuing.

"The next morning I called Danny at work and told him I wanted to come and visit. 'Liza and I were thinking of coming to you,' he said. 'Next weekend.' But I insisted on going there. He checked his calendar and he said, 'How about next Tuesday? A week from today?'

"That following Tuesday I caught the early train. The Acela. It arrived at Penn Station at eleven-thirty and I would take a taxi right to Danny's office. Danny and Liza worked just down the hall from each other. They were going to take me to lunch, I suppose to tell me their news. The train stopped suddenly and didn't start up again. We sat and sat, until finally I asked the man next to me if he thought something was wrong. He had his computer on and he looked at me, horrified, and he said, 'They've flown a plane into the World Trade Center.' Then the air crackled and the train's conductor spoke over the intercom and he told us the train had to turn around because terrorists were attacking New York City."

"They worked there?" Mary managed to ask.

"Both of them," Harriet said.

"I —"

Harriet put her hand out to stop Mary from speaking, put it right over her lips, gently. "There are no words. You lost your daughter. You know that, don't you? There are no words."

Slowly, her hand dropped. She went to the blinds again, to adjust them one more time.

When she returned, she picked up the pattern.

"Sew side, sleeve, and raglan seams," Harriet read. She rummaged through her knitting basket until she found a small pink tube of tapestry needles.

Mary stared at her hard.

"First, you sew the seams. I'll show you how. Then you need to make the neckband. Very simple. It's just knitting, after all. Not rocket science."

Harriet slipped yarn through the tapestry

needle and carefully demonstrated the back-stitch to Mary.

"Harriet . . ." Mary began.

"One step at a time," Harriet said, her voice even. "The side seam."

Mary took the needle from Harriet and slowly, slowly, sewed first the side seam, then the sleeves.

"See?" Harriet said. "It's just knitting."

10
THE KNITTING
CIRCLE

Mary came home from work and climbed into Stella's bed and fell asleep. At first, she could not bear to go into Stella's bedroom. Then she began to steel herself in order to enter it, standing in front of the door and pressing her hands to the wall outside for strength. Once she stepped in, she might open a drawer and gently touch her daughter's ballet tights and leotards, or the bright balls of colorful socks; she might open the closet and run her fingertips across the row of dress-up dresses hanging there; she might let her eyes scan the titles of books on the low pink bookshelf. Then she'd leave.

But that early September day, she'd come home and gone into Stella's room and been overcome by exhaustion. Even the walk out of the room and down the hall seemed impossible. Mary climbed into her daughter's bed, slipped under the purple and white quilt, and fell asleep, the way she used to when she'd put Stella to bed a lifetime ago. Back then she'd been tired from the abundance in her life. Now, it was the routine, the sameness, the smallness, of it.

With another Halloween, another Thanksgiving, the endless cycle of joy and holidays approaching, Mary spent every late afternoon asleep in her daughter's bed. The sound of Dylan coming home woke her. He stood in the doorway. "Does this help, Mary? Because I'm trying hard to understand and I can't seem to."

"I don't know," she said. "It makes me feel closer to her."

He stood there as if there was more to say. After that, he started coming home later more regularly.

It was wednesday. She would be late for knitting. She imagined Scarlet on that beach, Lulu in that park, Ellen alone in an Irish hospital, Harriet on the train heading south. The women's stories haunted her. Still, they got themselves up every morning, they moved through the world somehow, and on Wednesday nights they went to Big Alice's. She gathered her things and drove to the knitting circle.

Everyone was already there. Scarlet and Lulu and Ellen and Harriet and Beth and

Alice, all in their usual places. Yet something was different. An awkward air settled over the room.

"I thought you weren't coming," Ellen said as Mary went to her seat beside Alice. That was when she saw that Ellen's daughter Bridget was there, working on her long scarf.

"I fell asleep," Mary explained, embarrassed.

"That always happened to me when I was pregnant," Beth said. "I slept every afternoon for hours. Which was fine with the first one. But after that, I had toddlers everywhere. By the time I was pregnant with Stella, I had to bring the other three in my room and close the door. To keep them safe, you know?"

Shut up, Mary willed. She pulled out her knitting, a pair of fingerless gloves in orange, and jabbed one needle through the yarn. Beth didn't shut up, of course. Behind Beth's voice came a crackly noise, like water running through tubes. She droned until Mary snapped, "Well, I'm not pregnant. I'm just exhausted."

Beth looked at her, startled. "Sorry," she mumbled.

On a little wooden table lay a pink child's sweater with a yellow daisy knit onto the front. Mary could see that she was now knitting a slightly smaller yellow sweater, and would no doubt knit a pink daisy onto it for *her* Stella.

"Stella started ballet this week," Beth was saying. "You haven't lived until you've seen a five-year-old in a tutu doing an arabesque."

Mary put her knitting down.

"My Caroline is such a tomboy," Beth said. "She does soccer, T-ball, you name it. But my Stella —"

"Shut up," Mary said, surprising herself. "Just shut up."

She saw Beth's mouth open, then close.

"I can't even think straight with you going on and on about these things," Mary said. "And what is that noise?" she added, jumping up.

Of course, as soon as she said it, she saw what it was. Across from her sat Ellen, red-faced and staring down at her tiny needles tented together to form a sock. Beside Ellen, two tubes snaked out of her daughter Bridget's nose into a large green oxygen bottle that sat at her feet. Mary sat back down, embarrassed.

"You come here every week with this big chip on your shoulder and you expect everyone to coddle you," Beth said.

"I do not," Mary said, wondering even as she said it if in fact she did expect that very thing.

"You act like you're the only person with problems."

"No," she said weakly.

Big Alice stood up, her arms folded across her chest. "We've come here to knit," she said. "Can we do that?"

"And some people," Beth said, "might be bothered by the oxygen thing." Tears glistened on her waterproof-mascaraed lashes. "Some people don't want to be around that stuff, you know? It makes me uncomfortable." Beth's tears streaked the makeup on her cheeks. "Maybe I should go," she said.

At home, Mary was surprised to see that Dylan was still out. Mary dialed his cell phone, but hung up when she heard the familiar message. When a car pulled up, she rushed outside.

"Dylan!" she called out.

But it was Scarlet walking toward her.

"You followed me?" Mary said, embarrassed.

"What a night," Scarlet said.

Mary invited her inside. She opened a bottle of shiraz, and the two women sat on the sofa together.

"Ellen told us that Bridget is on the top of the transplant list now," Scarlet said.

"What?" Mary said.

Scarlet nodded. "She needs a heart. Soon," she added. "Then Beth walks in and immediately freaks out. Takes Alice aside and tells her she can't be around people who are so sick."

"Jesus," Mary said. "I hate Beth," Mary muttered. Her cheeks blazed red with shame for saying it.

They were silent a moment. Then Scarlet said, "Sometimes when I hear her going on like that, about those kids of hers, I think of my little Bébé. I wonder, doesn't Beth ever look away, even for a moment?"

"Why is Beth so fucking lucky?" Mary said.

"Sometimes I think about having another chance," Scarlet said. "With love, you know? But after you lose someone . . ."

Scarlet's eyes drifted to the mantel, where pictures of Stella, happy and alive, looked down at them. "She's beautiful, Mary," Scarlet said.

The ticket arrived in an Express Mail envelope. No note. Mary wondered if her mother realized the departure date was the day before Stella's birthday. Other grandmothers would remember such a thing. But her mother? Mary couldn't even guess.

Her mother's voice on the answering machine that night asked, "Did you get it? Did you notice how you fly direct to León from Logan? A car service will drive you right to my front door."

"I'm not coming," Mary told the answering machine, jabbing the delete button.

The ringing phone did not startle Mary awake, but blended into her dream. It was a fire engine, a police car, a burglar alarm. Then it stopped. Mary rolled over, toward Dylan snoring softly beside her. Early morning light was already casting shadows through the narrow blinds. Mary frowned, wondering when he had finally come home. When the phone began to ring again, Mary lunged for it.

"Mary? Mary?" a voice was saying.

"Scarlet?" Mary said.

"It's the Sit and Knit. It caught on fire last night."

"What?" Mary said.

"It burned down," Scarlet was saying. "It's gone."

■ ■ ■ ■

PART SIX:
SIT AND KNIT

■ ■ ■ ■

To leave your fingers untrained for anything beyond pushing, and perhaps twisting, is like leaving a voice without singing. It is a shame and a loss. Certainly knitting is not the only thing fingers can do, but it is a good thing . . .

— Anna Zilboorg,
Knitting for Anarchists

11
ALICE

Big Alice's Sit and Knit had saved Mary. She was certain of that. But she wasn't at all certain that she could help Alice. Still, she agreed to go with Scarlet to see Alice at her little cottage on the beach.

As they drove, Mary spotted a tree whose leaves had already begun to change color, revealing a glimpse of gold or red. Roadside farmstands boasted apples and pears and even pumpkins. The Westport River shone in the afternoon sunlight on their right. The Atlantic Ocean, white-capped and emerald green, lay ahead of them. Nestled between the river and the ocean, among rolling hills and tall cat-o'-nine-tails, sat Alice's weathered shingled cottage.

As they parked on the driveway made of crushed clamshells, Mary realized that she knew nothing about Alice's life. Other than a British accent that told her Alice was from England somewhere, and her gray hair and soft wrinkles that indicated she was probably close to seventy, and her love of knitting, Alice was a mystery.

"Is she married?" Mary asked Scarlet.

"I don't think so," Scarlet said, pausing a moment to take in the gorgeous view that stretched in every direction. "Funny," she said. "I don't know anything about her, really."

"That's just what I was thinking," Mary said.

The air was sharp and salty, the kind that begged for long walks. Alice was bent, working in the garden where the last of the zinnias had turned to dark reds and oranges. Marigolds flashed burnt orange and yellow, and feathery mums bloomed lavender and pink.

Alice turned at the sound of their footsteps, and wiped her hands on her plaid flannel shirt.

"A garden," she said to them, "can be a full-time job, if you let it."

Alice wasn't someone you hugged, and Mary had to resist the urge to throw her arms around her. But with Alice, you let her take charge.

"Well then," Alice said, "I suppose we should take stock of my disaster."

She led them right back to Scarlet's car

without even bothering to change her clothes.

"It's not a funeral," she said into the silence as they drove. "It's a shop, after all. Not a bloody person."

"Still," Scarlet said.

"Rubbish!" Alice said sharply. "I have insurance. If there's anything to salvage, we'll save it. If not, all that's left for me to do is decide if I should rebuild or not."

"But you will!" Mary said, leaning forward from the backseat. "You must!" Again, she almost grabbed Alice, but caught herself and clutched the side of the passenger seat instead.

Alice surprised her by taking her hand and patting it gently.

"Ah, darling," Alice said softly, "I'm seventy-eight years old. There comes a time when a person decides she's done with the responsibilities, the hours, all of it."

Mary chewed her bottom lip, unable to tell Alice how much the Sit and Knit meant to her. She felt oversentimental beside Alice's pragmatism. It's only a shop, Alice had said.

"We simply won't allow you not to rebuild," Scarlet said, her tone as matter-of-fact as Alice's own. "You know as well as we do that the Sit and Knit is more than just a shop. Especially for those of us in the knitting circle."

Tears of relief sprang to Mary's eyes.

"It's not the shop," Alice said. "It's the knitting itself that brings comfort."

"Yes," Scarlet said. "I suppose we could sit and knit anywhere." She laughed. "We do, in fact. But then why do you suppose we come every week to the knitting circle? It *is* the shop. And it's you and the people you've brought together. Like Mary here. You knew to invite her, didn't you?"

Alice sighed.

Scarlet turned down the curvy road that led to the store. "It's your magic formula, Alice, and don't pretend you don't know that."

When they saw the black and charred wood that just yesterday had been the store, they all gasped. One patch of roof remained, but topless now, the sun poured over what was left, illuminating how much Alice had lost.

"Oh dear," Alice said.

They got out of the car and stood in front of the shell of the building, squinting into the sunlight.

"I opened this shop in 1974," Alice said, folding her arms across her chest. "Thirty years. Can you imagine?" She forced a laugh. "My longest relationship."

Slowly she moved toward the store, stepping almost gingerly over what used to be the porch, and through the frame of the door.

"Oh dear," she said again.

Scarlet and Mary followed. Walking over the burned boards, Mary remembered the day a year ago she had stood here empty-handed, frightened. And how Alice had let her in.

Already Alice was looking through the rubble, moving things aside, busy.

"I need to make a list," she said, reaching into her pocket and retrieving a small notebook with a pencil tucked into its wire edge. "Brooms. Garbage bags. Boxes, in case we find anything to keep." She wrote as she spoke.

Scarlet had disappeared into what had been the main room. But now she joined them, grinning. "Buttons!" she said. "Dozens and dozens of perfectly good buttons."

"Thank God for plastic," Alice said.

"Did you know that knitting is hot?" Mary asked Eddie. She was leaning against his office door and he was at his desk, frowning up at her.

"I know that certain employees do it when

they should be working," he told her.

"Celebrities knit."

"Uh-huh," Eddie said. He had on an Italian soccer shirt, all bright yellow and black polyester.

"There are knitting cafés and knitting/yoga classes and someone even told me there were knitting pubs."

Eddie raised one eyebrow, a skill he loved to show off.

"In Canada," Mary added.

"Ah," Eddie said.

"I could write a piece about it."

"No," Eddie said. "But thanks for the offer."

"I could examine why it's so hot now — and it is, even though you haven't noticed — and the benefits of knitting and then do a roundup of the best knitting shops here."

"Is there any evidence for this big trend? Or is this just your own marvelous but narrow point of view?"

"I'm glad you asked," Mary said, and handed him her files of research.

"Is that review of El Coyote in here somewhere?" Eddie said.

"El Coyote is the worst Mexican restaurant in the world," Mary said. "They serve hamburgers."

"So it's in here?"

"No."

Eddie shook his head.

"Fine," Mary said. "Give it to Jessica. Let her go and eat bad bottled salsa and stale chips at El Coyote."

"You haven't even gone yet, have you?"

"You know me too well, Eddie."

Jessica appeared beside Mary. She had done something weird with her hair so that it flipped up at the bottom.

"Eddie," she said, "we need to talk. You know, alone?"

"I'll make you a deal," Eddie said before going into his office with Jessica. "Go to El Coyote tonight, give it to me tomorrow, and I'll think about it."

"What kind of deal is that?" Mary said. Jessica smelled of some spicy perfume that made Mary slightly dizzy.

"Otherwise I'm not going to read facts about knitting at all," Eddie said.

"Knitting?" Jessica said. "That's the hottest thing in New York. My cousin lives there and she goes every Sunday to a knitting group. Sox and Lox. Not that we have anything like that around here."

"Thank you, Jessica," Mary said, wiggling her fingers goodbye at Eddie.

"El Coyote," he called after her.

As Jessica pulled the door shut, Mary

heard her say, "I love that place, Eddie. You know I do."

Mary stopped right where she stood, between Holly's desk and Eddie's office. Holly's head was moving in time to whatever her pink iPod mini was pumping into her multipierced ears. Mary stared at Eddie's closed door. Shit, she realized, Eddie is sleeping with Jessica.

"Dinner?" Dylan said. "Tonight?"

Mary swiveled her chair in a slow circle, the phone crooked between her cheek and shoulder.

"Bad Mexican," she said. "What could be better?" She thought of La Rondalla, her favorite Mexican place in San Francisco, and sighed.

"I have this work thing," Dylan said, unconvincingly.

Mary frowned, an uneasiness settling in her. "Come to think of it," she said, "I haven't had dinner with you in a week. More."

"Work," Dylan said. "It's crazy."

From down the hall, she heard Jessica laughing.

"Go back to the office after dinner," Mary said.

"Okay," he said. "Great. I'll meet you

there."

Jessica walked by, wearing a bright orange coat that made her look like a pumpkin. She smiled at Mary. Mary didn't smile back.

She had read a statistic somewhere, in all the books and brochures she'd received since Stella had died, that fifty percent of couples who lose a child get divorced. Her own marriage had still felt new and uncertain when Stella was born. Dylan, in many ways, remained a stranger. His bright optimism made her cranky. So did his fastidiousness. She liked to spend weekends reading, making love, cooking decadent meals; he liked to wash the windows and take vigorous hikes. Sometimes she used to lie in bed, dreaming of her old life in San Francisco while Dylan vacuumed outside their bedroom door.

But when Stella was born, everything shifted. Together, they marveled at her for hours. As she got older, they both spent Saturdays at the RISD Museum with her, or at the corner playground. There wasn't time for their differences. There was just Stella.

Without her, where were they? Mary wondered. They both moved zombielike through their days, their marriage. They still found comfort in each other's bodies, but now Mary worried that in her daze of grief, she had not even noticed her husband moving away from her.

El Coyote smelled like onions and Lysol. Mary saw the familiar back of Dylan's head, the small stripe of skin between his dark curls and white button-down collar as he bent to study the menu. The menu itself was large and plastic. And sticky, she thought as she took one from the waitress and sat across from her husband. Her heart was beating hard. When he looked up and smiled at her, it sped up even more, filling her chest and throat. She loved him. In that instant she was more certain than ever.

"You," he said, pointing a tortilla chip, "are going to hate this place."

The menu described everything in great detail, even spelling the pronunciations phonetically: *quesadilla (kay-sah-dee-ah).* Green and red chile peppers with faces danced across the menu. Some of them even wore sombreros.

"Ugh," Mary said.

Dylan reached across the table and placed one of his hands over both of hers, casually. Everything's okay, Mary told herself. He was whistling through his teeth. Nothing was on his mind, she decided, except which bad combination platter to order.

She almost confessed her fears. Instead, she said, "Eddie is fucking Jessica. Can you believe it?"

Dylan didn't look at her. "Who would ever sleep with Eddie?" he said.

"Who would sleep with Jessica?"

"Eddie is not an attractive man," Dylan said.

"Jessica's a bitch! She likes this restaurant," Mary said. That nagging sense of unease had returned. "Would you sleep with Jessica?" she asked him.

Finally, he lifted his eyes. "I'm married," he said.

Dylan went back to work after dinner. For a crazy minute, Mary considered following him. The thought embarrassed her, and she went home, her stomach rumbling from the bitter taste of bottled enchilada sauce.

The last thing she wanted to do was talk to her mother. But when she sat down to knit, the phone rang and her mother's voice was on the other end.

"I'm going to Guanajuato for the weekend," her mother said, "so we won't talk before you get here."

"Mom," Mary said, "I'm not coming. I told you that."

"Nonsense! You have to come."

"I have work," she said. Even if she wanted to go, which she did not, she could never leave Dylan now, with these suspicious, ridiculous thoughts jamming her brain. "I have a husband."

"I so wanted to spend some time with you," her mother said.

Mary put down her knitting, surprised. Since Stella had died, she had not seen her mother at all, except for in those first horrible days right afterward. Even then, she had stayed in the background, allowing others to comfort her, to cook food and answer the constantly ringing doorbell and phone.

"Are you all right?" Mary asked.

"Of course," her mother said, disappointed. "It just seemed like time for us to have a visit."

"I'll use the ticket another time," Mary said. "Okay?"

Her mother was uncharacteristically silent.

"How about at Thanksgiving?" Mary said. "You were right. It would be better to get out of here for the holidays."

"That's fine," her mother said.

"Have fun in Guadalajara," Mary said.

"Guanajuato," her mother corrected.

After they hung up, Mary remembered she had wanted to tell her mother about the fire at the Sit and Knit. But when she called back, an answering machine picked up, her mother's voice telling her in Spanish that she wasn't available.

Mary panned El Coyote and Eddie gave her the assignment to write an article about knitting.

"See?" he said, leaning back in the chair at his desk. "You help me. I help you." He was growing one of those funny beards that just hang off the chin. Mary wondered if Jessica liked facial hair.

"That hair on your chin looks silly," Mary told him.

"Some women find it sexy," Eddie said.

"Aha!" Mary blurted.

He scowled at her. She could tell cold weather was coming because he was wearing one of his pilled, too-tight argyle sweaters.

"What's that supposed to mean?" Eddie asked her.

"Just aha," she said.

"You don't know anything," Eddie said, hunching over his typewriter.

"That's what you think," she said, standing to leave.

He narrowed his eyes at her. "What do you think you know?"

She grinned and walked out.

Alice had agreed to talk to her about knitting for the article. And to help her make the thumbhole on the fingerless gloves she was knitting. In the car on the way to Alice's house, Mary kept thinking of Eddie's face, and laughing to herself. Hadn't he once told her, "You don't shit where you eat"? That was back when a RISD graduate student interned one summer. Too skinny, with her hair pulled into two blunt pigtails at the nape of her neck, the girl had driven Eddie crazy. "Go out with her already!" Mary had told him, after weeks of hearing him go on about her talent, her intricate tattoos that snaked up both arms, her big clunky shoes. "You don't shit where you eat," he'd said sadly each time. Victoria. That was her name. Mary wondered if he had ever seen her after that summer. She wondered why he had broken his own rule now. With Jessica, of all people.

The ocean appeared in the distance, and Mary turned down the dirt road that led to Alice's small shingled house. Strange that Alice lived way out here alone. She didn't strike Mary as a lonely person. Just private, Mary supposed. Still, there was no town nearby. No neighbors, except the family who spent summers in the only other house on the road. Once, Alice had told her that she used to raise chickens that laid colored eggs. But they were too much trouble, Alice had said. I like to be by myself, doing what I want, when I want, she'd explained.

As soon as Mary pulled up the crushed-seashell driveway, the door to Alice's house opened and she stepped out. She wore her usual practical skirt and hand-knit cardigan, this one a periwinkle blue. Mary saw that she had on her trademark pink slippers; her gout must be acting up again. Her white hair was pulled back into a loose bun, and stray hairs fell down her neck. She tugged at those often when she talked.

Mary stepped from the car, remarking on the glorious day. It did feel glorious too. The week before had been a hellish week of hard rain, the remnants of a hurricane. Fitting, Mary had thought, for the week of Stella's birthday. But the storm had passed, and now the sun shone extra bright on the turning leaves.

"I grew up in London so I find the rain comforting, you know," Alice said, ushering Mary inside. "Always have."

The house was small, with too much furniture and too many knickknacks — porcelain cats and glass clowns and needlepointed everything. On a small side table Alice had set out tea, complete with small silver sugar tongs for the hard brown cubes. The teacups and saucers were bone china in a dainty pink floral pattern. A silver platter held small round scones, strawberry jam, clotted cream.

"Your mother loved coming here for tea," Alice said. "So I thought you might enjoy it too."

"My mother?" Mary said, surprised.

"She learned to knit sitting right in that chair," Alice said, pointing to an overstuffed powder blue chair with a needlepointed footstool in front of it. Alice sighed. "But that's another story, isn't it?"

Mary wished Alice would say more, but instead she busied herself fixing them each a cup of tea, preparing the scones just so, and settling Mary in that same powder blue chair. Alice sat on its pale pink twin, stretching her feet on the footstool there, also needlepointed with a picture of birds.

"So you want to know how it all began," Alice said after she'd blown on her tea, then sipped it daintily.

Mary clicked on her tape recorder. "Whenever you're ready," she said.

Alice sipped again, then said, "Did you know that knitting is one of the most ancient forms of handiwork? They found knit socks in Egyptian tombs. You can see them in the British Museum. In the Middle Ages, before the invention of the spinning wheel, girls used drop spindles that allowed them to spin even while they were watching their flocks, or simply walking. There are seventeenth-century woodcuts that show this. All of these aproned young women outdoors, knitting."

"So that's why you learned?" Mary prodded. "Girls were taught to knit."

Alice laughed. "I'm not quite as old as the seventeenth century." She nibbled her scone. "Are these too dry?" she asked.

Mary hadn't touched hers yet. She took a bite, savoring the sweetness of the jam with the slight tang of the cream. "It's delicious," she said. "Not at all dry."

"They're meant to be a bit dry, aren't they?" Alice said. "You go to a café here and what they pass off as scones is awful. Lemon goop or icing, even maple flavoring." She shook her head. "One thing the British get right. Scones." She lifted her teacup again. "And tea," she said, taking a satisfying sip. "Now. Where were we?"

"You were about to tell me how you learned to knit. As a little girl?" Mary prodded.

"So you would think. But I had three older brothers, all of whom played football. *Soccer,* as you call it. And all I wanted to do was play football with them. My mother grew so tired of mending the knees of my stockings! You have no idea. I would come home bloody and bruised. And triumphant. I beat the dickens out of those boys most of the time. And I would be coming down our street just when the streetlights were being lit, my skirt hem unsewn, the knees torn from my stockings, my hair wild, half in and half out of the careful braids my mother worked so hard on, and I'd have a big welt on my cheek, a little dried blood over my eye, and coming in the opposite direction were all the girls in my form who took dancing lessons from Mrs. Fish in the flat next door to us. We'd be eating dinner and the sounds of Mrs. Fish on the piano and all those girls dancing would fill our kitchen and drive my mum mad. 'What is wrong with you, Alice, that you cannot be over there learning to dance with all the other girls?' she would say.

"Then one day I came home from the football field, I must have been eleven or twelve years old, and my mother was waiting for me with a small case with a zipper closing. She unzipped it and pointed to the objects inside, naming each one. A tapestry needle. A yarn holder. A tape measure. 'But what do I need with all this?' I said, nearly in tears. 'It's for knitting. You will take this kit and go next door where Mrs. Fish will turn you into a lady. God knows I've tried without any success.'

"So every afternoon I went reluctantly to Mrs. Fish's flat to learn to knit. In the distance I could hear the boys playing football, making me even more miserable.

"That first afternoon, she sat me down, looked straight at me with her watery eyes, and said, 'Wool, of course, is the soft fleecy coat of the sheep.' I didn't even try to stifle my snort. 'Mrs. Fish,' I told her, 'I am a girl who already knows every country on the continent of Africa.' I was obsessed with Africa, and I was certain I would go to live there as soon as I possibly could. Mrs. Fish ignored me completely. 'After the wool has been through many refining stages of spinning and dying,' she continued, 'it is called yarn, and it is ready for our needles.' 'Can *you* correctly place the Belgian Congo on a map of Africa?' I challenged her. 'Or Rhodesia?' She handed me a hank of scratchy yarn the color of oatmeal. 'Winding a ball correctly is the first thing we shall cultivate,' she said. I stared down at the pile of yarn in my lap. Africa, I'm afraid, seemed very far away.

"I began to wrap the yarn, but Mrs. Fish stopped me. 'Never wind the wool tightly,' she reprimanded. 'This destroys the life of the yarn.' She positioned my hands just so. 'The strands should pass over all four fingers and thumb of this hand, while this hand guides the wool from the skein.'

"How I hated Mrs. Fish! Day after day I sat there, winding yarn, always too tightly, too sloppily, too everything. Until finally she said, 'Now you see how to do it properly, Alice,' and I jumped up to join the football game outside. She pushed me back down onto the small sofa. 'Every specialty has its own lexicon,' she said, 'and knitting is no exception to this rule. There are certain terms we must learn and certain symbols we must recognize.'

"I glared at her. 'When I live in Africa and hunt big game, I'll hang elephant tusks on my walls and make carpets of lions I shoot and skin myself.' I got the reaction I wanted — a look of complete and utter disgust. 'Ladies do not skin lions, Alice,' she said.

" 'I hate knitting,' I told her. 'Africa is tropical. Knitting is useless there.'

" 'Knitting,' she told me, 'is useful everywhere.'

"The strangest things occurred while I sat in Mrs. Fish's flat learning to knit. I developed breasts. When I played football, they bounced. And the boys noticed. Especially Rodney Harrison. Poor Rodney," Alice said softly, shaking her head.

She sighed. "So Mrs. Fish got her way and turned me into a knitter, if not a lady. I was still dead set on going to Africa and living in a hut. But the war came and got in the way. I got a job as a secretary, to do my bit. There were rumors that Churchill's War Rooms were right beneath us. But I don't know if that was true. Nice to imagine, of course. I do know that I slept too many nights in the Underground while the bombs went off all around us. Even down that low the walls shook. And pieces of cement and things crumbled around us. We girls would huddle together to feel safe. And for warmth too, of course.

"My one good friend, Beatrice Cooke, she was a secretary too. So beautiful, Bea was. Strawberry blonde hair, green eyes, like a cat. I used to lay my hand on her cheek just to feel her soft skin. The boys loved Bea. She would take me along to dances and the like, but they all wanted her. Circled her like sharks around a good meal. They brought her gifts all the time. Perfume from

France, chocolate bars — she'd share those with me. We'd laugh at those foolish boys and eat their chocolate. It was so rare to have chocolate. I gave her presents too. I knit her scarves, and warm gloves. Practical things. Things to keep her warm."

Mary watched how Alice's face softened while she spoke.

She hesitated, then said, "You were in love with her, weren't you?"

"A long story," Alice said, "and it doesn't involve much about knitting. The only other person who knows it is your mother," she added.

"My mother?" Mary said.

"Maybe that's why I feel comfortable telling you," Alice said. "Your mother was such a good listener."

Mary stifled a laugh. Her mother? A good listener?

Alice motioned toward the tape recorder. "Perhaps you can turn that thing off?"

Mary clicked off the tape. The sun warmed the room, and cast a golden light across it. In her pink chair, Alice sipped her tea, looking out the window as if she could see across the ocean, all the way to England and her past there.

"Poor Rodney," Alice said finally. "He was my fellow for a time. We'd go into the alley and, how should I say this politely? Make love is not right, but for lack of a civil term, I'll say it. We'd make love there. And he would burst with passion while I traveled in my mind to Africa and set up house there. I would kiss him when he was done, and share a cigarette with him. That part was nice. Afterwards. Having a smoke in the late hours with a nice fellow. We'd talk about the war, where the Germans were advancing, what Hitler was up to. Sometimes he'd say, 'When we get married, we'll do such and such,' and I'd tell him flat out that I wasn't going to marry him, or anybody. 'Alice,' he'd say, 'you don't do what we just did and not marry the fellow. That would make you a whore.' " Alice chuckled. "Isn't that the most ridiculous thing you've ever heard? But he was so serious when he said it that I couldn't laugh.

"Then he went off to the war, of course. They all did. Before he left he blathered on about love and marriage and all his plans. I let him talk. After all, that was the thing girls did for boys about to go to war. We gave them hope. Something to look forward to. Something to think about while they were out there.

"I got my secretary's job and my desk right beside Beatrice's. She showed me

261

around the place, taught me the shortcuts, how to win favor and stay out of trouble. There must have been twenty or thirty of us girls sitting at rows of desks, doing our part for the war effort. Filing and stamping papers. Typing and mailing. Tedious stuff, but the days passed pleasantly. Except for the air raids. Those were frightening. At first, anyway. But eventually they became part of the day too. Type these letters. Make tea. File these papers. Run to the Underground until the planes pass.

"Bea and I became fast friends. We'd go together to the picture show and link our arms or even hold hands and cry if it was a sad one. Right off, I recognized that all of those feelings I hadn't had for Rodney, I did have for Bea. I remember one night, I walked her to her flat, and we stood on the steps out front whispering together, and our faces came close and it seemed we might kiss and I thought I would surely die from joy if my lips actually touched hers. Then the moment passed and she turned and went inside, quickly. She stopped at the door, and looked at me, amused. 'Good night, darling,' she said, as if testing the word. Or the idea that I could be her darling. She ran inside, but I stood there, paralyzed.

"Sometimes on Friday nights, Bea and I would go to these dances and then let a couple of boys buy us dinner after. Both of the men only had eyes for Bea usually, but I didn't care about them. I just wanted to be near her. At the end of the night we'd let them kiss us a little, because they were soldiers and going to die probably. One of them who was especially crazy about her was an American. From Hartford, Connecticut. She let him kiss her an awful lot and it made me jealous. So I told her I hated him. Beatrice said, 'You're jealous of Pete, aren't you? Admit it.' I was speechless. 'Pete is a bore,' she said. 'A big American bore.'

"It wasn't long after that night on her stairs, we'd gone to another picture and I'd walked her home, that she invited me upstairs for some tea. 'Pete brought me a canister of sugar,' she said wickedly. Bea lived with two other girls, but one was in the infirmary with the measles, and the other had gone to the sea for a few days with an American GI. It was colder in the flat than it had been outside, and I rubbed Bea's arms to warm her. She let me for a bit, then moved away abruptly and put on the kettle, chattering the whole time about the funny American ways. Then she took a small silver canister and held it out to me.

'Sugar,' she said."

Flushed, from embarrassment or memories, Mary could not guess, Alice got up and went to the window, holding her cup in both hands, staring out at the sea.

"She was my lover for the next two years," Alice said without turning around.

"But what happened to her?" Mary asked. "To the two of you."

"She married Pete," Alice said flatly.

"Pete?" Mary said, confused.

"The American from Hartford, Connecticut. He came back and for two weeks she saw him, crying in my arms every night when she got home. Apologizing for being such a coward. Until one night, she didn't come home. I sat by the window, waiting, knitting the sweater I was making for her. I knit the whole night, not letting myself think, just knitting. Finally, the next morning, I heard the door open. I had dozed off in the chair and I opened my eyes and watched her come in. She knelt right at my feet, and put her head in my lap. 'Darling,' she said — her voice was hoarse, from cigarettes and no sleep — 'I'm going to marry him and go and live in America.' "

Mary jumped to her feet, clattering the teacup and saucer. "But that can't be!" she said.

"Why not? Doesn't life surprise us like that all the time?" Alice said, smiling wryly. "When Pete came for her, his friend Emmett was with him, to help with the bags and the passport and all of the details. Emmett remembered me from the dances and asked if I'd join him later for dinner, after they'd gone. I said yes, out of loneliness, I suppose. Or maybe out of revenge. One dinner led to another and then to another and in three or four months' time I was marrying Emmett and on my way to America myself. He bought us a little house outside of Boston and for a time I tried being a wife. But it didn't work."

"You left him then?" Mary said, struggling to write a happy ending for Alice.

"I'm afraid I was too much of a coward for that. I found comfort in drinking instead."

Of course, Mary thought, there are no happy endings. She tried to remember when she had been a woman who believed in them, but that woman was a stranger to her now.

"Like your mother did," Alice said.

Mary swallowed hard. "Did she ever tell you why she drank?" she asked.

Alice shook her head. "But there's no shame in it, Mary." She stopped. "That's all that really matters. Why, I was drinking sherry instead of tea in the afternoon and a martini with Emmett when he came home and wine with dinner and then a little Drambuie before bed. Before long, it was sherry in the morning and my martini for lunch and the day was just one long blur.

"Then, one afternoon, this was in June of 1970, I was sitting in my kitchen, drunk, which was how I was most of the time anyway, and I heard this rapping at the door, a light sound, and I stumbled toward it and there stood Beatrice, the summer sunshine all around her, like an angel. She was still beautiful, even all those years later.

" 'Do you want me to go away?' she said right off. She looked so American, in a way that's hard to explain. But she had on these blue jeans, one of those T-shirts with a pocket, a white one, and her hair was pulled back into a ponytail. Like an American teenager, except there were the loveliest crinkles around the corners of her mouth and eyes. She wore these silver hoop earrings, and lots of silver bracelets up one arm.

"I stepped aside to let her in, and the kitchen was a bit of a mess. Everything around me was a mess. I couldn't get things organized or accomplished. But what she saw was my knitting. I had a poncho half

266

finished, with orange and green stripes, on the kitchen table. 'You still knit,' she said, smiling.

" 'Let's go somewhere,' I said. 'It's about cocktail hour, isn't it?'

" 'God, yes,' Bea said. 'I could use a good stiff one.'

"She drove a big dark blue Mercedes-Benz to a bar nearby, talking the entire way. Remember the sugar? she said. Remember the reams of paper we filed? Then we were inside the bar, sliding across the red vinyl booth to sit close, knee to knee. We both ordered gin and tonics. It was one of those dark bars where drunks go, or people having affairs meet. It was attached to a motel called the Red Rooster. All around us sat businessmen who'd gone to seed, or married men with their lovers.

"When the drinks came, Beatrice clinked her glass to mine, then took a long sip. 'I was so nervous coming here,' she said. She took out her wallet to show me pictures. Three sons, big tall American boys. Only one looked like her. The strawberry blonde hair, the cat eyes.

"She kept chattering about Pete, his business, those sons. I ordered another drink. They lived in West Hartford, she told me, and described the big lawns, the leafy trees.

"She was nursing her drink, but I ordered a third and then asked her, 'Why did you come? After all this time?'

"Beatrice finished her drink. 'Have you done it with anyone else?' she said, sucking on her straw. She glanced around again, and lowered her voice. 'With another woman, I mean?'

" 'No,' I said.

" 'I have,' she said, fishing out an ice cube. Her hand was trembling. 'I meet someone and we spend a few months together. You know, at my house or at her house. Then I get worried that people can tell. That somehow Pete will know, or a neighbor, and I break it off.' Her accent was practically gone, I noticed. 'Until the next time,' she said.

"The air conditioner came on noisily, as if it had to work very hard to send out cold air.

" 'The thing is,' she said, 'I'm still in love with you. And I wanted to come and see if that feeling was real, you know? Because with all of these other women, I never felt the same.'

" 'I'm a mess,' I said. 'You can see that.'

"Beatrice looked at me finally. 'What is it?'

" 'I'm a drunk,' I said, and I laughed,

268

inappropriately. But it was the first time I'd said those words out loud. 'That's what I do. I sit at home and I drink. I make plans for the garden, or the ironing, but I never quite manage it. Emmett comes home and I try to act sober and busy. I make us martinis, some dinner if I can manage that, and then it's gin and television.'

" 'Pete and the boys are camping in the Berkshires,' she said. 'They won't be back until late Sunday night.'

"That weekend we stayed locked in that motel room at the Red Rooster and it was as if no time had passed. I called Emmett and told him I needed time away, time to think. And I lost myself in Beatrice.

"But of course, Sunday afternoon came. I watched her dress to leave me again, sliding the bracelets up her arm, carefully putting on the silver hoop earrings.

" 'It was real after all,' she said.

" 'I won't go back to Emmett,' I said. 'Not after this.'

"She came and sat beside me. 'I'll talk to Pete about a divorce.'

"I had told her that Emmett and I had a cottage on the beach in Rhode Island. I would go and stay there. I wrote down the address for her and told her to come as soon as she could."

Alice sat again in the chair across from Mary.

"She never came, did she?" Mary asked her.

Alice shook her head. "But she saved my life."

"She broke your heart!"

"I divorced Emmett and he gave me the cottage. I opened the store. I stopped drinking."

"Did you ever fall in love again?"

"In love? I don't know. I've had some wonderful relationships. I've been happy, in my own way."

"You never drank again after that weekend?" Mary said.

Alice laughed. "Oh no, it doesn't work quite that easily. Even now I would like nothing more than to get good and blotto. But I joined AA and, well, you know that already."

Mary looked at her, confused.

"Why, that's where I met Mamie. Your mother. I was a few years sober by then, and I became her sponsor. I sat her down right where you're sitting and I taught her to knit."

"You met her in AA?" Mary said.

"You never knew that?"

Mary shook her head no.

"I told her to store up energy for a day when boredom and grief cannot touch you. Then get some old wool and needles and play with knits and purls."

Later, as Mary drove home in the dusk, down that driveway and then the dirt road, leaving the ocean behind her, moving west toward Providence, she began to cry. Who was this woman that Alice described? A desperate woman, needing help, sitting in a powder blue chair by the sea, learning to knit. Her own mother. Mary remembered the dozens of tiny hats, carefully knit, then wrapped in tissue paper and boxed to be sent to the hospitals. *I hate you!* Mary had screamed at her mother. *You're crazy!* Her mother had just sat, quietly, desperately, knitting.

12
THE KNITTING
CIRCLE

Weeks passed and Dylan came home late most nights. "Meetings," he explained. "Over wine?" Mary asked him, tasting it on his lips when she kissed him good night. Was it her imagination, or were they really making love less often? She thought back, trying to gauge frequency, intensity, interest.

"Half of the marriages of people who lose a child end in divorce," she reminded him one October afternoon as he worked diligently on the crossword puzzle from that day's newspaper.

He looked up at her, then went right back to the puzzle.

"Since when do you do crossword puzzles?" she asked him.

"I used to do one every day. It's good for the brain," he said, tapping his pen against his temple.

"When was that?" Mary said.

"A long time ago," he told her. "Before I knew you."

Mary frowned. "Were you an entirely different person before I knew you?"

"We both were different people," he said, shrugging. He turned back to the crossword puzzle and carefully filled in the squares.

Mary watched him, remembering the small details he had told her so long ago about his first wife, how she didn't use enough laundry detergent and his clothes never smelled clean; how she liked to sew and made the curtains for their house, and her own skirts and summer shifts; how she always served Jell-O salads at dinner parties, with cut-up fruit inside and a dollop of mayo or sour cream. She had sounded like a woman from the 1950s, with her sewing and her Jell-O.

"What?" Dylan said, looking up at her now.

"I was just remembering things you told me. Trying to figure out who you are."

"You know who I am," he said, irritated.

"Of course," Mary agreed. But really, watching him like this, she felt like there were many things she didn't know.

Mary's mother didn't ask questions. When Mary tried to tell her how much she missed

Stella, how long her days had grown, how sad she was, her mother suggested she knit more, travel more, join a book group, take a class. Mary knew her mother was still stung from her refusal to visit back in September, but she'd promised Thanksgiving, and reluctantly intended to keep that promise.

She and her mother had had exactly two visits alone together, both disastrous. Back in college, her mother had come for a weekend and Mary, out of nervousness or anxiety, had gotten drunk and thrown up in the rental car. The next day she'd been too hungover to sightsee with her mother. And, over their final dinner, her mother had lectured her about the dangers of drinking and driving, of taking drugs, of having sex with too many boys. She'd talked about gonorrhea and unwanted pregnancies until Mary had told her to please be quiet and go back to her hotel.

The second trip was back when Mary had lived in San Francisco. Her mother came for a week, sleeping on the futon in the living room. She'd complained about all of the things that Mary loved: the steep hills, the brisk air, the endless variety of people. At the airport her mother had said, "I don't know how you stand it here. Too touristy." "Mom," Mary had told her, "you are the first person I have ever met who doesn't like San Francisco." Secretly she was relieved; maybe her mother wouldn't come back.

Now she was facing the prospect of Thanksgiving with her, eating Saul's turkey mole and missing Stella.

"When we're in Mexico —" Mary continued, interrupting Dylan's crossword puzzle again.

"Mexico?" he said. "Oh, hon, I'm sorry. I thought I'd go to my sister's, like we did last year."

"You're not spending Thanksgiving with me?" Mary said, shocked. "We always spend the holidays together."

"Okay," he said, raising his hand like a cop, "if it's important to you."

"If it's important to me? Why isn't it important to you?" She heard her voice growing shrill, and shuddered.

He slipped the cap on and off his pen a few times. "It just doesn't matter without Stella," he said finally. "Remember that song she used to sing at Thanksgiving?"

Tears sprang to Mary's eyes. She nodded, hearing their daughter's voice as if from a great distance: *Turkey and stuffing on the table, sweet pumpkin pie is mighty fine, mother and father, aunts and uncles, Thanks-*

giving is a family time!

"It all seems so pointless," Dylan said softly.

"But *we're* not pointless," Mary said, wiping her face with the back of her hand. "Are we?"

Was it her imagination, or did he wait too long before he said, "Of course not." And did he hesitate before he put down the newspaper and went over to her to wrap her in his arms?

Holly sometimes made a pot of strong dark roast, and everyone kept a mug by the coffeemaker, just in case. Mary rinsed out hers, filled it, and took a slice of Holly's pumpkin bread. Holly was too busy moving in time to her iPod and typing away on the computer to hear Mary's "Thank you." It would have been good to have company, even for a few moments. This morning she had called her mother and made excuses to not visit her at Thanksgiving. Her life felt too precarious to leave for even a few days, especially to spend time with her mother, who would somehow manage to make Mary feel even worse.

Mary leaned against the wall, sipping her coffee and listening to the peculiar sound the wind made as it whistled. The building, a former mill, still had elevator shafts and closed-off areas that did funny things with sound. Combined with the distant sound of Holly's music played so loud Mary could almost catch it too, Mary settled into the high-pitched noise and thumping bass.

Mary straightened. She walked around the corner and saw it wasn't just wind and rain and the Black Eyed Peas. Eddie and Jessica were fucking in his office, right against the closed door.

Why did this upset her so much? Mary wondered as she hurried back to her own office. Holly came in right behind her and closed the door.

"I know," Holly said. "It's like gross, right? What's that thing Eddie always says? Don't pee in my pool?"

"Don't shit where you eat," Mary said.

"Right," Holly said, nodding.

Mary slipped on her shiny yellow raincoat and put her computer to sleep.

"I'm going home," she said.

"Got a party or something tonight?" Holly asked brightly.

Mary shook her head no.

"I'm going as a black widow spider," Holly was saying. "I made this great costume out of black velvet with all these arms that I can manipulate with strings."

"Sounds great," Mary said, suddenly crying. She bent her head so Holly wouldn't see, and walked as fast as she could out of the office to the elevator. Incense from the yoga studio downstairs filled the little waiting area. Mary jabbed the down button several times, hard.

When she turned, Jessica was standing there.

"The mayor," Jessica said. "He's hosting this thing at his house."

She had on a black trench coat belted tight so that it showed off her tiny waist, and knee-high black boots. Mary thought of Nazis, of hostile invasions and takeovers.

Jessica smiled, smugly, Mary thought.

"You're off to do this knitting story?" she said.

Mary nodded. The elevator arrived with a creak and a sigh, the door sliding open slowly. They rode down together in silence.

At the door, Jessica opened a pale blue umbrella decorated with white puffy clouds.

"By the way," Mary said, pulling her hood up, "that El Coyote is probably the worst Mexican food I've ever had."

Jessica raised her tweezed eyebrows. "Really?" she said. "Eddie loves it."

Mary watched Jessica's skinny self go downtown. Despite the rain, Mary walked slowly. Eddie was, after all, just her boss. But somehow she felt alienated now, unable to drop in his office and talk, or to speak freely about assignments, about Jessica herself.

The umbrellas in the outdoor patio at Jake's dripped rain onto the empty tables. This was one of Dylan's favorite places. Hamburgers stuffed with blue cheese and two-dollar pints of beer. Maybe they would come here tonight, Mary decided. She looked at the Halloween decorations in the windows, big cardboard witches and scarecrows.

She stopped.

There, at a window table between a witch and a scarecrow, sat Dylan, his head leaned forward toward a woman. Mary stared at them. The woman, with her blonde wispy hair and wire-rimmed glasses looked familiar. Then she remembered — it was the woman from that party, the one who had told the boring story about her year studying in Florence. The one who had stood by Dylan's side, in his cluster.

She watched her husband sip his beer. He was smiling in a way that made Mary start to cry all over again. The woman was talking, was making him laugh now. She also held a pint of dark beer.

Mary took a few steps toward them, watching as the waitress appeared with food. That hamburger for Dylan; a big bowl of something for the woman. But they didn't seem to notice. They stayed like that, heads bent across the table, almost touching, talking and laughing in the way people did when they were . . . Were what? Mary asked herself. Having an affair? Or simply having lunch? She glanced at her watch. It was three-thirty. Too late for lunch.

Then Dylan reached over and wiped a strand of that wispy blonde hair out of the woman's eyes. Mary's stomach lurched. Without thinking what she would say, she walked into the dimly lit restaurant, dripping water on the floor as she moved.

"What a coincidence," Mary said as soon as she reached the table.

They both looked up at her. The woman still smiling, Dylan expressionless.

"I was walking by and I was thinking that we should come here for dinner tonight," she said. She imagined what a mess she looked with her rain- and tear-streaked face, her silly yellow coat. Everyone else — Jessica with her trench coat and this woman in her black pantsuit and Dylan with his tie loosened and his shirtsleeves rolled up — looked like grown-ups. She just looked ridiculous.

"I'm his wife," Mary said.

The woman said, "I'm Denise."

Mary nodded. "Denise. I've heard nothing at all about you, which makes me even more nervous."

Dylan was getting to his feet, reaching for his wallet. "I'll take you home," he said.

But even as he was putting his hand on her arm to move her away, he was talking to Denise. She had thin lips, and pink lipstick, and eyeliner on the top and bottom of her eyes.

"No, no," Mary said, shrugging out of his grasp. "You don't need to take me home. Stay and finish your lunch. Or dinner. Or whatever it is."

Denise had the vegetarian chili. A vegetarian with pink lipstick and glasses. This was who her husband was having an affair with.

Dylan was urging her away from the table. Could a person be more embarrassed? Mary wondered. More heartbroken? What is left? she was thinking as she walked away from them. She slipped on the wet floor, but didn't fall. Instead, she kind of glided out. Like an ice skater, she thought. She could hear Dylan's voice, but she wasn't sure who he was talking to. Mary didn't stop to find out. She just kept going, out the door, into the rain.

When he finally came home, Mary was in the bathtub. It was dark out, still raining. Her skin was wrinkled, and the bathroom was steamy. When the water cooled, she emptied it and refilled the tub with more water as hot as she could bear it. She wasn't sure how long she'd been doing this when Dylan opened the bathroom door and moved through the steamy air to the edge of the tub, where he sat.

"I'm not sure I want to have this conversation while I'm naked," she said.

He nodded, but didn't leave.

"So," Mary said after a moment, "you're having an affair. You're having an affair with Denise." The woman's face floated across Mary's mind and she closed her eyes tight against it.

"Not an affair exactly." Dylan cleared his throat. "I haven't slept with her," he said.

"Yet," Mary said, opening her eyes to look right at him.

"Yet," he said.

"You're at what?" she asked him. "The groping stage? The making-out-in-the-car-and-stopping-yourself-before-you-do-anything-more stage?"

"Yes," he said.

Mary swallowed hard. "You've groped her?"

"Yes," he said.

"Wow," Mary said. "You're not even denying it."

She didn't know what to say next.

"I can't lie to you. I love you," he said, and Mary laughed.

"Obviously," she said. "I mean, kissing and groping another woman is always a sign of love for your wife."

"She's happy," he said.

"Happy about what?"

"No," Dylan said. "Just happy. She comes to work every day and she looks good and she smells good and she's smiling. When I talk to her, she tells me happy things. Like something funny about her dog. Or about her garden or, I don't know. She's just happy."

"Good for her," Mary said. The water had turned cold and she was starting to shiver. "I guess her little girl didn't die. It's easy to be happy when you haven't lost everything."

"I know," he said.

"I'm sorry I'm not happy enough for you," Mary said, her teeth chattering now.

"It's just good to be with someone who doesn't have a clue. Who is just fucking happy."

"I want to get out of the tub now," Mary said. "And I don't want you in here. Okay?"

He nodded again, but he still didn't leave.

"Dylan?" Mary said.

"I won't see her anymore," he said. "If that's what you want. I mean, it's not anything. We haven't even slept together."

"Could you go now, please?" Mary said.

He stood. The ass of his pants was wet. Mary waited until he'd gone, closing the door behind him. Then she got out of the tub and dried off, rubbing the towel hard on her skin. She wondered if he would still be here, in the house, when she came out. She wondered why she felt so numb, like something inside her had grown cold, or disappeared altogether.

When she opened the door and stepped out, she saw the glow of the television, the back of Dylan's head. He was still here. Mary went to the sofa and sat beside him, not too close. Larry King was interviewing the parents of a woman who had been murdered by her husband.

"Don't get any ideas," Mary said.

She said, "I don't know if I'll ever be happy again. If it's happy you want, you're probably in the wrong place."

The woman's parents were crying now. Mary couldn't watch them anymore. She got up to go to bed.

"I don't want to leave," he said.

"I don't care," Mary told him. "I wish I did."

She lay in bed, still hearing the dead woman's parents crying. In movies, the wife finds out about an affair and cries and throws things. But here she was, unable to do anything. She remembered that morning when Scarlet called to tell her that the Sit and Knit had burned down, how she had wondered what more she could lose. Now she saw that she could, truly, lose everything.

"It's a stitch a month," Alice was explaining on the telephone. "In a year you have a blanket."

"Okay," Mary said.

It had been three days since Dylan had told her about his happy girlfriend. Mary hadn't gone to work since then. She and Dylan had eaten mostly silent dinners together. They had played a game of Scrabble. He'd slept in the guest room.

But tonight, the third night, dinner had come and gone and Mary was sitting alone knitting the fingerless gloves she was making everyone for Christmas. It was still raining out, but now the rain was mixed with snow so that when Mary looked out the window it sparkled in the streetlight.

"And by then," Alice was saying, "we'll be in the new Sit and Knit."

"Great," Mary said.

"We'll meet on Wednesday," Alice said. "The usual. But we'll meet at Beth's house. She's under the weather and it will be easier if we all go there."

"A stitch a month," Mary said. "Beth's house. Wednesday."

Alice paused. "Honey?" she said. "Are you all right?"

"I'm not happy," she said.

"No," Alice said.

"But I'm glad we're meeting. That's a sign of good things to come."

"We'll see you there," Alice said. "On Wednesday."

Dylan came home very late. Mary heard him come in, and when he stood in the doorway of their bedroom she pretended to be asleep. The next night, when he came home even later, she was waiting for him.

"Let me guess," she said, her throat dry and aching. "You've moved past groping."

"I'm thinking," Dylan said, "that I should move out."

That numb spot vanished. Emotion rose in her, hot and enormous. Here it comes,

286

Mary thought. Even as she cried, she thought it amazing that a person never ran out of tears.

■ ■ ■ ■

PART SEVEN:
MOTHERS AND
CHILDREN

■ ■ ■ ■

I thought it would never do to present myself to a gentleman that way; so for want of kids, I slipped on a pair of woolen mittens, which my mother had knit for me to carry to sea . . .
— Herman Melville,
Redburn

13
BETH

The pattern was called "textured rib."

Bottom border: K 6 rows.
Row 1: K3, (p2, k2) 12 times, k1.
Row 2: K5, (p2, k2) 11 times, k3.
Row 3: K3, p46, k3.
Row 4: K.
Repeat rows 1–4 until block measures 12".
Top border: K 6 rows.

Alice brought large loops of vivid-colored yarn, spun and hand dyed by women in Uruguay. The knitting circle, hungry to knit together, to knit something new, dropped their hands into the wool as if it were jewels, something precious to hold. Even the names of the colors were exotic — jungle, lava, wildflowers, flame.

Mary picked up a skein, felt the way each thread moved from thin to thick and back, making an uneven diameter that stretched like the awkward lines of back roads on a map. Looking around at the women choosing a skein to begin, Mary remembered her first night at the knitting circle, when each of them had been a blank to her. Now those blanks were filled in. There was Scarlet, her long red hair pulled back today in a low ponytail, in an ivory sweater with one thick cable running up the front and faded jeans over an old pair of Frye boots. The soft lines etched around the corners of her eyes and mouth were the only sign of the tragedy she held inside her.

And Lulu, spiky platinum hair topping black roots, plucked at some yarn, her eyes darting over it. She discarded one, picked up another, plucking at the wool. These nervous habits and the sense of discomfort with her surroundings probably came from what had happened to her back in New York. Even when she smiled at Mary, like now, the smile was tight and quick, as if it might hurt.

"Flame," Lulu said, brandishing the bright orange yarn. "Hubba-hubba."

Lulu's urban bravado usually made Mary smile, but today she winced. She turned back to the yarn, the hot pinks and electric blues and maraschino cherry reds.

"I like all these whites," Ellen said. "So

many shades of white." Her fingers lightly skimmed several skeins, all white: the blue-white of ice, the stark white of snow.

Mary knew that Ellen's daughter was not doing well. On the way here, Scarlet had said she was in bed now, waiting.

"For?" Lulu had asked.

"A heart," Scarlet had said simply, and Mary's own heart had gripped tight on itself.

"You like the reds?" Alice asked Mary, her voice painfully kind, as if she knew that Dylan had moved out, that Mary really had nothing.

Mary looked down at the yarn she was holding. Poppy. "I guess so," she said.

Alice held another shade of red against the one in Mary's hand. She studied them, nodded, and added a third.

"In three months," Alice said, "you'll have three squares done. A row."

And three months will have passed, Mary told herself. Poppy, Cherry, Brick. The colors sounded like characters from a soap opera: Brick leaves Poppy after their daughter Cherry dies. Tears welled up in Mary's eyes. She pretended to care about the blanket that these squares would become, these colors.

But Alice saw through her. She squeezed

her hand and whispered, "If you ever need to talk."

Mary nodded again, felt Alice waiting beside her, but she didn't look up again until she heard the soft shuffle of her slippered footsteps walking away. She could not tell anyone that Dylan had moved out, that she was left with nothing.

The yarn needed to be rolled into balls. Mary took it into another room and sat there alone, mindlessly winding it. From somewhere she heard voices, the clatter of dishes. Beth's house, in a subdivision not far from Harriet's, was an ordinary center-hall colonial: white with black shutters, a brambly wreath dotted with orange berries hanging on the front door. Nothing at all special. Mary took some comfort in this, the dullness of Beth's surroundings.

The dining room, where the yarn spilled across a glass-topped table, had straight-backed chairs covered in white fabric, tied with bows at each side, as if Beth had dressed the chairs in dinner jackets.

"Beth made these," Harriet had beamed.

Mary had to stifle a comment. No shit, she thought. They looked homemade, someone's idea of sophistication.

The family room where she sat now had a fireplace made of brick with a short wooden mantel crowded with pictures that Mary avoided looking at. The room itself was overflowing with toys that had been shoved into corners and plastic bins, a hasty effort at order. Mary sat on a green and white plaid couch, its slipcovers probably also hand-sewn by Beth, like the striped ones on both easy chairs. On the coffee table, magazines stood in neat piles. A small dish of candy corn and a remote control dressed in a green knit cover were placed at perfect angles to each other.

Behind her, Mary could make out Harriet's low voice. She thought of Harriet's son and his wife, the careful control with which Harriet lived her life. Beth was the only one who still remained a blank to Mary. Perhaps this was by design, on both their parts. Mary had no desire to hear about Beth's homemade life, her daughter Stella, the best way to bake a pie or sew a hem. And she had no desire to tell Beth — or anyone — anything about her own pathetic life.

Mary picked up her yarn, put the two still-unrolled skeins in her bag, and followed the rise and fall of the women's voices to the living room across the front hall.

Past the polished wood of the banister and the small table where mail and keys and telephone directories all lived in their own clearly marked boxes, Mary entered the living room last. Everyone was already seated and beginning to cast on. She glanced at the colors snaking up each number nine needle: calypso and juniper, bramble and mist, autumn and jade. A rainbow of yarn.

Beth took up most of the pale blue velvet sofa, where she half lay, half sat beneath a dark green fleece blanket. At her feet, wedged into the corner at the opposite end of the couch, was Harriet. They were meeting here because Beth wasn't feeling well. Under the weather, Alice had said on the phone.

Mary took a seat on the ivory carpet and began to cast on.

"Fifty-two stitches," Alice reminded her.

"How are you feeling?" Mary asked her.

"Not so great really," Beth said.

Mary looked up from her knitting, surprised. Of course, Beth was already ahead of everyone else. Her block was a good six inches long, the pattern already revealing itself with small puckers of pink squares alternating with soft valleys between them.

Harriet tsked. "She'll be just fine," she said. She didn't look up. Instead, she kept knitting, her lips silently shaping the stitches: *purl, purl, knit, knit, purl, purl, knit, knit.*

"Cancer," Lulu said in the car as they drove back to Providence.

"What?" Mary said from the backseat. She leaned as far forward as her seat belt would allow. "Beth has cancer?"

"When I first started going to the knitting circle," Scarlet said, "she had just gotten a clean bill of health. Alice taught her to knit when she was undergoing chemo the first time."

Mary swallowed hard. "You mean this is a recurrence?"

Lulu twisted around to face Mary. "She's probably going to die," she said.

"Lulu!" Scarlet scolded. "Don't catastrophize."

"What?" Lulu said. "You think bad things don't happen? You think mothers with four little kids don't die?"

"God," Scarlet said, "I need a cigarette."

Lulu looked back at Mary again. "Breast cancer. Metastasized."

Mary's hand flew to her mouth, as if to keep something back.

"She's had what? Four good years?" Lulu said, settling back in her seat.

Scarlet rummaged in her bag and pulled

out a pack of cigarettes.

"Now you're going to get cancer," Lulu said.

"Stop!" Scarlet told her.

The lighter made a small popping sound. Mary watched the soft red glow at its tip as Scarlet moved it to the cigarette dangling from her lips. She inhaled luxuriously.

"We're all going to get cancer," Lulu muttered.

Mary sat back and watched the blur of headlights as they sped down the highway.

"Every one of us," Lulu said.

Mary was surprised when she saw Beth, bald beneath a red chenille knitted hat. Beth's cheeks were a surprisingly healthy pink, and Mary thought for a foolish instant that maybe she had been cured. Beneath the smell of furniture wax and banana bread lingered the sour smell of vomit.

"She looks good, doesn't she?" Harriet said cheerfully, squeezing Beth's face tenderly. She placed a cup of weak tea on the coffee table.

The house was dressed for Christmas. A jolly Santa on the lawn. A fat wreath with a red velvet bow on the front door. Inside, poinsettias on tabletops and candles in every window glowing white. A Christmas tree in the room where they gathered stood ceiling high, a gold star glistening at the very top, and white ornaments on every bough.

"She does another tree for the kids," Harriet beamed. "In their playroom. That one has crazy stuff on it. Trains that chug and balls that play music and reindeer that spin."

"This year —" Beth began.

"This year you supervised," Harriet said, waving her hand dismissively.

Beth smiled, but it seemed to take all her energy to do it.

Alice cleared her throat. "Block two," she said. "Everyone, I assume, finished block one?"

She passed around a finished square so they could see the pattern. "It's a zigzag," she said. "Same bottom border. Knit six rows. Then it gets complicated."

Mary wrote down the pattern as Alice spoke:

Row 1: K8, (p3, k3) 7 times, k2.
Rows 2, 4, 6, 8 —

"Who do we appreciate?" Lulu cheered.

Alice rolled her eyes. "There's always one wise guy."

"And it's always Lulu," Scarlet chuckled.

Rows 2, 4, 6, 8, 10, and 12: K3, p46, k3.
Row 3: K7, (p3, k3) 7 times, k3 . . .

Mary glanced around the room, grateful to be here, in the company of these women, just knitting. Her eyes moved from Alice to Scarlet to Lulu. Ellen was not here tonight. Instead she was with Bridget, both of them waiting for that call to come with a new heart. She settled her gaze on Harriet, who was ignoring Alice's instructions and knitting away furiously. Then Mary looked over at Beth, who probably had already finished her zigzag and was on her way to spiderweb or dashes.

To her surprise, Beth was sound asleep. Her mouth slightly open, her knitting resting on her chest.

"And finally," Alice was saying, "the top border is only five rows."

Somewhere, Dylan was with happy Denise doing happy things. Mary imagined a large golden dog. A garden in bloom. She imagined them blissfully groping each other.

"Mary?" Scarlet said.

Mary saw that they were all looking at her.

Scarlet pointed to Mary's knitting, which had fallen completely off one needle, her square unraveling in her hands.

The thing about knitting, Mary thought,

was when it fell apart, it was easy to fix.

"Need help?" Alice asked.

Yes! Mary screamed in her head. I need a life raft. A lifeline. I need my life back.

But she said, "I'm good. Thanks." Carefully she picked up her knitting, and began the slow process of slipping her stitches back on the needle.

In Mexico at Christmas a statue of the Virgin is paraded through the town. Villagers dress like wise men; children dress like Jesus. There is a bazaar so large and full, it takes days to visit all the sellers' booths. Nativity figures can be had for a few pesos. Tamales are sold steaming from carts in the streets.

Mary's mother told her they would do all of that and more. Why, she said, if you'd like, we can even fly to Puerto Vallarta. Rent a car and drive on to Sayulita, where the beaches are perfect moons of sand and clear blue water.

"I want to be home for Christmas," Mary had told her, and even as her mother continued talking, trying to convince her that this trip would be good for her, Mary had realized how truly sad it was that she would rather spend Christmas alone than with her own mother.

In the attic sat boxes, red with green lids, and inside those boxes were Christmas stockings, *Dylan, Mary,* and *Stella* written in silver glitter across their tops. There was a Santa who danced to "Rockin' Around the Christmas Tree" and a Nativity set her mother had sent them from Mexico on which Stella had colored over all the painted figures in red marker.

At the Christmas party at the office, Holly wore a Santa's hat and earrings that blinked on and off like Christmas lights. Eddie and Jessica wore matching accessories: Eddie a bow tie with martini glasses and olives, Jessica a matching scarf. He kept his arm around her waist and spoke into her ear, conspiratorially.

Mary left the party, got in her car, and drove out of town. She was still dressed in her red miniskirt, her black hose with candy canes climbing up her calves, and her holiday high heels. On the seat beside her was her Secret Santa gift, a rubbery fish that lifted its head off its mounting and sang, "Don't worry, be happy."

Four hours later, she was somewhere in Maine, on the ocean Route 1. She was tired. It was nine o'clock and she'd only eaten two Christmas cookies all day. A rambling white B and B appeared around the next corner, and Mary pulled into its driveway and parked.

Inside it smelled like cinnamon and evergreen. The place was hushed, low-lit. She could hear a piano. She could hear the crashing of waves. It was Christmas Eve, and Mary could see that families and couples in love were all gathered here.

She would have walked out, but a woman appeared dressed in a red plaid ankle-length skirt and a big Christmas tree brooch. Her gray hair was tied into two braids, like Mrs. Claus. Mary smiled to herself, and asked if they had a room.

"You alone?" the woman asked in a flat Maine accent, narrowing her eyes.

Mary nodded.

The woman glanced around the small overheated room.

"No luggage?"

Mary shook her head.

"Well," the woman said finally, "we've got a room all right. The dining room's closed but we could probably find you a turkey sandwich or some such thing."

"That sounds fine," Mary said.

She followed the woman into another overheated room. There was a long wooden bar and red stools. The bartender stood, looking bored. The Christmas music was louder here.

"Get Miss . . ." The woman raised her eyebrows at Mary.

"Mary."

"Get Miss Mary here something to eat. And a glass of wine." She raised her eyebrows again.

"That would be great," Mary said. She sat on one of the stools, relieved to slip off her high heels.

The woman touched her shoulder gently. "Merry Christmas then," she said.

"You too," Mary said.

The bartender brought her a thick turkey sandwich with cranberry sauce and stuffing in it. He poured her a big glass of chardonnay, then stepped back and watched her eat.

When she pushed the plate away, he said, "Alone on Christmas Eve?"

Mary sipped her wine.

He refilled her glass, poured himself one, and left the bottle on the bar.

"There's only three reasons a person is alone on Christmas," he said.

She looked at him, waiting. He was handsome, she realized. Longish sandy hair, a stubbled face, broad shoulders.

"Thrown out," he said, holding up his fingers to count off the reasons. "Lost. Or running away."

She almost said, *Lost.*

"Running away," she said.

"From a jealous husband?"

"Hardly," Mary laughed. Dylan had called her to talk about Christmas. He had said he would be away over the holiday. Could you be a little vaguer? she'd asked him before she hung up.

"What then?"

"Ghosts," she told him.

"Ah then," he said, "we have something in common." He stuck out his hand. "I'm Connor."

They didn't say any more about it then. Instead, he came and sat beside her and they talked about the safe things that strangers discuss: snowfall amounts and recent movies and what a person liked in a bottle of wine. They drank that bottle, and before it was finished Mary heard herself flirting with this man whose knee pressed against hers gently. His smile was easy to like. In another lifetime, she had been a woman who might meet a man like this, in a bar, and talk of nothing with him while something built up between them. She had been a woman who might go home with a stranger, who would take pleasure in a man's large hands running along her body, a tongue on her breast, the newness of lips kissing her for the first time.

Connor pointed to the large window behind her, and she turned to see lacy snowflakes falling outside it.

"Let's go and catch some on our tongues," he said, taking her hand and leading her out. They stopped to put on coats, and he took a long scarf from a peg and wrapped it several times around her neck.

"You're in Maine, you know," he said. "Got to bundle up."

Then he tugged on the two ends, pulling her toward him. When they started to kiss, Mary felt all the sad things melt away. For an instant, she thought about Dylan, and wondered if this was why he had left her. For such moments when it was easy to forget.

They kissed and kissed like that, until Connor was unraveling the scarf now, pulling it and her coat and hat off. Mary did the same, removing all of the outer layers he had so carefully buttoned and tied a moment ago. The Christmas music had stopped, and the only sounds were the fire crackling and their breathing, hard and fast, as they continued undressing each other, her skirt hiked up high, his shirt and pants open now. Mary reaching for him desperately.

When he entered her, the shock of feeling someone different than Dylan inside her excited her. Perhaps she should feel guilty; the thought drifted across her mind but got lost in the passion between her and this man she didn't know. For this brief time, nothing mattered except the two of them on this worn Oriental rug in this inn in Maine.

When it was over, he propped himself on both elbows, looking down at her with that easy smile of his.

"Whatever it was that sent you out on Christmas Eve," he said, "I'm glad it sent you my way."

"I haven't done something like this in . . ." She laughed.

Slowly, he eased out of her, and kissed her full on the mouth.

"I'm taking you home with me," he said.

"You don't even know me," Mary told him.

Connor pulled her to her feet, and slowly began to put her back together, until once again he was tying the scarf around her neck, and tugging her toward him to kiss.

"I'm damaged goods," she said.

He laughed. "Who isn't?" He nodded toward the window. "Snow already stopped. Let's go and make snow angels."

■ ■ ■ ■

Later, sitting on a blanket in the snowy field beyond the inn, the ocean pounding behind them, Connor asked her what those ghosts were. "Or who," he added.

"My daughter died," she said. She rarely spoke those words, and she shivered when she said them. "She was five."

His arm was already draped around her shoulders, but now he pulled her even closer. His down jacket was cold against her cheek. It was so black out, the streetlights so distant, that Mary could believe they were the only two people in the world right then.

"I came here," Connor said, "from Boston, after my wife died. I used to work in television news. A reporter. You know, the guy who stands outside in the middle of hurricanes. Now I tend bar in Maine."

Mary nodded into his chest.

"We never had kids," he said. "I can only imagine."

Clouds obliterated the moon and the stars, drifting in a milky dance across the black sky. When Connor bent to kiss her, Mary lifted her face to meet his. He could be anyone. They could be anywhere. It was as if she were floating in space, untethered.

Mary stayed. She never even went upstairs to the room at the inn. Instead, she followed Connor's old yellow Jeep down icy curving roads to his apartment on the second floor of an old Victorian facing the ocean. The radiators hissed and creaked. The windows shuddered against the wind. She lay naked beneath layers of blankets with this man she did not know, as if she were trying on a new identity. Or finding an old one.

They didn't speak of their losses again. Instead, they just brought comfort to each other with their bodies. Once, so long ago it was just a whisper to her, Mary remembered doing this with Dylan — the long days in bed, their bodies sore as they explored each other. Connor made them instant soup in chipped diner mugs. He told her funny stories about working as a reporter. He played the banjo for her, and sang songs she had never heard before. They took baths together in his old claw-foot tub, Mary soaping up Connor's husky body, her hands learning someone new.

One night he rolled a fat joint and for the first time since college she got so stoned she had giggling fits that wouldn't end. To laugh, even with the help of that strong pot he said he'd brought back from Hawaii, felt so good Mary thought she might die from the feeling.

The next night she asked him to roll another joint, but he refused. "Sure, you'll go home a drug addict and your husband will come and find me and beat the shit out of me."

"I do have a husband," she said.

It was dusk and the sky beyond the bedroom window was blue-black.

"I figured," Connor said. He hesitated, then said, "You told me you were damaged goods. But since my wife died, I can't connect any more than this. Than what we have here."

Relieved, Mary said, "Eventually I have to figure out if it's really over between him and me."

"You'll figure it out," he said.

The inn was closed between Christmas and New Year's, so they spent a week together, taking walks along the empty beach, building fires in his fireplace, talking little about each other's lives or plans. They were two people without futures, Mary thought more than once. Two people living in a kind of limbo.

New Year's Day, when she finally got into her car to leave, Connor waving goodbye from the wraparound porch's steps, Mary thought it was entirely possible that she'd never return to Providence at all. She imagined driving south and not stopping until the warm air and palm trees of Florida came into view. Or perhaps she would turn the car west and find a small town somewhere, with a good bookstore, a café that roasted its own coffee beans, a group of strong women who met for coffee and knitting and talk. For a while, the possibilities seemed endless.

But then Maine turned into New Hampshire, New Hampshire to Massachusetts, and then the WELCOME TO RHODE ISLAND sign appeared and Mary knew that she was not going to do anything but go home, where the pieces of her marriage lay, where Stella's room sat empty, where the image of her daughter still brought her both comfort and pain.

"I've gotten ahead," Mary told Alice. She was grateful they were speaking on the telephone rather than in person so that Alice couldn't see her blush. "I was up in Maine and I kept knitting and knitting and I finished my zigzag block."

"Good for you," Alice said. "But I can't help you with the next one. I'm going home to England for a couple of weeks."

Mary fingered her next skein of yarn: brick. Scarlet and Lulu had gone to Costa Rica together for New Year's. "If you weren't married we'd invite you along," Lulu had said, and Mary had pretended that she was indeed married and full of holiday plans. Ellen had moved into an apartment near Boston Children's Hospital with Bridget while they waited for news of a heart. Even Harriet was off on an Elderhostel trip to the Galápagos Islands.

"Beth is way ahead," Alice was saying. "You could ask her."

Mary swallowed hard. "I don't want to bother her," she said, a half lie. She didn't want to bother her, that part was true. But she also didn't want to be around someone sick like that.

"I think she likes company," Alice said.

"How is she?" Mary asked.

"She's dying," Alice said.

"But there's always something that can be done," Mary said.

"She keeps trying, God bless her. Chemo-therapy and surgery. She had one right after Christmas on her lungs. But they only found more tumors."

"Oh," Mary said, tears welling up in her eyes.

312

"She'll be glad for the distraction," Alice said before she hung up.

Beth's husband answered the door. Mary was immediately struck by how young he looked, how flushed with fear.

He reached out a hand for her to shake, saying, "I'm Tommy."

Mary surprised herself by moving past his offered hand and hugging him instead. Tommy seemed used to it, and accepted the hug readily.

"She was so glad you were coming," he said, taking Mary's coat and hat and scarf and leading her into the kitchen. "The holidays, you know," he said. "Everyone's away. Even Aunt Hennie."

"Aunt Hennie?" Mary asked.

Tommy blushed. He had a shock of very dark hair and a very white face with pink cheeks, a red bow of a mouth, a nervous Adam's apple.

"Sorry. Aunt Harriet," he said. "We always called her Hennie."

"Harriet is —"

"My aunt," Tommy said. "My mother's sister."

"Your mother's Viv then," Mary said, more to herself than to Tommy.

"You know her?" Tommy asked, surprised.

"Harriet's mentioned her," she said.

Everything fell so neatly into place. Beth was the niece who did everything so perfectly: the picnics and the Thanksgiving dinner, all of it.

"Harriet is crazy about Beth," Mary said, remembering that Beth was the kind of wife Harriet had wanted for her own son.

Tommy's Adam's apple jumped a few times, then he turned from her, moving about the kitchen, lost.

"Beth would have scolded me by now for not offering you a drink. Eggnog, maybe?" Then he added apologetically. "It's the store-bought kind."

"Nothing. Thanks."

Tommy held out a platter of Christmas cookies.

"I'm all set. Thanks," Mary said.

Tommy nodded, but didn't put down the platter.

"The kids are at my mother's," he said. "She doesn't like to take all four of them, but . . ." His voice trailed off and he swallowed again, hard. Then he looked at Mary hopefully. "The doctors are going to see Beth on Monday. There's something new they want to try. We're sure it'll work. You know, back when this all first started, one doctor told her she'd be lucky if she lived a year. And look at her. Four and a half years and there's still something they can try. On Monday," he said again, "we'll go to Boston and we'll see."

"Is Beth in the living room?" Mary asked.

Tommy frowned. "No, no, she's staying in bed mostly these days. Just until she feels a little better."

It was too hot in the house. Mary felt sweat trickling down her ribs. No wonder Tommy was wearing a short-sleeved shirt, a yellow one with a small light blue pony on the front.

"Come on," he said. "I'll bring you upstairs."

Mary followed him, listening to the smack his bare feet made on the floor as he walked.

Upstairs, the hallway was carpeted in pale green. It smelled of children — fruity shampoo and sweaty socks and baby powder. One room had bunk beds, a table of LEGOs, a wooden train set in various stages of completion. Across the hall a room with lilac walls and a light shaped like a bouquet of colorful tulips. Then another girl's room, this one pink and scattered with stuffed animals, baby dolls, a pair of ruby slippers.

"Hey, hon," Tommy said softly. "Look who's here."

Mary stood in the doorway of Beth's

bedroom. Beth was propped up with a se:
of pillows behind her in bed. She had on
that same chenille knit cap, and a white cot
ton nightgown. When she saw Mary, she
smiled.

"Come on in," she said.

Tommy rushed ahead of Mary and moved
magazines from a chair by the bed. "Here,"
he said. "Sit right here."

He asked Beth if she needed anything
More water? Some hard candy? A pill?

But she shooed him away.

"Just let us knit for a while," she said.

She had grown thinner, her cheeks hollov
beneath the sharp angles of her cheekbones
Mary stumbled over her own thoughts
Ridiculous, she knew, to ask Beth how she
was doing. Too many people had asked
Mary that in the months after Stella died
and she was too aware of how that question
could not be answered. With her own hus
band gone, Mary felt awkward in the pres
ence of this marriage. She watched a
Tommy smoothed Beth's blanket and ben
to kiss her forehead before he left the room
Was Dylan performing such tender gesture
with Denise? Mary wondered, her hus
band's touch already fading.

Beth tapped the seat beside the bed. "Si
down."

Relieved, Mary sat and busied herself with taking her knitting needles and yarn from her bag.

"All business, huh?" Beth said. Her breath smelled like peaches that had gone bad.

Mary laughed nervously. "No. Not at all. I just don't want to tire you."

"I'm tired all the time. All I do is sleep. Once I recuperate from this last surgery, I'll be up and around again."

Mary looked away from Beth's optimism.

"It's complicated," Beth said.

"It must be. You have to keep trying things. But there must be a part of you that is ready to say enough."

Mary realized that Beth had pushed herself upright, her eyes wide. "I, I meant the pattern," Beth said.

"Oh," Mary said.

There was an awkward silence.

Then Beth said softly, "You know, the day I got my original diagnosis, I looked at that doctor and I told him, 'I have a baby who's not even two yet. And a three-year-old and a four-year-old and a son who just finished first grade. I've got a lot of work to do.' "

"I'm sorry," Mary mumbled.

"I know this woman who fought her cancer for fourteen years when the doctors told her she only had six months to live.

Then, fourteen years later, her oldest son got married and her youngest son graduated from high school and her middle son got into law school and she died that summer."

Mary's fingers trembled around her knitting needles, her palms grew sweaty.

"A mother can't leave her children," Beth said. "You don't have children, do you?" Beth said, studying Mary through narrow eyes.

Mary hesitated, then said, "No."

"Only a mother can understand maybe," Beth said thoughtfully.

"During this last operation," she continued, "I was out, you know. Under anesthesia. And I saw this really fuzzy . . . something. Like a world or something. I had to squint to make anything of it, but there were gardens and people and sunlight, but it was just out of reach. I kept trying to get there but I couldn't. Do you think that was heaven?" Beth said suddenly.

Shaken, Mary stammered, "I don't know."

"You seem like someone who reads a lot. I thought maybe you'd read about it —"

"About heaven?"

Beth shrugged. She picked up her own knitting, and Mary saw that she was almost finished with her blanket, each square neatly finished, the various patterns perfectly knitted.

"Spiderweb," Beth said, examining each square. "Here it is."

She held it out for Mary to see.

"I lied to you," Mary said.

Beth looked at her, surprised. "When?"

"Just now," Mary said. "I had a daughter. Stella," she said, choking on the name. "She died last year, suddenly, and she was only five years old." She was crying now, and dimly aware that she should not burden a dying woman with her own grief, but somehow she needed to tell Beth this one thing, so that Beth would see her differently.

Beth was half off the bed, taking Mary's hands into her warm ones. "Oh, oh," Beth was saying, as if she were in pain.

"That's why I've been such a bitch," Mary said. "Every time you talk about your daughter, or knit her a sweater, or show her picture, I'm reminded of what I don't have."

When Mary's eyes cleared of her tears, she saw Beth's bloated stomach, the smell of rotting fruit hanging over her.

"Let me help you," Mary said, guiding Beth back into bed. Her bones were sharp beneath Mary's hands.

The effort of sitting up had worn her out. Beth lay with her head deep in one of the pillows, her eyes closed, her breathing shallow.

Mary waited a few minutes, then quietly stood to leave.

"No!" Beth said sharply. Her eyes opened and she had a feverish look about her.

"Stay," she said more softly. "It would be nice to talk a bit."

Mary hesitated, then sat back down.

"It's hard," Beth said. "Tommy can't bear to hear what I want to say."

"I don't know if I'm —"

Beth put her warm hand on Mary's knee. "Sometimes, someone you don't know well is the best listener."

Mary thought of all the stories she'd listened to since she'd joined the knitting circle. Hadn't Alice told her that the listener finds solace in the act of listening?

Beth sank back against the pillows. "It's hard for some people to understand," she said, "but all I wanted was to be a mother. I look at some of the women in the knitting circle, like Scarlet and Lulu, and I try to imagine what it would be like not to have any children. To have this successful, glamorous life, you know?"

"Glamorous on the outside, maybe," Mary said. "But everyone has their secrets."

"I know," Beth said. "I had mine, didn't

I? Until it came back with such a vengeance." She chewed her already-chapped lips. "Don't laugh, but I met Tommy when I was seven years old. He hated me. But I knew then that I was going to marry him. Second grade! He'd always yell, 'Beth Armstrong, you get away from me!' And I would. I'd walk away. But deep down I knew that someday . . . well, here we are, right?

"In middle school, he went out with my best friend, Leah. It practically broke my heart. But my mother said, 'Somebody is going to marry Tommy Baker and that somebody could be you.' So I took a deep breath and dug my heels in. Sure enough, by the time we got to high school, Leah was with another boy, Ronnie Blackhall. The worst kid in school. And she got pregnant. And she dropped out of school and they live in this terrible run-down house in Warren."

She paused, satisfied.

"One day, at a football game, Tommy and his friends came up and sat right behind me and my friends. I still remember exactly what I had on. This puffy pink coat with white fake-fur trim around the hood, and white mittens with pink zigzags on them, and light blue corduroys. And my heart was beating so fast I thought I was going to pass out or something. Tommy never said one word to me until the game ended and we all got up to leave. Then he leaned close and said, 'You look pretty in pink.' My mouth went absolutely dry and I was afraid if I tried to talk my tongue would stick to the roof of my mouth, so I just smiled and felt grateful that my braces had come off two weeks before. 'Want to meet me at Billy's party tonight?' he said, and I nodded again and smiled some more and that was it. I met him at Billy's party and we've been together ever since. I don't know, Mary. I always thought I was blessed with this perfect life. And now this."

Mary noticed a tube of Chap Stick on the night table and she took off the cap, slowly rolled up the balm, and held it out to Beth.

"Thanks," Beth said, tilting her face upward so that Mary could roll the Chap Stick across her dry lips.

"I used to tell Tommy that I wanted six kids. Three girls and three boys. Even when we were in high school, I knew that. I was an only child and I remember sitting all by myself in the late afternoon, lonely, and imagining my future. There would be fancy dinners. Lamb chops, maybe. Fettuccine Alfredo. And there would be china dishes, white ones with pink flowers around the rims. And linen napkins. Oh, and there would be children. Lots of them. And they would have freshly scrubbed faces and bright eyes and OshKosh overalls. They would help me set the table and pour milk in the glasses and at dinner they would talk. Loud. And all at once. There would be beautiful, joyful noise.

"And then there would be soccer practice and violin lessons and ballet recitals and homework. We would do these projects. Like at Thanksgiving we would trace our hands and make turkeys from them, each finger a brightly colored feather and our thumb the turkey's head. Or we'd cut hearts with scalloped scissors and string them together, all red and pink and white, for Valentine's Day. And in summer we would go to the beach and build elaborate sand castles, with deep moats.

"I could see it all so clearly. Then it was actually real. Six days before our first wedding anniversary, I had Christopher, and then they just kept coming. I thought it was strange that I didn't get pregnant right off after Stella. It just happened, every time. So when Stella was two and I still wasn't pregnant again, I started to worry. Tommy said I was crazy. Maybe we're not having enough sex, he said." Beth rolled her eyes. "Honestly, to me that was just the way to get another baby. I didn't *not* like it. But I didn't understand why people spent so much time thinking about it."

Beth blushed, her pale cheeks burning pink. "I don't think I ever, you know," she whispered.

Mary considered. "You mean you never had an orgasm?"

Beth giggled and blushed some more. "Right," she said.

"But you must have," Mary said, lowering her voice too.

Beth shrugged. "Wouldn't I know?"

"Sure," Mary said. "But it isn't always as dramatic as it is in movies. It can be just like, something building up, then falling away."

"Nope," Beth said. "Not that it matters."

"It does matter," Mary said. "You deserve that. Four kids. Married, how long?"

"Twelve years," Beth said.

The door opened and both women jumped, startled and guilty.

"Need anything?" Tommy asked.

Beth laughed, hard.

"What?" he said.

"Nothing," she said, gasping.

The laughing, or maybe all the talking

seemed to have worn Beth out. She closed her eyes again and her breathing grew shallow and even.

"Don't go," Beth said. "I just need to rest."

"Okay," Mary said.

After a few minutes, Beth spoke again, without opening her eyes. Mary leaned closer to hear her.

"That day I found it," Beth said, "it was summer and warm and beautiful. The kids were running through the sprinkler in the backyard, Stella in just her diaper and the others in their bathing suits, everyone in blue and green, like the ocean. And I was in the shower, soaping up, and reveling in the sounds of them laughing and squealing, the spray of the sprinkler hitting the side of the house. I had my eyes closed and I was smiling and so happy. And my hand on my breast felt it. Round and hard and big. I imagined a clogged milk duct. I imagined a mistake. But it was there. That was how my mother died, when I was in college.

"I dried myself, and put on a summer dress and sandals and walked outside, calling my babies to me. I kneeled down in the wet grass and opened my arms, hugging them, holding on, not letting go. Until Caroline said, 'Mama! Let's make lemonade!' And Nate said, 'Mama! Can we have hot dogs on the grill for supper?' I let them go then. I had to. They were squirming, moving away from me. Then I lifted my face and looked up at the cloudless sky."

There was silence. Then Beth mumbled something Mary could not make out. Her breath rasped in her chest and throat, and she frowned against it.

Mary walked out of the room as quietly as she could. Downstairs, Tommy was in the kitchen pouring teriyaki sauce on chicken breasts.

"She's sleeping?" he asked.

Mary nodded.

"Thanks for coming today," he said. "Some people, well, it's too hard for them to see her like this."

Mary watched him as he began to tear lettuce leaves and toss them into a salad bowl.

"Once she recovers from this latest surgery . . ." he said. But he didn't finish the sentence.

He began to slice plum tomatoes into quarters, frowning as he worked.

"I forgot something," Mary said.

She went back upstairs, and into Beth's room. Kneeling beside the bed, she whispered Beth's name.

Beth's eyes fluttered open. She smiled, a little confused. "Have I slept a long time?"

"No," Mary said.

Relieved, Beth closed her eyes again.

Mary lightly touched her shoulder. "Beth?"

Her eyes fluttered open again.

"Do you and Tommy ever . . . you know?"

"Back to that, huh?" Beth said. She shook her head no. "Not lately. But when we can, we will."

"When you do, you should get on top, and lean back a little and move up and down. That's the best way."

Beth's feverish eyes sparkled at Mary. "It works?"

"All the time," Mary said.

Beth closed her eyes. "I'll let you know," she mumbled.

Mary watched as she faded back into sleep, before she went downstairs again.

Tommy was slicing cucumbers into thin rounds.

"All set?" he said.

"All set," Mary told him.

She gathered her coat and hat and mittens. Something caught her eye on the wall behind him. Six turkeys, drawn from hands of all different sizes, the fingers all brightly colored feathers, the thumbs smiling turkey faces. Beneath them, in perfect calligraphy, Beth had written each of their names, the children's and hers and Tommy's.

Tommy saw what she was looking at.

"Beth," he said, his voice so full of love and pride that Mary had to turn from him, and from those six happy turkeys.

14
THE KNITTING CIRCLE

The wedding invitation was hot pink. The wedding was on Valentine's Day. *Come watch Jessica and Eddie get hitched!* There was a vague country western theme about it, a choice of ribs or chicken for dinner, a reference to a band with the word "Rodeo" in its name. Mary fought a desire to toss the thing in the trash.

But when she glanced over at the growing mountain of trash — neatly bagged, she reminded herself, but trash just the same — she decided it would be futile. Instead, she squeezed it into the drawer where her unused ticket to Mexico still lay, along with ten-dollar-off coupons at Old Navy, offers for new credit cards, notes she should have answered months ago.

Sometimes, she heard the answering machine picking up, the voices of her worried friends in San Francisco and here in Providence telling her they were thinking of her, just checking in on her. Dylan called, sounding almost sheepish. He wanted to meet for coffee, or to take a walk, or something. Once he even choked out an "I miss you." Connor called too, twice. The first time just to be sure she'd made it home all right. The second time was more of a good-bye call. "If only we'd met at a different time. Like in a few years," he'd said. Mary smiled, knowing what had happened between them had been necessary, but it was over. Like all the others, when his message ended, she pressed the delete button.

Her life grew smaller still. She slept on the sofa under a fleece blanket that also smelled slightly sour, the television blared ads for unneeded kitchen appliances all night. She knit on the sofa too, and ventured downstairs only to make coffee. Or used to, until she broke the glass carafe. That sat in the sink, amid spilled grounds and broken shards, empty cartons of ice cream, the remnants of some pasta from several days ago.

Somewhere in her mind, Mary remembered a warning from just after Stella had died. Once the shock wears off, the real depression begins. Was that what was happening to her? She had left Beth's with an overwhelming sense of how unfair life was.

Even the cliché of that thought had not diminished her feeling of giving up. If she could lose her own daughter, if Beth's young kids could lose their mother like this, if Bridget could die while waiting for a new heart, what was the sense of anything?

Somehow Mary still dragged herself to the office every day. Not early. Not even close to on time. But she showered and dressed, and until the coffeepot broke, gulped down some coffee, even a piece of toast. She managed to sit at her desk, staring at her computer screen, compulsively researching knitting. When Eddie poked his head in, frowning and concerned, she always threw a new fact at him.

"Did you know that in the Aran Islands families developed their own patterns for sweaters so that drowned fishermen could be identified?" she'd say brightly.

"Uh-uh," Eddie would say, frowning even more.

Then she'd pretend to get back to work, her files on knitting growing fatter with facts about cultures that used knitting to express grief or oppression.

"How does this fit into the piece you're doing about knitting here?" Eddie asked her after she gave him a lengthy explanation about knitting and the Incas in Peru.

"You'll see," she'd say, forcing a smile.

Jessica smirked. She was hanging in the doorway of his office, like a snake. "Maybe you should write a whole book about this stuff," she said.

Later, Mary walked in as the two of them ate lunch at Eddie's desk, Jessica perched on one corner, her long legs folded up like origami. Couldn't the woman simply stand up or sit down? Why did she have to drape herself over everything?

"In Riga," Mary said, popping her head in the office, "they knit celebratory mittens for weddings."

Eddie's office smelled so much like soy sauce, Mary felt thirsty.

"Great," Eddie said.

Jessica looked down, embarrassed, her chopsticks poised like daggers.

Mary tapped her folder on Latvia. "Good stuff," she said.

A person who had really, finally, lost it wouldn't be able to learn so much, to Google so long, to follow the links and paths that led her around the world of knitting. Would she?

The Chef Bobby Flay was cooking dinner for all the firemen in a fire station in the Bronx. The Food Network showed this same episode all the time. Yet Mary still watched as Bobby Flay shopped on Arthur Avenue for good Italian groceries, and spiced slabs of steak, and kidded with all the firemen.

The sound of a bell ringing seemed to fit right in with the noisy Bronx background. Mary burrowed deeper under the sour fleece blanket. She imagined the steps involved in actually doing laundry: the gathering of the clothes from various floors, the separating of colors and whites, the measuring and pouring of the detergent, and choosing the load size, the water temperature, whether these clothes needed a gentle or vigorous washing.

It was too much. Today she had worn to work a pair of denim overalls that had gotten her through more than half of her pregnancy and, beneath them, an old fraternity T-shirt of Dylan's with a picture of a drunken man in a hammock and Greek letters across the top. They were all clean, which is what she pointed out to Jessica when she looked at Mary in disgust.

That bell rang again.

"Mary?" someone called from inside the house.

Mary wondered if she could hide somewhere, feign sleep or a coma or worse. Who walked right inside someone's house, anyway?

"Mary," the woman said again, closer.

Mary heard footsteps climbing the stairs. She closed her eyes.

When she opened them, Scarlet was standing in the center of the living room, looking around, horrified. Yarn, empty bags of microwave popcorn, scattered mail covered the floor. And there was Mary herself, in those overalls, wrapped in that blanket.

"I've been working really hard," Mary managed to say, even though her voice seemed stuck in her throat. "On a piece about knitting," she added. "Maybe it'll even be a book. That has been suggested to me."

"Oh, honey," Scarlet said, crunching her way over the popcorn bags and catalogues on the floor to the sofa.

"Did you know that a year or even longer after you lose someone you love, you can take a turn for the worse?" Mary heard herself saying. "Yes. It's true. The shock wears off and some people get even more depressed."

Scarlet was looking her right in the eye. "We need to get you cleaned up, and then to clean up around here a bit, and then have a good long talk. Okay?"

Mary laughed. "Don't be silly. I go to work every day, you know. I'm fine. Sure, I'm not the best housekeeper, but that's because I'm so busy."

"Where's your husband?" Scarlet asked gently.

"Oh, that." Mary laughed again. "He moved out."

"What? When?"

"Let me think, uh, that was before Thanksgiving."

Scarlet was starting to look worried. "You've been here alone for two months?"

Mary pushed on her temples with her fingertips. "I guess so." She blurted, "Except I went to Maine and I had this affair, I guess you'd call it."

"That's okay," Scarlet said, her voice soft and soothing. "Hell, if your husband left, right?"

"For another woman. A happy woman." Mary could feel the tears pouring out of her, but somehow they seemed disconnected from her.

"You know, honey," Scarlet said, "your door was wide open. I think you forgot to pull it closed behind you. I was just coming by to see if you wanted to go to knitting with me."

"The stitch-a-month. Dashes?"

"I think so," Scarlet said, getting to her feet. She began to pick up the things that littered the floor. "That's all right," she said. "We can catch up. We'll do dashes on our own this month and then next month we'll go with everyone else. Okay?"

Mary closed her eyes, still feeling that rush of tears. Around her, Scarlet moved, quietly cleaning.

Mary was surprised when she woke up and saw bright sunshine and fresh snow. The house smelled yeasty, like freshly baked bread, and of flowers and laundry detergent. The television was turned off, and a quilt she didn't recognize was over her, squares of ivory and white and pale pink, each square tied at the corner with a bit of ribbon or lace.

"Hey there, Sleeping Beauty," Mary heard, and she turned to see Lulu in the doorway holding a tray with three mugs of coffee and the cinnamon rolls you could only find at Rouge. Lulu put the tray on the coffee table. Mary saw that her weeks of clutter had been cleared. She caught a whiff of the faint scent of lemon furniture polish.

"Tell me my whole last year has been a dream," Mary said, taking one of the mugs and sipping.

"I wish I could, baby doll," Lulu said. "You slept something like nineteen, twenty hours." She sat beside Mary on the sofa. "When I first got out of the hospital," Lulu said, "all I did was sleep."

"Beats the real world," Mary said.

Lulu took Mary's hand in her own and squeezed.

"Feeling better?" Scarlet asked from the doorway, a basket of freshly washed and folded laundry balanced on her hip like a baby.

"A little."

"The real world got to her," Lulu said.

Scarlet put the basket down and kneeled beside Mary.

"After Bébé drowned, my therapist told me that grieving is very hard work. It's exhausting. I remember feeling like my body was made of lead. I would look at a stairway, or down a street, and know that I could not make it to the end."

Without warning, an image of Dylan came to her: minutes after Stella was born, and he was watching Mary hold their newborn daughter. She had never seen such happiness on a man's face before.

"I have nothing left," Mary managed to say.

Lulu grabbed her by the forearms. "Don't

say that. You do. I know what it's like to lose everything, to feel so hopeless. But you have to keep going."

Mary let herself be wrapped in Lulu's arms.

"He left me for someone else," Mary said into the warmth of Lulu's shoulder.

At night, it snowed. But every morning the sun emerged and glistened on the bright whiteness that covered everything. The trees shone with ice. The air stayed crisp.

Mary called in sick for the last two weeks of January. She RSVP'd *Yes* and *Ribs* to Eddie's wedding. At home all day, she baked banana bread and cranberry bread and froze the extras, lining her freezer with the silver-foiled loaves. She bought a new coffeemaker. She ordered Major Dickason's Blend coffee from Peet's in San Francisco. She put her yarn in plastic bins and labeled the bins with a magic marker. She cleared her answering machine of all those messages: her mother chastising her for not calling, for not using that ticket to go to Mexico and visit; her friends checking on her from San Francisco, from here in Providence, and her knitting friends; even Connor called several times from Maine, his voice strange to her ears. She pressed the delete button and watched the blinking red light finally come to rest.

"Row one," Alice said. "Knit three, purl four, then knit two, purl four seven times."

Mary bent her head, silently counting off her knits and purls. When she was finished, she looked up, waiting for more instruction.

Lulu was frowning, counting, swearing under her breath, and pulling out stitches. Scarlet was still knitting, her fingers lifting as she counted, keeping track. Ellen's seat was still empty, and Mary sent a silent wish to her that Bridget would get a donor soon.

"Knit the final three," Alice said.

Quickly and easily, the yarn the color of persimmons smooth beneath her fingers, Mary knit the last three stitches in that row.

She looked up again, and her eyes settled on Beth this time. Out of bed, dressed in jeans and a fisherman's sweater, her chenille cap on her head, Beth had improved after all. As if she felt Mary's eyes on her, Beth looked up too, straight at Mary, and grinned.

"Mary," she said, "that advice you gave me?"

"Advice?" Mary said.

"Shit," Lulu muttered, and pulled out more stitches.

"You know," Beth said. "The advice." Her eyes twinkled and her cheeks were flushed.

Mary laughed. "Oh," she said, "that."

"You were right," Beth said. "It works. Boy, does it work."

"Ssshhh," Lulu said, counting the stitches on her needle.

Beth gave Mary a thumbs-up sign, then looked back at her knitting.

"Row two," Alice said, "just knit your knits and purl your purls."

■ ■ ■ ■

PART EIGHT:
KNITTING

■ ■ ■ ■

What? You can't knit in the dark? Stuff
and nonsense; anybody can. Shut your
eyes. Knit one stitch. Open your eyes and
look at the stitch; it's all right. Shut your
eyes and knit two stitches. Open them.
Shut them. Knit three stitches . . .
— Elizabeth Zimmermann,
Knitter's Almanac

15
Roger

There were hearts everywhere. Sparkling ones dangled from the ceiling, strings of cutout chains of pink and red hearts hung on the walls, shiny red-foil hearts were sprinkled across the tabletops, and dishes of conversation hearts sat as centerpieces. *Kiss me. I luv u. Let's I M!*

Standing amid all the happiness, all the hearts, all the possibility that weddings held, Mary wondered if she would ever again be able to recapture her own heart's capacity for joy. Instead of opening, her heart squeezed tightly shut when Jessica and Eddie said their vows and gave each other big sloppy kisses.

That morning, on the *Weekend Today* show, Campbell Brown had interviewed a research doctor who had found that stress speeds up the aging process. This is why I look so bad, Mary had decided. Lately, when she looked in the mirror, she surprised herself. Her face had grown slightly jowly, her hair had lost its sheen, and she'd gone up a full size in her jeans, mostly because her ass seemed to have spread.

Mary grabbed another Corona from the silver tub of beer and sidled over to Holly, who stood watching Jessica and Eddie and a bunch of people Mary didn't know doing the Texas two-step. Jessica wore elaborately designed cowboy boots under her wedding dress, and a white cowboy hat instead of a veil.

"What do you think?" Mary asked Holly.

"Only she could look that good dressed so stupidly."

Mary sighed. "No stress in her life," she said.

They watched the dancing some more. Then Mary said, "What's in that jar anyway?"

"Uh," Holly said, "lemonade. Made from real lemons."

Mary frowned at her. "You're drinking lemonade."

Holly laughed nervously.

"At a wedding?" Mary said. All of a sudden, it was as if Mary were seeing Holly for the first time. Her face was slightly puffy, and she had breasts instead of her usual flat chest. "You're pregnant," Mary said, that lump in her throat back again.

"Uh," Holly said. "God. Well. Yes." She grabbed Mary's arm. "I didn't want to tell you. I was afraid it would make you sad again. And you've seemed, not happy exactly, but less sad. You know?"

"You don't even have a boyfriend," Mary said.

Holly ran her fingers through her choppy hair. "I know. Isn't it crazy?"

"So how did it happen?"

"Jeez, Mary. The usual way. I just don't know who the father is. I mean, I have some ideas, but, you know me. I kind of like variety. It's the rice of life, right?"

"Spice," Mary said.

"You are sad now, aren't you?" Holly chewed her bottom lip, worried. "I've made you sad."

How could Mary admit that weddings and babies made her depressed? Especially to Holly, who was like a big open heart with her skinny-armed hugs and her gooey cakes.

"No, no," Mary heard herself saying. "I'm happy."

Scarlet had the next knitting circle at her loft. The smell of sugar and vanilla filled the air, even in the hallway that led to her apartment. They were all making a baby sweater that day. As it turned out, each of them had a pregnant friend and Alice decided to have a baby-sweater knitting circle. "Then our gifts will be finished!" she'd said.

Mary rang the bell and heard Scarlet shout, "It's open!"

Inside, Scarlet was heating milk for cafés au lait, pouring it into colorful oversized mugs of hot coffee. Warm cinnamon knots and elephant ears dusted in sugar were carefully laid out on a red and yellow tray. Mary watched Scarlet fill one cup with just-steamed milk, then add some almond syrup to it.

"Beth's here," Scarlet said. She held up the warm milk. "This is for her."

Mary took the cup and brought it to Beth, who sat in the living area, dwarfed in the overstuffed chair. But despite being so thin, she looked remarkably well. She'd put on frosty pink lipstick, and was dressed in jeans and a pale pink sweater. She wore a white knit hat with a crazy trim of sparkly pink, red, and silver yarn.

"Hey, beautiful," Mary said.

Beth laughed. "I'm trying." She took the cup from Mary and sipped.

Mary sat on the sofa and began to unpack her knitting bag. "How are you?" she asked Beth.

"I'm good. In a couple of weeks I get another scan and I know the tumors are gone. I can feel it. This was a scary one, but I'm almost back one hundred percent."

Women's voices grew louder and Scarlet, Lulu, Harriet, and Alice all walked in with their coffee and knitting.

"So," Alice said, "who knew this would turn into a celebration of sorts."

"What are we celebrating?" Beth said.

The women all settled themselves, Scarlet placing the tray of pastries on the wide coffee table.

"Ellen's girl, Bridget," Alice said. "Even as we speak, she's getting her new heart. They got the call at four o'clock this morning."

"Thank God," Beth said.

Mary swallowed hard. She thought of Stella in that hospital room, the doctor's stethoscope pressed to her chest. Around her, the women were talking about organ donors, about Bridget's bravery and Ellen's dedication to her daughter.

"How simple," Alice said gently. "A one-skein cardigan. We'll be done in a few hours."

The yarn was thick and lush, with variegated colors. Mary had chosen purple and green and blue for Holly's baby, and even as she cast on, the colors revealed them selves vividly.

Other than the clacking of needles and Alice's instructions from time to time, the room was quiet. For once, Beth knit slowly her fingers swollen and sore from treat ments.

"Who's your sweater for?" Beth asked Lulu.

"My sister is pregnant again. Both of my sisters spit out babies like crazy."

"How about you, Scarlet?" Beth said.

Scarlet kept knitting. Already the back of her sweater was on stitch holders, and she had marked the places for the sleeves with pins.

"Scarlet?" Beth said.

Scarlet carefully laid the front on her lap its rich pinks and magentas bright agains her black pants.

"I guess," she said, "it's kind of for me. just got approval from China to adopt a baby girl," Scarlet said, as if she couldn' quite believe the news herself.

Mary watched as Lulu and Alice ran over to hug Scarlet. She watched Beth's face break into a smile. Even Harriet gave a reluctant nod of approval. Slowly, Mary go up and joined Alice and Lulu by Scarlet's side.

"You really did it," Mary said.

Scarlet squeezed her hand.

It grew dark outside as they sat knitting their sweaters. Scarlet turned on lamps and made more café au lait. Each woman had a front and a back and two small sleeves and now knitted the right front band, making careful buttonholes. Except Beth. She had fallen asleep, and Scarlet had taken the sweater pieces from her and placed a quilt over her. She breathed heavily in her sleep, her face pale in the glow of lamplight.

"She's remarkable, isn't she?" Harriet said softly.

Alice patted Harriet's knee. "Yes," she said. "Of course she is, darling."

Then they were silent again, interrupted only by the sound of Beth's breathing. When the phone rang, Lulu jumped, startled, and dropped a few stitches.

Scarlet took her baby sweater with her as she went to answer the phone.

"It's Ellen!" she said to everyone. "Bridget is doing great. The operation was successful."

The women cheered and called hellos and good wishes to Ellen while Scarlet held out the phone so she could hear them. Mary let them believe that, like all of theirs, her tears were from happiness. How could she ever

let anyone know how stingy her heart had
become? She wanted Bridget well, and alive
and Ellen to have her daughter. But she
wanted her Stella more.

"Of course," Harriet said after Scarlet had
hung up and they had all returned to their
sweaters, sewing up the sides, adding the
buttons — flowers on Lulu's, fish on
Mary's, antique silver ones on Harriet's
and small pink hearts on Scarlet's — "of
course, these things don't always work out.
Sometimes the body rejects the new heart.
Sometimes —"

"Sometimes," Alice said, holding up her
finished tiny sweater, "sometimes everything
goes perfectly."

Dylan had moved out four months ago, and
even though he still called her once a week
— "Just checking in," he'd say — her work
had finally managed to keep her from thinking too much about him and their mess of a
marriage. This was what he had been able
to do after Stella died — work so hard that
he could lead a life again. Mary understood
that now. She wondered if he understood
that she had not been able to help herself
until now.

Sitting at her desk with her computer
humming and her brain finally working, she

thought about calling him. But she couldn't. From her office, she watched Holly and Jessica whispering by Holly's desk. Lately, she'd felt the two of them had grown fond of each other and her sense of betrayal had deepened. Even now, the way their foreheads bent close together, the secretive smiles on their faces, Jessica's hand placed possessively on Holly's arm, made Mary uncomfortable and a little jealous.

It was hard enough watching Holly's stomach grow bigger seemingly every day. With the warmer weather, she had taken to wearing thin baby-doll dresses that showed off her pregnancy. She looked ridiculous, Mary decided as she watched them. Holly began to dig around in the big bag she toted everywhere, pulled something from it, and gave whatever it was to Jessica.

Holly had been Mary's ally against Jessica, and suddenly here was Mary alone. On today of all days. She found herself wishing for Dylan, the way he knew the right things to do, his good self.

She gathered her things and headed out for lunch. A new restaurant had opened on Thayer Street, with the unlikely and inappropriate name Takie-Outie Sushi. Mary avoided Thayer Street if she could. It was full of chain stores and restaurants and too many students clogging the narrow street sipping oversized, overpriced Starbucks coffees. But she needed to get out of here and it was a far enough walk to get her some good exercise. She'd managed to lose almost ten pounds since January.

When Mary walked into the foyer, Holly and Jessica stopped talking, stepping away from each other guiltily.

"What's up?" Mary asked before she could stop herself.

She saw Holly glance sideways at Jessica before she said, "Oh, you know."

"I'm pregnant," Jessica said.

Holly let out a little gasp. "Jess," she said firmly.

"Twelve weeks. We thought it would take a while but we were wrong."

Mary saw what Holly had handed Jessica: a bottle of prenatal vitamins from the natural-food store.

"Congratulations," Mary said, hoping Jessica couldn't tell how dry her throat had grown.

"Well, off to a new sushi place," Mary managed. "Any takers?"

There was a moment of awkward silence before Jessica said, "We can't. No raw fish."

"Right," Mary said, walking away from them. Behind her, their voices once again rose in that excited and anticipatory way that pregnant women have with each other.

The news at the next stitch-of-the-month club was that Bridget was coming home from the hospital that weekend. Last month, Alice had taken donations and made up a knitting basket for her: soft pastel yarns and a variety of needles, a measuring tape shaped like a woolly sheep, and a simple pattern for a hat. Scarlet and Alice had delivered it to the hospital themselves, and reported that Bridget looked healthy, healthier than she'd ever looked. Ellen was, of course, exhausted, but her cautious optimism could not be hidden.

Now Bridget was coming home with a good prognosis. The transplanted heart was pumping as if it were her own, and she could breathe easily, even doing light exercise.

In between working on this month's stitch, the chevron, everyone discussed a welcome-home party for Ellen and Bridget. When they chose a date, Mary lied and said she couldn't make it.

"We'll reschedule then," Alice said, opening her appointment book again.

"No, no," Mary insisted. "I'm so crazy with work. You'll never get there if you wait for me."

She didn't look up into their silence. With her head bent and her focus on her knitting, Mary could avoid considering how ungracious she had become. The world around her was full of babies about to be born, daughters whose lives got saved, triumphs over adversities. Mary carefully paid attention to the row she was knitting. *Knit five, purl four, knit two . . .*

The day of Bridget and Ellen's welcome-home party, Mary drove an hour south to the small seaside town of Westerly. A movie theater had opened there a few months earlier that showed old movies and served soup and panini, wine and espresso. She'd been meaning to review it, and by going today she felt slightly less guilty for avoiding Ellen.

Mary glanced at her watch and saw she was just on time. She hurried inside, ordered a mozzarella and tomato panini and a beer, then entered the already-dark movie theater. Although Mary had expected to be alone at a matinee on a sunny afternoon, there was only one empty table. She sat and began to eat her sandwich just as the screen came down and *Mrs. Miniver* began to play.

By the time the credits rolled, Mary had

fallen in love with the place. What a comfort to escape into a darkened theater for an old movie. She watched the faces of the people as they left and knew they felt the same way. Back in the lobby, she waited in line for dessert and coffee beside a tall, balding man who — like Mary herself — was still teary from the film. He saw her watching him and shrugged apologetically.

"I can cry over anything," he said.

Mary studied his face a moment, finding him familiar. "I think I know you," she said finally.

He shook his head. "I just moved down here. I'm opening a knitting store across the street."

"Knitting?" she asked.

"Men knit, you know," he said, his blue eyes sparkling. "Fishermen invented it from the knots they used to repair their nets."

Mary took a step back to better see his face. "That's how I know you. From Big Alice's."

His smile froze, then disappeared.

Mary put her hand on his. "I'm sorry," she said. "I was there that night you finished the blanket."

"Ah," he said.

"Roger, right?"

By now they both had their desserts and

coffees. Roger motioned to an empty café table. "Want to sit awhile?"

"I do," Mary said.

Roger pointed across the street. "My store," he said. "The Sit and Knit Two. Alice is my not-so-silent partner."

"I had no idea," Mary said, surprised.

"She knew I needed to get away, to do something different. After what happened, all I did was sit at home and knit. I have a lot of sweaters, let me tell you."

When they finished their desserts, Roger suggested a walk by the river that flowed noisily behind the theater.

"I bought that building," he continued as they walked, "and spent the winter making the upstairs livable, and now I'm getting ready to open the store."

Mary pointed toward her car. "This is me," she said.

"Matinees every Thursday," he said.

"Maybe I'll see you next Thursday then," Mary told him.

Roger grinned at her. "See you then," he said.

The next Thursday, after *Tea and Sympathy*, Mary told Roger about avoiding Ellen.

"Me too!" he said. "God knows I wanted that child to make it. But then I felt so

356

riddled with jealousy that I can't bear it. I sent an overly extravagant flower arrangement. It had guilt written all over it."

"So did I!" Mary admitted.

Roger wagged his finger at her. "We're transparent."

"Ellen's going to be at the next stitch-of-the-month meeting. I have to visit before then," Mary said.

Roger leaned close to her. "We'll go together. What do you say? Two broken-hearted cowards."

Mary saw that he had tears in his eyes. "All right," she said.

"But not next week. Next week is *The Days of Wine and Roses.* We can't miss that."

"All right," Mary said again.

"You'll stay for dinner afterwards," Roger told her.

Mary took a breath and then said, "Since my husband moved out to pursue a happier life, I happen to be free for dinner."

"Oh, honey," Roger said.

"It has to start getting better, right?"

"It already has," Roger said.

The walls of his loft were the purple of eggplants, and religious folk art hung from them: oversized silver *milagros,* ornate paintings of the Black Madonna, heavy wooden crucifixes and bright *retablos.*

"We collected them," Roger explained. He was mixing a pitcher of Cosmopolitans — "the best ones you've ever had," he'd told Mary. "We traveled in Mexico quite a bit. Central America. Peru. His Spanish was excellent."

Mary took the frothy pink cocktail he offered her.

"Is it the best you've ever had?" Roger said.

"The best," she agreed.

Roger flopped onto the red velvet couch. "Wasn't Lee Remick so beautiful? So tragic?"

"Those Brandy Alexanders," Mary said, shaking her head. "They did her in."

"That's what I should have made," Roger said. "In honor of the movie."

"No, this is perfect," Mary said. "May I tell you how awful it is to work with two pregnant women and one expectant father?"

Roger refilled their martini glasses, then leaned back into the cushions. "Every time I see two men walking down the street together, I want to run them over. Honest, I do."

Mary considered a moment, then she asked him, "But you're okay, aren't you?"

"Yes," he said quietly. "But sometimes I

curse even that."

Mary went and sat beside Roger on the couch. Its cushions were so soft they seemed to swallow her up. "I have thought that too," she said. "Wouldn't it be better to be with Stella than alone here without her?"

"We don't get to choose," Roger said.

"Dylan chose," Mary said. "He chose to leave me."

Outside the apartment's large bank of windows, it had grown dark. But he made no move to turn on any lights other than the small lamp beside the sofa and the soft globe light still on in the kitchen.

"Do you think there's anything afterwards? Heaven or anything?" Mary asked.

"I don't know," Roger said. "I want there to be. But I just don't know."

"I want there to be too," Mary said.

It was one of the things she feared most, that Stella was simply gone forever. She would not ever again hold her daughter, or see her soft round face. In the hospital, she remembered praying for Stella to call out to her, to say "Mama." And Stella had said it. She squeezed her eyes shut against the memory.

"Have you done the medium route?" Roger said, his voice returning to its playful self.

"No. A friend wanted to take me once, but I just can't buy it. You?"

"Alice came with me once. 'Rubbish,' she said before it even started. 'A bunch of rubbish.' " Roger sighed. "I suppose it was," he said.

Mary held out her glass and he got up to refill them.

"Okay," Mary said, "here's a totally sexist question."

"How did I ever start to knit?" he laughed.

"You are the only man I've ever seen knitting," she told him.

"Being homosexual isn't a good enough reason?"

She shook her head.

"I learned probably for the same reason you did. To save my life." He rubbed at the stem of his martini glass absently. "We had these few idyllic years. Gave up our tiny tiny apartment in the West Village and moved to this eighteenth-century farmhouse. Totally restored it. Opened a nursery. The plant kind, not the kid kind. Made friends. Like Alice. And we had fabulous dinner parties on our big wooden table with white candles dripping wax on it and good wine. People still talk about our New Year's Eve party. We used to say that we felt like we were living in a Ralph Lauren catalogue.

"Then he goes for a routine physical and we're not even worried. I mean, if you were a gay man in New York City in the eighties, you have had your AIDS test, believe me. That was part of our charmed life. That we had escaped it somehow. Then one night I'm standing at the stove making spaghetti carbonara. I've got the pancetta browning and the spaghetti cooking, I'm working on a big glass of a very nice Barbera, and the light from the garden is coming in the window just so that it casts a small glow on him at the table. The phone rings. He leans over and picks it up. And zap! our life ends.

"It took eight more years before he died. But we stepped out of that catalogue and into hell right then. Our world became T-cell counts and bottles of pills and late-night emergency trips to the hospital. One morning, early, I'm having coffee at her house after another night spent in the ER hoping they can save his life one more time, and Alice comes around the corner with these knitting needles the size of batons and this gorgeous Rowan chunky yarn and she says, 'Just sit here and knit.' She showed me what to do, and I sat at that table for four hours and then I had a scarf finished. My hands stopped shaking along the way and my heart stopped pounding and all I

361

thought about was putting one needle into one loop of yarn and pulling it out.

"Next thing I know, she's got both of us knitting. You wait in enough doctors' waiting rooms, or spend enough hours in hospitals, and you can knit a whole fucking wardrobe. Pretty soon, we're going to the Wednesday night knitting circle. Different people back then. But Ellen was there. Bridget was only seven or eight.

"That's how I became friends with Ellen. She understood. I met her at the knitting circle and she had the same life as I did. Everything was about keeping the person she loved alive. Everything. But I couldn't do it and she could. I failed."

"No!" Mary said. "Medicine failed."

"I've got to go see her," he said. "Ellen, I mean. Talk about a lousy friend. I've been trying to figure out if all that time we both were helping each other through these medical emergencies and navigating these horrible conditions and watching our loved ones failing, were we expecting them both to die? Or to live? Because I keep feeling like one of us didn't keep our promise to the other. I'm just not sure which one it is, her or me."

"We'll go tomorrow," Mary said. "We'll bring something really decadent. Expensive chocolates or champagne."

"When your husband comes back, are you going to drop me?" Roger said.

"He's not coming back," she said.

"He'll come to his senses," Roger said.

"I won't drop you," Mary told him.

The next day, another beautiful sunny spring day, Mary and Roger drove together to Ellen's apartment. Even her bleak neighborhood looked bright. In the park, Hmong families were having a party of some kind. Families dressed in elaborately embroidered outfits played music and ate food spread on folding tables. The sound of children's laughter split the air. Two men walking identical pugs passed by, then a group of women pushing babies in strollers.

Mary carried an oversized bottle of Veuve Clicquot and Roger had a balloon bouquet and a box of handmade chocolates wrapped with a giant gold bow. They went inside, up the stairs, to Ellen's door, which was slightly ajar.

Right outside it, Roger paused to hug Mary. "We are happy," he whispered to her. "Remember that."

Then he pushed open the door.

"Ta-da!" he shouted in his biggest voice.

Bridget came running into the room, pink-cheeked and bright-eyed, healthy. She ran into Roger's arms, giggling. Ellen came in right behind her. Mary watched her face light up when she saw that Roger had come.

"Honey," Roger said, studying Bridget at arm's length, "that new heart of yours has done wonders for you. Why, you're positively gorgeous!"

It seemed to Mary that Ellen looked stunned by the turn of events in her life.

"Mary," Roger said, "what in the world are you waiting for? Pop that cork!"

Mary let the sweet foam of champagne spill down her hands and arms, in celebration. Ellen ran to get glasses, and returned with a collection of Winnie-the-Pooh jelly jars, holding them out for Mary to fill.

"To life," Roger said, looking directly at Mary.

"To life," she repeated.

16
THE KNITTING
CIRCLE

By summer, the knitting circle met in the empty new frame of Big Alice's Sit and Knit. Without a roof, sunlight poured into the shell. The women sat on beach chairs, slathered sunscreen on their arms and faces, and knit with cotton yarn: floppy hats, light lap blankets for cool summer nights. Someone always brought a pitcher of cocktails. Someone always brought snacks. They met earlier, while the sun was still bright, and knit until dusk. Even then they sometimes stayed on, sipping the last of their drinks, watered down from melted ice, and running their fingers across empty platters for the crumbs and bits left behind.

At first, Beth arrived for these Wednesday nights with crab Rangoon or rounds of baguettes smeared with sun-dried tomatoes whipped with cream cheese. Her blond hair was short and chic, wisps of pale curls that showed off her angular cheekbones and deep-set blue eyes. She had end-of-the-year school pictures of her kids, all in their school uniforms — white shirts and blue ties for the boys; Peter Pan collars and plaid jumpers for the girls. Even Mary admired the straight parts and neat braids Beth had made. Holding the pictures, staring into a child's gap-toothed grin, Mary remembered what a failure she had been at pigtails and braids, how slippery and impossible Stella's hair had felt beneath her hands.

Mary heard herself gasp. Scarlet's eyes met hers, but there were no words to describe how in that moment her memory had become something pleasing instead of painful. Remembering the baby-shampoo smell of Stella's hair, envisioning the flesh on the back of her daughter's neck, had almost felt good, Mary realized. But right on the heels of that realization, she saw how her hand trembled when she passed the pictures to Ellen.

It was Lulu who brought the tiki torches. She set them up in the dirt outside the frame of the store. Even though walls were going up, there were still enough empty spaces to let the flicker of the lights filter in. Then Scarlet hung red Chinese lanterns across the trees, and Harriet brought in an oversized silver candelabra — "a twenty-fifth wedding anniversary gift," she explained, setting it on the small green plastic table that someone — Ellen, maybe — had picked up at Wal-Mart one afternoon.

In July, after the Fourth, when everyone had returned from a long weekend of cookouts or trips to the beach, Beth came empty-handed.

Harriet settled into her chair with the margarita Lulu offered her, and immediately began talking about the barbecue Beth had hosted.

"She grilled portobello mushrooms," Harriet boasted. "They were this big, weren't they, Beth?" she said, holding her hands together to form a large circle. "So many vegetarians these days," Harriet said, shaking her head. "You always have to serve an alternative entrée. Not that I would necessarily. But Beth thinks of everything. Absolutely everything."

As Harriet spoke, Beth remained still, staring straight ahead and out the empty doorway.

"The cake," Harriet was saying, "was like a flag. White frosting. Strawberry stripes and a field of blueberries for the stars."

"It's back," Beth said. "My cancer."

The late afternoon sun poured through the roofless building, lighting each of the women, the reds and golds of their hair and the shine of sweat on their foreheads.

"They used the word 'palliative,' " Beth said. "I went this morning, Aunt Hennie, and they were all there, waiting for me, with their somber faces. I can read their faces, you know. And I knew this news wasn't going to be good."

"Oh no," Alice said.

"Don't!" Harriet said, glaring at Alice. "Just seven months ago they were all so certain she couldn't beat that. And did she? Of course she did!"

"Auntie," Beth said. But that was all.

Ice cubes tumbled in glasses, knitting needles clinked against each other, but otherwise the women were silent into the evening.

Three weeks later, on an overcast Wednesday afternoon, Beth arrived leaning heavily on a cane, Harriet supporting her under one elbow. A week earlier her husband had brought a chaise lounge, a long redwood one with brightly striped cushions and a back that could be raised and lowered several notches. She eased onto this now and closed her eyes briefly while Harriet settled into the chair beside her. Harriet pulled out her knitting and began working in rapid sharp motions.

Slowly, the other women got back to their own work. Ellen hummed softly. This was something she had started doing after Bridget came home. The sound was pure and lilting, and comforting somehow.

After a while, Mary saw that Beth wasn't knitting. Her eyes were open, her face impassive.

"Did you have a treatment this morning?" Mary asked her.

Beth had been getting chemo most mornings ever since she gave them the news.

"They've stopped them," she said.

Harriet looked at Beth. "Already?" she said.

"It's not working, Auntie," Beth said. "It's just making me sick. Too sick to hold my babies. Too sick to go to a Little League game or for an ice cream cone."

"But you can't stop the treatments," Harriet said, her eyes wild. "You have to keep going."

Mary noticed then that Beth's left arm was grotesquely swollen and purple. She cradled it tenderly with her right arm.

"You're a brave one," Alice said, her accent thick and strong. "You are a brave, brave woman."

The next two Wednesdays it rained, and

the knitting circle didn't meet. Mary used the time to finally visit Holly. She'd had her son Jasper a few weeks earlier. He was ten pounds, red-faced, and angry-looking. Mary brought him the sweater she'd knit that spring, and gerbera daisies for Holly. But even the vivid blue and green yarn and bright pink flowers did not help Holly's spirits.

"I'm not quite getting why this is considered such a wonderful experience," Holly said. "I mean, it hurt like hell, my tits are leaking like crazy, and I'm sore."

Mary glanced around the apartment. All of the shades were drawn, and the sharp smell of diapers hung over everything. Mary looked at the unmade bed, the stack of dirty dishes, the pile of laundry.

"First thing," she told Holly, "we open the shades and let in some light. Then you're going to point me in the direction of the Dumpster and the washing machine." Mary remembered how Scarlet and Lulu had done these things for her. How they reached out to rescue her. "And then," she added, "you are going to take a shower, put on clean clothes, and get out of this apartment."

"Yeah. Right," Holly said. "Yesterday I washed both of us and got us dressed and got as far as the car before he pooped all over me. It isn't worth all the work."

"It is," Mary said softly. "You'll see."

She walked around the small apartment, carefully opening each shade. By the time she'd emptied the diaper pail and put in a load of laundry, Holly had put the daisies in a makeshift vase.

"Well, it looks better and it smells better in here," Mary said. "Now get out. I'm giving you an hour all by yourself."

Holly handed Jasper to Mary.

"I don't know how I can thank you —" she began. But Mary shooed her out the door.

When Mary held Jasper, she was surprised by his heft, how solid he felt in her arms. She remembered as if she had dreamed it, how fragile Stella had felt. Again, the warmth of the memory washed over her, before the pain cut into her.

The next Wednesday, the diaper pail was clean and the shades were up, rain splattering against the windows noisily. Holly was already showered and dressed, grinning as she eased Jasper into Mary's arms.

The rain left hotter, stickier air. The knitting circle met, grateful that the roof was half done and now blocked out a good deal of the August sun.

Lulu poured margaritas, chattering about the best tequila and the importance of using fresh limes. Scarlet set out platters of empanadas and Ellen brought bowls of chips and salsa.

All the Mexican food made Mary think of her mother who had called just before she left, inviting her to come for Labor Day weekend. "Four days," she'd said. "A short little visit." "Sorry," Mary had told her. She hadn't had the energy to tell her mother about Dylan, to hear herself try to sound like it was fine that he was gone, to make light of her marriage falling apart.

The sound of something large and noisy arriving forced Mary out of her thoughts.

Harriet was pushing Beth in a wheelchair across the graveled and bumpy ground. Beth's head lolled oddly, and Mary stepped outside, walking quickly toward them to help.

As she moved closer, she saw that something had happened. Beth's eyes were both glassy, but her left eye drooped and that side of her mouth drooped as well. Her arm was even more swollen and discolored, and she seemed to be having trouble holding up her head.

"I told her not to come until she felt better," Harriet said. "But she insisted."

Beth said something but her speech was too garbled for Mary to understand. Mary kneeled at Beth's side. "What, Beth?" she asked her.

"To say goodbye," Beth managed.

Mary squeezed Beth's hand, unsure of what to say. She straightened and told Harriet, "Let me push her."

"It's bad," Harriet whispered, grabbing hold of Mary's arm and clutching it tight. "It's in her brain. Look what it's doing to her. They're giving her morphine, but they say that's all they can do."

Mary hugged Harriet close to her, surprised by the older woman's strong arms.

"We have to hold ourselves together," Mary said softly. "Why don't you go ahead and prepare the others? I'll take Beth from here."

Harriet took a deep breath and nodded.

"Ready, Beth?" Mary said, bending close to her.

Beth looked up at her with her one good eye. Tears spilled down her cheeks. "My babies," she said. "I don't want to leave them."

"I know," Mary said, willing herself not to cry.

"Summer," Beth said with great difficulty.

"Summer?" Mary repeated.

"Not good to die in summer." She worked hard to get her words out so that Mary could understand. "Summer should be good memories," she managed. "Fun. Ocean. Popsicles."

"Do you need help?" Scarlet called from the shop.

Mary stood to give her a thumbs-up sign.

"Beth?" she said, kneeling beside her again. "You have given them a lifetime of memories."

Mary thought of all those matching snowflake sweaters, the handmade Halloween costumes and the wall filled with turkeys made by their hands.

"Those memories will be painful at first. But over time" — she stopped to hold back her own tears — "over time," she continued, "they will bring them happiness. They will remember you, and they will smile."

"Promise?" Beth said.

Scarlet was running down the path toward them.

"Promise," Mary said.

The next wednesday was even hotter and more humid. Ellen set up a machine she said emitted carbon dioxide that kept mosquitoes away. Alice passed around bug spray. "With DEET," she said. "That's the only thing that works."

No one mentioned that Harriet and Beth hadn't come.

"That Beth," Alice said, "can knit circles around me."

After the Chinese lanterns were lit and the tiki torches blazing, a car pulled up. Enough of the shop was built by now that the lights outside did not illuminate very much. In the still, hot air, the women paused to listen to the sound of one car door slamming shut and footsteps hurrying up the path that led to the shop.

When Harriet appeared in the doorway she was a vague silhouette, lit dimly by the candles and the torches and the lanterns. She stood for a moment in the gaping doorway, then stepped into the half-finished room.

"She's gone," she said softly.

Ellen began to cry.

"She suffered so much these last few days," Harriet said.

Alice wrapped her arms around her.

"We'll all go to the house tomorrow," Alice said finally, stepping away from Harriet. She took her by the arm and led her to the chaise lounge, adjusting the back slightly.

"I've lost everything now," Harriet said.

Mary heard herself saying that she still had her son, her home, her friends. The very words people had been telling her in her own bleak desperation. Were the words true? Mary wondered, even as she said them to Harriet.

Scarlet poured a glass of the cold chardonnay she'd brought, and carried it over to Harriet.

Then they sat, and slowly, each in their own time, returned to their knitting.

"Aye," Alice said, "that one could knit."

Everyone agreed.

It grew darker, but they kept knitting. After a while, Ellen began to sing an old hymn, her voice lifting upward into the summer night.

■ ■ ■ ■

PART NINE:
COMMON SUFFERING

■ ■ ■ ■

Grief and sadness knits two hearts in
closer bonds than happiness ever can;
and common sufferings are far stronger
than common joys.
— Alphonse De Lamartine

17
MAMIE

From her office, Mary watched Jessica waddling down the hall. Jessica favored the new look in maternity wear: instead of hiding her belly, she flaunted it. At five months pregnant, even Mary had thought Jessica looked almost cute. But now that she was eight months pregnant, Mary found it unattractive. Even embarrassing. Today, Jessica was wearing low-cut black pants and a short sweater. Mary could see that her belly button had popped. Why didn't she go on maternity leave already?

Sighing, she swiveled her chair so that she faced the window instead of Jessica and her belly. When Jessica had announced a few weeks ago that she was definitely having a boy, Mary had been flooded with relief. Baby boys she could take. She could even enjoy them. Whenever Holly's sister couldn't babysit, Mary was happy to watch him for a while. But baby girls, little girls,

girls in general, broke her heart.

Her mind drifted to Beth's children standing solemnly at the funeral two weeks earlier. She had noticed how the youngest girl's braids were uneven, the surest sign to Mary that Beth was really gone. Standing there clutching a well-worn stuffed tiger, Beth's Stella had looked terrified rather than sad. But Mary knew that soon Stella would be playing on the swings in the backyard, making friends in school, having tea parties and sleepovers and, eventually, boyfriends and college roommates. Life was like that. Time kept moving and swept you right along with it.

Mary hit the print button on her computer and watched as her latest restaurant review came out. Then she picked it up and carried it down to Eddie's office, where Jessica teetered on too-high heels in front of his desk, complaining about the mayor.

"Are you taking any time off? At all?" Mary asked her.

"I don't believe in it," Jessica said.

Up close, Mary could see the blue veins running along her belly. She looked away.

"Have you read *The Good Earth?*" Jessica was asking.

"I guess so," Mary said.

"Then you know that in China, women

work in the fields, go inside and have their babies, and get right back to work."

"I'm sure they do," Mary muttered. She placed the review on Eddie's desk. "Sayonara," she said.

"Don't go," Eddie said.

Mary realized Jessica made him uncomfortable too, and she grinned. "Actually," she said, "that's the name of the restaurant. It's awful."

"Do you ever like a restaurant?" Jessica said.

"She has good taste," Eddie said.

Surprised, Mary looked at him. He needed a shave. And a haircut. He was wearing a polyester striped shirt with a run down the front.

"Why, thank you," Mary said. "Now if you two lovebirds will excuse me, I'm going home."

"Hey, Mary," Eddie said. "I think it's time we revisited that steakhouse you like so much."

"Really?" Mary said. "You want to come?"

"Yes," Eddie said.

"Not tonight," Jessica said. "We have our Lamaze class."

"How about those people in *The Good Earth?*" he asked her. "They didn't have to take classes, did they?"

"I'm leaving before you change your mind," Mary said.

"Don't leave me," Eddie said.

When Mary walked in the house, the phone was ringing. If it was Dylan on the other end, asking to come back, what would she say? This was a game she sometimes played these days, ever since he'd called and told her that he was not with Denise. "Why? Did she have a bad day or something so you had to dump her too?" she'd said.

"Do you have to be so mean?" Dylan had asked her. "Maybe it didn't work out because she's not you," he added.

Mary chewed her lower lip.

"Mary?"

"You had me," she said finally. "Remember?"

"Yes," he said.

He hadn't said he wanted to come back. He hadn't even called again. But if this was him and that's what he wanted, she would say no. She would say we have lost too much now.

"This is Saul Byrd calling from San Miguel, Mexico," a man said when she answered the phone. "Your mother's in the hospital. She's had a pretty bad heart attack. You should come right away."

The trembling began somewhere deep inside Mary, then quickly spread throughout her body so that it was difficult to hold the telephone or to speak. She had felt this before, that night in the hospital when the doctor had looked at her and said that Stella was not going to make it. Now, like then, a buzz sounded in her head, constant and persistent, as if her brain was short-circuiting.

Saul was giving her flight information and Mary wrote it down on the palm of her hand. Ridiculously, she reminded herself that she needed a pad to keep by the phone. Then she started to cry.

Remarkably, Mary made the flight. Remarkably, she slept the entire way. Perhaps her whole body had short-circuited. Like a sleepwalker, she changed planes in Houston and then went right back to sleep.

Mary took her own small overnight bag from under the seat, then she followed the crowd off the plane, through Customs, and into the fluorescent lights outside the airport.

The sky was ink black, but the glare of the lights made everyone look ghoulish. When a small blond woman touched Mary's arm, Mary actually yelped.

"I'm Kay," the woman said. "Your mother's friend."

Was everyone her mother's friend? Growing up, Mary had never known her mother to have even one friend. She didn't go out to lunch or play bridge or even sit around a neighbor's kitchen table sipping coffee and eating doughnuts like all the other mothers. Suddenly, she had friends.

Kay patted Mary sympathetically. "She'll be okay," she said unconvincingly.

They drove out of the airport into the darkness. A large factory spewed foul-smelling smoke.

"Hold your breath! Toxic fumes!" Kay said.

Obediently, Mary did.

Along the road, teenage girls hitchhiked in short skirts.

"They work at the factory," Kay explained.

Then, miles and miles of nothing. Mary looked out the window anyway. She thought of her mother. Not of the mother she was about to see — she didn't want to imagine that. No, she thought of her beautiful mother.

Like Grace Kelly, everyone used to say. Your mother looks just like Grace Kelly. To Mary, she looked like a princess, which was the same thing. Shiny blond hair, smooth white skin, blue eyes the color of a summer sky. In her mother's bottom dresser drawer lay carefully folded sweaters, arranged by color. Hidden beneath them was her wedding album: ivory, heavy, monogrammed. If Mary turned a small silver key, a music box inside played the song "Always." Mary was afraid to turn the key, afraid her mother would hear the tinny song playing and get angry at her.

Still, there were times when Mary could not resist and she turned the key and mouthed the words to the song. When the music box wound down, Mary replaced the key, her heart beating hard against her chest until it was safely put away.

Inside the album were pictures of her mother looking like a princess, in a wedding gown with a long train and other beautiful women carrying that train. The photographs had vivid unnatural color, so that the women's cheeks were too red, and their velvet gowns too green. But they still all looked lovely to Mary. And her mother looked the loveliest. Exotic flowers formed a wreath on her hair. No matter how hard she studied those flowers and searched her *Little Golden Book of Flowers,* she could never identify what they were. Just rare, exotic, beautiful things, like her mother herself.

Mary used to wonder what had become of those women. They never visited or sent Christmas cards. Instead, they seemed to exist only in the heavy ivory album. Mary's mother did not like for her to ask questions. But sometimes, if her mother seemed calm or nice, Mary would ask. She would start with something small and harmless.

"How did you meet Daddy?" she'd say.

Often, her mother would shoo her away. "I don't have time for that nonsense," she'd say. Her mother was certainly always busy. She dusted and washed and ironed and mopped, constantly.

But sometimes she'd get a far-off look in her eyes and sigh and say, "We met at a dance. At the country club. I was the guest of my friend Violet Addison and he was visiting her brother. They were roommates at Amherst College." Then her mother would sigh again and get back to work.

"Did you get married in winter?" Mary might ask, remembering the velvet dresses, the possibility of snow out the church windows.

"December ninth," her mother would say, if Mary was lucky.

"Was Violet Addison there?" Mary once

asked, pushing her luck.

Surprisingly, her mother had gotten teary. "Yes, she was. And Brenda Devine and Barbara MacNally. All of my friends from school were there."

Then when Mary stared at those pictures, she tried to figure out who was who. Who had a brother who went to Amherst and roomed with Mary's father? Who had the Veronica Lake wave in her hair? Who was the sultry dark-haired one? Of course, that was when her mother still talked and cried. Over time, she retreated. She drank more and more and went into rages or passed out on the sofa.

"We're here," Kay said, touching Mary's arm gently.

Dawn was cracking the dark sky, showing streaks of pink and lilac. But stars still glowed beside a crescent moon.

"You want me to go in with you?" Kay asked. She had a nose that looked like it had been changed, made smaller perhaps, and now it didn't seem to be on the right face.

Mary shook her head. "Thank you," she said. "But I want to go in alone."

"Room 208," Kay said. "That's where she is."

Kay leaned across the front seat and

hugged Mary. She smelled of roses.

Mary thanked her again, and got out of the car. She stood in front of the hospital, counting two floors up, guessing which window was her mother's and wondering what she would find when she went inside.

Kay rolled down the passenger window and called to Mary. "You want me to take you in?"

"No," Mary told her again. "Thanks."

Then she turned away from the car and from Kay, and began to make her way toward her mother.

All hospitals smelled the same, Mary thought as she navigated the dim corridor that led to Room 208. A hospital in San Miguel de Allende, Mexico, smelled exactly like the children's hospital in Providence. The smells made her shudder, sending goose bumps up her arms.

This hospital was run by nuns in white habits with pointed white hats that made them look like angels from behind. Whenever Mary passed one, the sister bowed her head and avoided eye contact as if it were rude to look directly into the eyes of a patient's family member.

At the nurses' station, a nun dozed. She sat in a chair behind the desk, her head thrown back, her mouth open, snoring lightly. A second nun tapped away on a computer. As Mary rounded the desk she saw that the nun was playing a computer game in which a slow-moving hook attempted to pick up what appeared to be nuggets of gold.

"Shit," the nun muttered.

Room 208 was right across from the nurses' station. The door was half open, and Mary walked in, afraid of what lay on the other side.

The familiar sound of machines — the steady measurements of heart rate and blood pressure, the hiss of oxygen — made her weak-kneed, and she sat immediately in the cracked vinyl chair beside the bed. The bottom cushion let out a low hiss.

Her mother was gray-faced and still, but other than the two slender plastic tubes delivering oxygen in her nose and an IV hookup with a fat bag of clear liquid slowly dripping into her arm, she seemed surprisingly all right. Flashes of the ICU, the bright lights, the multitude of machines and tubes and staff, made Mary shiver again and she rubbed her bare arms to warm herself and to erase the images.

Soft footsteps approached. Mary turned, expecting one of the nuns. But instead, a round-faced woman with long salt-and-pepper hair stood in the doorway.

"Mary?" the woman whispered in a stage whisper.

Mary stood nervously, as if she had done something wrong.

"God," the woman said, "I haven't seen you since you were a baby." She had the voice of someone who had been smoking forever. "You look just like your father," she added after studying Mary up close.

Another friend of her mother's, Mary thought, and shook her head. Miss Popularity all of a sudden. "So I've been told," Mary mumbled.

The woman took Mary's hand in hers and shook it firmly, sending the collection of bracelets that lined her arms into a noisy jangle.

Mary glanced at her mother, but there was no response.

"Coma," the woman said matter-of-factly.

Mary heard her own sharp intake of breath and the woman gave a throaty laugh. "Sounds worse than it is. They expect her to come out of it. It's like a restorative coma."

Again, Mary glanced at her mother, watching the even up-and-down of her chest.

"Let's get some coffee," the woman said.

Mary followed her past the dozing nun, down the corridor and two flights of steps, and outside. The woman had on a purple gypsy skirt and a white embroidered blouse. Leather sandals. All those bracelets. She jangled up a short steep hill and into a café that was just opening.

"Buenos días, Violet," a young woman sweeping the floor said.

"You're Violet Addison!" Mary said. "I can't believe it! When I was a child, I used to fantasize about you. My mother had this wedding album and there was a picture of her with her friends, her bridesmaids." Mary shook her head. "Not that she showed it to me or anything."

Violet spoke sharply. "Your mother never recovered. I don't know if I could have."

Mary frowned at her. "Recovered? From the drinking, you mean?"

Violet didn't answer right away. "Of course," she said finally. "The drinking."

Even when Mary pushed her to explain, Violet just said, "No, no, of course. I'm sorry."

On their way back to the hospital, Violet told her that she had moved here in 1959. "Right after you were born," she said. "My second husband was an artist, and we moved here in 1959 and never left. Well, *I* never left. He up and died on me. Drowned in the hot springs. Seems like a lifetime ago, but at the time, it was pretty awful. Everyone told me to come back home. Except your mother. She said, 'Violet, if I could pick up and leave and move to Mexico, I'd be right behind you, girl.' So when she could, after you were gone and your father died, she came. Just like old times, having Mamie down here with me."

"I wondered why she wanted to move so far away," Mary said.

Morning had arrived while they had breakfast. The small streets were crowded with children on their way to school and small carts selling fried dough and tamales and flowers.

"You go on in," Violet said to Mary. "The rest of us will come later." She squeezed Mary's hand. "She's been wanting you to come. I guess I know why now."

"Do you mean she knew she was sick?" Mary said.

Violet laughed. "Oh no. This heart attack surprised the hell out of your mother."

Even the nurses' station outside her mother's room was noisy and active. When Mary went to open her mother's door, a hairy hand stopped her. A doctor began speaking to her in Spanish.

"I don't understand!" Mary said.

"Ah! You are Señora Mary Baxter's next of kin?" the doctor said, grinning. His teeth were yellow and stained with nicotine.

It had been so long since she had heard anyone call her mother Mary that she paused before saying, "Yes, I'm *Mamie* Baxter's daughter."

The doctor looked down at the clipboard he held and made a note. "Mamie," he said under his breath. When he looked back up, he grinned again.

"Your mother, *Mamie* Baxter, she's going to live," he said. "Yesterday, I'm not so sure. Last night, I think probably. Now I know yes."

Mary grabbed both his hands. "Thank you," she said. She imagined a different mother waking up. One who would come home. One who would take her in her arms and comfort her. She imagined the mother she'd always hoped for.

"You go inside," he said, nudging her forward. "We'll talk later."

Mary stepped into the room, expecting to see her mother awake, sitting up in bed. But she looked exactly as she had a few hours ago. The machines, the IV, the gray skin.

Once again, Mary sat in the vinyl chair.

The chair hissed. Mary sat, and waited.

"So this is what a person has to do to get you here," her mother said. "Have a heart attack." Her voice was raspy, but not weak.

Mary had fallen asleep after two nuns brought in lunch. "How about some water?" her mother said.

"I'll get some out of the bathroom," she said when she couldn't find any.

"Not from the tap, Mary," her mother said. "You're in goddamn Mexico."

"You sure sound like yourself," Mary muttered.

Her mother squinted out at her. "Isn't that a bottle of water right there?"

Mary poured some into a paper cup and held it to her mother's lips to drink.

"So," her mother said when she was done, "they accepted the ticket?"

Mary nodded.

She sat back down and the chair hissed. Even though it happened each time, Mary giggled, out of relief perhaps.

"Don't be so silly," her mother said.

"Violet was here," Mary told her.

When she didn't answer, Mary continued. "I remembered her name from a long time ago. Remember how I always used to ask you about your wedding? And you told me that you met Dad through Violet Addison's brother?"

Mary stared down at her mother. She had gone back to sleep.

"Hello, beautiful!"

Mary knew immediately it was Saul Byrd standing in the doorway shouting. He held a big bouquet of flowers and did a fancy dance step toward her mother.

"Saul!" her mother said, suddenly awake.

Mary had read three *People* magazines from 2001, the only English-language magazines she could find, while her mother slept. Bored, she'd even done the crossword puzzles in the back.

"You look so good," Saul said. Then he noticed Mary. Immediately, he gave her a hug. He smelled like pipe tobacco and hair tonic.

"You're not at all what I expected," he said. "I thought you'd be blonde. Like your mother!"

"She looks like my late husband," Mamie explained. "He had that same mouth."

"Thanks for arranging everything," Mary told Saul.

"What do you need?" he asked her mother. "Those tamales you like? The ones María Domingo makes?"

"That sounds good," Mamie said, smiling.

Saul took a small notebook from his shirt pocket and scribbled in it. "How about some chocolate?"

"Not yet," Mamie said. "The tamales will be good."

"Just tamales?" he said, the pencil poised in midair.

"For now."

He pinched her cheek affectionately. "You scared the living daylights out of me, Mamie," he said, his voice softer.

"But I'm still here!" Mamie said.

"Mary, you'll stay with her while I go get those tamales?" Saul said.

"Of course," Mary said.

"Good girl," he said. "Don't look so I can smooch your mother."

"What?" Mary said.

But Saul was already bending over and kissing her mother right on the lips.

As soon as he was out the door, Mary said, "That guy's your boyfriend?"

Mamie shrugged. "Friend, boyfriend. Whatever. I'm getting a little tired of him, actually."

"He kissed you!" Mary said.

"I'm sorry I have a life," Mamie said. "A nice life, finally."

"You could have had a nice life with us, when I was a kid, you know," Mary said.

Mamie studied her daughter's face.

"Say something," Mary said.

"I wanted you to come," she said.

"All right, I know. I'm a bad daughter. You finally decided you wanted me to come and I didn't. But you have no idea the hell I am going through."

Mamie patted the bed beside her for Mary to sit there.

"I do," she said quietly. Mamie patted the bed again. "Come here," she said.

Reluctantly, Mary got up and sat beside her mother on the bed.

"I always got everything I wanted," her mother said.

"I guess so," Mary said.

"I did. I was beautiful."

"Like Grace Kelly," Mary said.

Mamie laughed. "A beautiful girl walks into a store or onto a train or anywhere, and people want to help her. I learned that early. I figured it out and I used it and I had a lovely spoiled life.

"Men? I could have any man I wanted. It was actually boring it was so easy. I sailed through life on my beauty. I was smart enough. I was nice enough. I knew how to have fun. But it was being beautiful that got me places. Violet and I spent a summer abroad and we got absolutely anything we wanted. Champagne. Jewelry. Steak dinners. Chanel perfume. Anything. All I had to do was pay attention to a man and we were set. 'You are my greatest asset,' Violet said. We both knew it.

"American men were afraid to try to have sex with me. Don't blush, Mary. Do you think I didn't know what you and that foolish boy were doing in your bedroom when you were in high school? Sex is a natural thing, Mary. But these American boys were afraid of me. So when Violet and I went to Europe, I thanked these men appropriately. Having sex with an Italian is something one remembers her entire life. Oh, pardon me, maybe you've had sex with an Italian, Mary?"

"Mom!"

"We finally have a girl-to-girl chat and you're embarrassed?"

"Fine," Mary said. "No, I have never had sex with an Italian."

"Well, you must. Violet was so mad at me. We laugh about it now but she was an absolute prude. She flirted and kissed, but she honestly believed in being a virgin on her wedding night. I, on the other hand, slept my way across Europe."

"Mom! Do they have you on some kind of drugs or something? Honestly. I don't want to know."

Her mother laughed. "When we got back, Violet was sure no one would marry me. We finished our senior year at Mount Holyoke, and it's true I was one of the few who wasn't even pinned, never mind engaged. But then I went to that dance with Violet, and her brother was there with your father."

"Did he know about your European trip?" Mary said sarcastically.

"He said to me, 'I never date beautiful women. I admire them. But I would never marry one.' And of course right then I knew I would have to marry him. After all, I always got what I wanted. It didn't take long either. You know, we hardly knew each other. I thought that was a good thing. All of my friends had proper courtships, and long engagements. But once I got your father to fall in love with me, that was it. We got married. It all happened so fast. Nineteen fifty-two. Right before Christmas. And I was pregnant by Easter."

"Mom," Mary said, "why don't you sleep? I think the drugs are making you loopy."

"I don't think so. I feel quite all right. Just tired. And happy you're finally here."

"But Mom," Mary said, "you didn't get

pregnant for seven years. I was born in '59."

Mary could not remember the last time she saw her mother cry. Maybe it was back when she was drinking and had those angry rages. Or maybe she had cried when Stella died and Mary simply hadn't noticed. But she was crying now. Not sobbing. Just tears falling down her cheeks.

"This is what I've been wanting to tell you. Why I needed to talk to you," Mamie was saying. "In those days, they took your pee, your urine, and they injected it into a rabbit, and if the rabbit died you were pregnant. Isn't that silly? It was right before Easter and your father would come home every day and ask me, 'Did the rabbit die?' and I'd say, "The doctor still hasn't called.' But I knew I was pregnant. 'How do you know?' he asked me, and I said, 'Because I want to be pregnant.' How naïve was I? Then the doctor called, and I said, 'The rabbit died, right?' And he said, 'You're absolutely right, Mrs. Baxter. The rabbit died. And by Thanksgiving you'll have a beautiful baby.' Do you know what I said, Mary? I said, 'I know.' That's how smug and confident I was. I said, 'I know.'

"I had the best pregnancy. I bought all of these maternity clothes with matching hats and shoes. Your father, unlike other husbands, thought that I was even more beautiful pregnant. He snapped so many pictures of me. He even took some very racy nude ones, very artsy, you know, with me cradling my stomach, or my arms folded over my breasts. Tasteful. He said that I was so beautiful pregnant that we should have a dozen children. But I told him, no. I wanted just one. So that I could absolutely adore that child. I didn't want to share my affection. I couldn't.

"All of my friends were throwing up and fainting, but I never felt sick even once. Everything was perfect. Thanksgiving morning I woke up and my water broke and four hours later she was born. My mother had told me, 'Mamie, if it's a girl you must name her Mary. Every generation has a Mary in our family.' She was Mary Wall but she went by Polly, and my grandmother was Mary Irons, but she went by Maisie. And of course I was Mary Baxter. Mamie. I was so spoiled, so certain of everything, that I said, 'I'm going to name her Susan. Susan is a beautiful name, not old-fashioned like Mary.' So we named her Susan.

"God help me, Mary, in my darkest hours I wondered if she was cursed because I broke the tradition. Isn't that ridiculous? But you know how your mind works. If I had only done this thing instead of that, she would still be here."

"You had a child? Before me?"

"That's what I've been wanting to tell you, Mary. About my Susan. After Stella . . . I thought I would lose my mind for you, because I knew the pain of losing a child like that. And I couldn't bear to watch you go there."

"What happened to her, Mom?" Mary said. She was crying too now, even as she wiped the tears from her mother's face.

"She was three years old. So beautiful. And smart. I would buy us these mother-daughter outfits, for special occasions, you know. Not every day.

"This one day, it was a beautiful summer day and I took her to the park, and she played with other children there. In the sandbox, and going down the slide. I always wonder if we had stayed home, maybe she wouldn't have gotten it."

"What?"

"Polio. The thing we all were so afraid of. I never thought it would happen to me. To Susan. That night we went for ice cream, and she wouldn't eat hers. She said she was too tired. She ordered raspberry, in a cone. And she sat there holding that cone, with the ice cream melting all pink down her arm. I reprimanded her for that. 'Don't be so messy!' I said. I hate that I said that to her.

"I threw the ice cream away and we walked home, except she said her legs were too tired so your father carried her, up on his shoulders. 'Isn't she getting too big for that?' I said, and Susan said, 'I'll never be too big.' Can you imagine that? Like she knew something.

"I gave her a nice bath and then I put her to bed with some children's aspirin. Your father thought she felt warm. He thought maybe she had a cold. 'You don't get colds in summer,' I said. It was later, sometime in the night, that I woke and heard her crying. I went to her room and touched her forehead and she was burning with fever, and her hair and her nightclothes were drenched with sweat. I called for your father to get the doctor. But when he came in, he said, 'Let's take her ourselves to the emergency room rather than wake the doctor.' We bundled her in dry clothes and we got in the car. I was holding her on my lap. And something happened. I've never been able to quite explain it. But there was an instant when something changed and I screamed for your father to pull over. He did, and I looked in her beautiful face and I saw right away that she was gone. My Susan. The most unthinkable thing in the world had happened, and it had happened to me."

Mary was crying harder now, her face resting on her mother's stomach, her mother stroking her hair.

"I was sent away for a little while. To a sanitarium, they called it. A fancy nuthouse was what it was. They told me the best thing for me would be to have another baby, straightaway. This time, it took years for me to get pregnant. I felt as if all my luck was gone. Used up. The only thing I still had, ironically, was my beauty. And it meant nothing. Eventually I did get pregnant, of course. And I had you. But God forgive me, I never had joy again. It died with Susan. And this is for you to forgive someday, Mary. When I realized I wasn't going to feel that joy, that something had died in me, I resented you. I resented your laughter and your love for me.

"I used to make your father a martini every day when he came home from work. Since we were first married, I'd mix it for him. And one day I made the martini and I looked at it and I understood that it offered me an escape. I'd been drunk before. I loved the feeling, the fogginess, the numbness. So I drank that martini straight down. You were five or six, and you came in with a drawing of our house. That martini made me able to smile at you and look at your drawing and tell you it was wonderful.

"It's like I woke up ten years later and you had grown up and your father had grown distant and I had grown older. Ten years, in a fog that enabled me to stay alive. I drove down to a church where they had AA meetings and I stood up and I said, 'My name is Mamie and I am a drunk.' That night they assigned me to a sponsor, a British woman who owned a knitting store."

"Alice," Mary said.

"The next week, after the meeting, she invited me to her house for tea. I went because I was desperate. She sat me in a chair and she handed me two knitting needles and a ball of yarn. I had knit as a young girl. But I didn't remember how exactly, so she showed me. While I knit, she told me her story. That day, I just listened. But I went back every week. And after a few months, while the two of us sat knitting, I said to her, 'You know, I used to always get everything I wanted, because I was beautiful.' "

18
THE KNITTING CIRCLE

Mary stayed with her mother over the next few weeks, through blood tests and stress tests and echocardiograms.

Sitting in a wheelchair, her hair loose around her and her skin still pale, her mother looked oddly young, and beautiful. She watched the flurry of activity around her. She smiled up at a doctor who walked past, his stethoscope swinging with authority. But he paused when he saw her.

"Are you still here, Mamie?" he said, grinning beneath his Don Ameche mustache.

"Trying to leave," she said. A flush of pink dotted her cheeks as she flirted with the doctor. "Want to take me home with you?"

The doctor chuckled. "Of course I do," he said. "But my wife wouldn't be very happy." He leaned in close enough for Mary to smell the tobacco on his breath.

A sullen technician appeared, shuffling up

to them. She spoke in Spanish to the doctor.

He pressed Mamie's hand, a bit too tenderly, Mary thought. Where was that other, hairy doctor anyway?

"Mina will take good care of you, Mamie," he said. He took the clipboard that hung from the back of the wheelchair and perused it. "Everything looks fine," he said. "I hate to let you go, but I'm afraid that I will have to release you soon."

"How soon?" Mary asked impatiently.

The doctor straightened and adjusted the knot of his tie.

"Excuse me?" he said.

"How soon will you release her?" Mary said.

The doctor glanced down at her mother, raising his eyebrows.

"My daughter," Mamie said. "Mary."

"I would never have guessed," the doctor said, surprised.

He extended his hand and shook Mary's authoritatively. She thought of how tenderly he had held her mother's hand, how sweetly he had spoken to her.

"Your mother is recovering beautifully," he said in a doctorly voice. "She can resume normal activities over the next few weeks. Of course, we'll keep a very close eye on her," he added in a softer tone.

Once again, the doctor pressed her mother's hand into his own, then bid them *adiós* before walking away, his stride confident, the stethoscope swinging.

"What is wrong with you?" Mary hissed as she followed the wheelchair toward the lab. "Flirting with the doctor like that?"

"Why are you so angry?" her mother said just before the technician shoved the wheelchair through the doors.

The doors swung shut lazily. Mary watched her mother disappear through the fingerprint-smudged Plexiglas. A small turquoise vinyl sofa was pushed into a nearby alcove, and Mary dropped onto it.

Her mother was right. She was angry. Not about the flirting. Her mother always flirted, with policemen and gas station attendants and waiters and valets. The power of her beauty had not diminished with age. In a way, it had intensified. Her voice had grown more sultry over time, her body was even leaner and tighter than when she was younger.

Now that it was clear her mother would survive, Mary was beginning to absorb the story she had told her that first day. Anger that had been dormant in her for her entire life came to the surface. Her mother's aloofness, her chilly love.

She wondered about this other mother, a woman who had loved another child with warmth and enthusiasm. She tried to put a face to this child, her lost sister. But only her mother's face came to her.

She heard the whoosh of the doors opening and the rattle of wheels.

"I have been poked for the final time," Mamie announced triumphantly.

Mary looked over at her mother. She wanted to hate her. But somehow couldn't. Mary got to her feet and walked over to the wheelchair, already on its way back down the corridor.

"Great," Mary said without conviction.

But her mother was too far ahead to hear her. Quickly, Mary hurried to catch up, chasing the golden back of her mother's head.

Mary stayed in Mexico for two more weeks. She took her mother home from the hospital and got her settled into her crooked little house with the bright blue door. She opened that door over and over through the course of a day as her mother's friends arrived with colorful bouquets of flowers, baskets of tamales, presents of hammered tin and *milagros* of hearts in all sizes. Finally she could go back to her own life. She had made decisions while she was here. She would ask Dylan for a divorce. She would sell their house and move to an apartment, something the right size for a woman living alone.

It did not make Mary happy to know what she had to do now. But it was time. Despite drinking and knitting and fleeing to Mexico, her mother had never moved through her grief. She had simply avoided it. Mary refused to do the same.

At the airport, she and her mother sat and drank coffee as they waited for Mary's flight to board. Mamie looked even healthier than she had before her heart attack.

Her hair was pulled back into its usual chignon, neat and blond and lovely. Her blue eyes twinkled again, and the silver jewelry at her neck and ears made her skin glow. The waiter admired Mamie openly, bringing her a small plate of cookies dusted with powdered sugar, smiling at her warmly.

"You look great, Mom," Mary said.

"I feel pretty damn good," Mamie said, grinning at the waiter.

A staticky voice called for the boarding of Mary's plane.

"That's me," Mary said, relieved to finally be going home.

Mary stood, but her mother reached for

her across the table, the powdered sugar dusting her hand.

"There is so much I want to explain," Mamie said.

Mary squeezed her mother's hand briefly. "You don't have to explain anything," she said. She pulled the handle up on her travel bag and placed her shoulder bag on top of it, then angled the suitcase to wheel it away.

Again, the loudspeaker crackled.

Mamie rushed to Mary's side. "I wasn't a good mother to you. I know that. Or a good grandmother to Stella."

"It's fine," Mary said.

"It's not fine. All these years and I never got over losing her. That's the truth," she said.

Mamie kept pace with her as she rushed toward the line at the security gate. She took Mary's free hand and held on tight. "I never got over her, and so I lost so much more. The joy of that little Stella. The joy of you."

At the gate, there wasn't a line so much as a crowd, everyone pushing forward to make their way through. Mary gave her mother a quick hug, but Mamie was not ready to go. She opened her arms and took Mary into her embrace.

"I don't expect you to forgive me, Mary-la," she said. "But I hope someday you can

411

understand." She had pressed her lips right against Mary's ear, and after she spoke, she moved them to her daughter's cheek and kissed her the way a mother kisses a daughter goodbye. "I love you, Mary-la," she said.

Before Mary could speak, her mother was pushing her way back through the crowd.

Mary stood and watched her go. A woman in a bright purple dress kept jostling her to get by, but Mary stood still, watching until her mother disappeared completely. Then she joined the crowd moving toward security.

When it was her turn to place her bags on the conveyor, Mary found the neatly folded envelope her mother had slipped into her hand. She shoved it into her pocket, then collected her bags and walked hurriedly toward the plane that would take her home.

The knitting circle was meeting at the Sit and Knit Two in Westerly. Roger had sent invitations to everyone for a knitting party on opening night. On her way there, Mary stopped at Dylan's office and left him the divorce papers, small Post-its flagging all the places for him to sign.

By the time she pulled into the parking lot, everyone else had already arrived and the champagne had been opened.

Roger greeted her at the door.

"Finally home," he said, planting a big kiss on her cheek.

Inside, she was blinded by color. Roger had arranged the yarn by color rather than brand, so that hills of orange spilled out of containers in one corner, every shade of blue dominated another, the pinks rose against one wall and the greens against another.

"I like what you've done with the place," she said. Her eyes settled on the familiar faces of the other women and she at last began to relax.

Mary lifted her bag and announced, "Presents!" She pulled out the yarn she'd bought in Mexico from a small group of women who raised their own sheep and spun and dyed the wool.

Soon, she was surrounded by Scarlet and Lulu and Ellen and Alice and Harriet. They hugged her and cooed over their presents.

A man stood behind Harriet, hanging back shyly.

Harriet took his arm and pulled him forward.

"This is my son," Harriet said, her eyes downcast. "My son David. Remember? I told you about him?"

Mary smiled. "I do remember."

"I'm going to teach David how to knit," Roger said. "My first victim. I've got an all-men's knitting class on Friday nights, and a Sunday morning knitting brunch."

Alice shook her head. "He's offering knitting and yoga," she said. "How do you knit in downward dog, that's what I want to know." She beamed proudly at Roger. "You just need the knitting. That's what I told him. But he's got ideas."

Roger winked behind David's back. "Yes, I do," he said.

Later, at home, Mary stood in her bedroom, remembering how she and Dylan had waited out her pregnancy in here, the two of them snuggled in this bed, reading books of names, dreaming about all that their future held. Dylan used to place headphones on her belly and play Beatles songs from his Walkman. "She's got to love the Beatles," he'd say. This was where newborn Stella used to sleep, in a cradle by their bed, the two of them awake all night listening to her baby sounds. Soon a new family would live here, and put their own imprints on this room.

Sadly, Mary began to undress, slipping off her shoes, shrugging out of her jacket. As she folded it, she felt the small tight square of paper she'd put in the pocket at the security gate in León.

Mary retrieved the envelope and went downstairs. In the living room, she turned on a lamp and sat, carefully opening the envelope.

There were two sheets of paper. The first was dated the day she'd left Mexico. In her perfect penmanship, her mother had written simply:

Mary-la, Even in my darkest days I wanted to let you know how I felt. But I have never been very good with words, like you are. I give you this now. It is what I wrote to you in one form or another every day of your young life. I offer it not for forgiveness, but for understanding. With all my love, Mom

Mary put the paper down and looked at the other one, also written in her mother's perfect penmanship. This one was undated. It read:

Daughter, I have a story to tell you. I have wanted to tell it to you for a very long time. But unlike Babar or Eloise or any of the other stories that you loved to hear, this one is not funny. This one is not clever. It is simply true. It is my story, yet I do not have the words to tell it. Instead, I pick up my needles and I knit. Every stitch is a letter. A row spells out "I love you." I knit "I love you" into everything I make. Like a prayer, or a wish, I send it out to you, hoping you can hear me. Hoping, daughter, that the story I am knitting reaches you somehow. Hoping, that my love reaches you somehow.

■ ■ ■ ■

PART TEN:
CASTING OFF

■ ■ ■ ■

So you've knit a good, long strip and you want to get it off the needles and secure it so it doesn't unravel. This process is called casting off.

— Kris Percival,
Knitting Pretty

19
Mary

Mary stood at the window in her small office and looked down at the street. It was two weeks before Christmas. The bar across the street had fat colored lights strung above its windows and drooping over the door. They blinked on and off in the early evening. A lazy wet snow fell, melting before it even hit the ground. Eddie had bought some strange collection of Christmas carols and it played endlessly in the outer office. Mary could make out the Chipmunks' nasal singing.

She had a fiber-optic snowman on her desk and it glowed eerily, changing colors with the slow creepy movement of a lava lamp. Walking past the antique shop on Wickenden Street, Mary had seen this funny snowman dripping colors across its popcornlike skin, and bought it immediately. She carried it to work, careful not to break its fake stick arms, and plugged it right in. Then she stood back to admire it. Even then it didn't occur to her that this was her first act of celebration since Stella had died.

That came later, when she got home and dug out her Andy Williams Christmas CD. Mary put it on while she cooked a complicated stew, humming along with Andy as he sang "Winter Wonderland." She paused. Her kitchen smelled of onions caramelizing and the crisp freshness of just-chopped carrots and celery. Small white lights twinkled in the windows. She could catch the smell of the heat that gurgled through the radiators. All that was missing, she thought, was everything else.

Mary had stood, still holding the long wooden spoon, looking at her life. Dylan had agreed to bring the divorce papers back to her quickly. No Dylan. No Stella. Instead, this new life, so different from the one she had been living.

Now she tried to count her blessings: New friends. Knitting. She faltered. The Chipmunks. The fiber-optic snowman. Mary closed her eyes and made herself remember every detail of Stella's lovely face. Stella, she added to her list of blessings. Still, always, Stella.

"Uh," Holly said from the doorway. "Are

you like, meditating or something?"

Mary opened her eyes, her heart oddly full. "Just thinking," she said.

"I like the snowman," Holly said.

Holly had lost all of her pregnancy weight. Her hip bones jutted against the blue miniskirt she wore, and her skinny legs poked out beneath it. She'd stopped breast-feeding, and her breasts were small and flat again, boyish beneath her Clash concert T-shirt.

Mary frowned at Holly's clothes. It was December and snowing and she was dressed for summer. But she didn't say anything. Jessica was always reprimanding Holly — she hadn't breast-fed long enough, she didn't play classical music tapes in the car, she needed more black and white toys. All of Jessica's ideas made Holly even wearier. Jessica and Eddie's baby, Waylon, was only a month old but had a regular routine of stimulation. Mozart, tapes of Dr. Seuss books read aloud, scary pictures of black and white faces. Holly didn't have to hear Mary telling her she was dressed inappropriately.

"Are you going home?" Mary asked Holly.

She felt sorry for her. Holly was in over her head. She'd imagined a playmate, not a baby. Sometimes, Mary babysat Jasper so that Holly could go out. She would come home drunk long after Mary had put Jasper to bed, her makeup smeared and her miniskirt all twisted. Mary would put her to bed too, Holly mumbling her thanks.

"Um," Holly said, her heavily lined eyes gazing at the snowman's changing colors. "No. Going to a party. I met this guy the other night? When you babysat?"

Mary lifted her eyebrows. "Really? That's great."

"Um," Holly said again. "Yeah. So far. I haven't told him yet. You know."

"Don't worry about it," Mary said. "Just have some fun."

"Right," Holly said. Her eyes shifted to Mary, then back to the snowman. "That's what I'm thinking."

"Did Eddie go home?"

Holly rolled her eyes. "He took Waylon to a fucking swimming lesson. I mean, the kid can't even sit up yet."

"Go on your date," Mary said. "I'll lock up."

"Thanks," Holly said, relieved. "He's cute, this guy. Rocco."

"Rocco?" Mary laughed.

"Yeah. He kissed me and it was like, zap! You know?"

"You be careful," Mary said. "Zap got you

in trouble."

Unexpectedly, Holly gave her a quick fierce hug. "Thank you," she said. "I left you something at my desk," she added when she let go.

"Like a Christmas present?" Mary said.

Holly brightened. "Yeah," she said. "Like a Christmas present."

"But the party's not until tomorrow."

Holly shrugged helplessly. Then she walked away quickly, the heels of her boots tapping against the hardwood floor.

It wasn't until after Mary heard the ding of the elevator arriving to take Holly away to her date that she wondered who was babysitting Jasper. Maybe Holly's sister had agreed to do it. If it were possible, her sister Heather was even less reliable than Holly herself. She didn't even like to hold Jasper. "Too squirmy," she'd said. "Makes me itchy, like I'm holding a worm or something."

Mary unplugged her snowman and put on her coat and the gloves she'd knit. That was what everyone was getting for Christmas this year. Just last night, she'd laid them all out on the dining room table, a dozen pairs of wool tweed gloves in rich jewel colors, topaz and garnet and emerald and amethyst. Her own pair was a deep ruby with flecks of pink and purple.

In the outer office, the silver aluminum tree with pom-pom-tipped branches glittered in the fluorescent lighting. Eddie had brought it in the other day in a long skinny box that smelled of mothballs. Mary and Holly had helped him stand up its spine and stick the branches into its holes. They'd hung blue balls on every branch. Those balls reflected Mary's own face now, distorting it. She hit one lightly, watching it spin.

Eddie's CD was playing a song by Tiny Tim now, and Mary happily turned it off. After she checked that all the doors were locked, she stood in the silent office a moment and watched the fake tree glisten before she flicked off the overhead lights and went out to the elevator.

One came quickly. But as soon as the door slid open she remembered that Holly had left her something. She could just get it tomorrow, she supposed. But Holly seemed so fragile lately that Mary was afraid she'd be disappointed if she came to work in the morning and saw that Mary had left the present there, unopened.

Mary dug the keys from her coat pocket and went back, unlocking the two locks on the main door, then flicking on the lights again. They hummed, then blinked on. For some reason, the tree had lost its glitter and looked ridiculous, a stick with peeling aluminum branches and chipped blue ornaments.

Mary remembered that when she bought the snowman, she'd seen one of those old color wheels, the ones that looked like a Trivial Pursuit playing piece, all filled in with colored wedges. You plugged it in, and it splashed color across trees like this one. She decided she'd buy it for Eddie's Christmas present and give it to him at the party tomorrow. She'd already bought too many Baby Einstein products for Waylon, but this gift was too perfect to pass up. In fact, she'd go to the store on her way home.

For now, though, she didn't see any present on Holly's desk. Just the usual chaos of papers and Post-its and tubes of cheap lipstick. Holly had probably taken the thing with her. Mary could sympathize with her spaciness. She remembered too well how a new baby seemed to gobble up your brain cells. That, combined with lack of sleep, had left her in a fog. A pleasant fog for Mary. But Holly was doing it alone, and working full-time.

Something caught Mary's eye on the floor behind Holly's desk. A big red bow. She hoped Holly hadn't spent too much money on her, an extravagant thank-you for babysitting for free. That would be like Holly. She could barely pay her rent but she still bought expensive shoes and vintage clothes. She probably went overboard on presents too.

Mary walked around the desk and wheeled the chair out of the way.

"Holy shit!" she said.

There, asleep in his jumpy seat, was Jasper. Taped to the top of the seat was a card with a big red bow.

Careful not to wake the baby, Mary leaned over and quietly pulled off the card. On the front was a candy cane with cat hair stuck all over it. Despite the fact that Holly had just left her baby with Mary, she smiled. Holly's entire apartment was covered in cat hair.

Underneath the printed holiday message inside, Holly had written:

You're a good mother. I know. I saw you do it. And I suck at this. Why should someone like you be deprived of your baby? Why should someone like me deserve one? Keep him. Make sure he knows I love him but I just couldn't do it. I know you'll do better. Your Friend, Holly Patterson

"Holy shit," Mary said again, after she'd read the note three times to be sure she understood it.

She grabbed the phone and punched in Holly's cell phone number. But she didn't answer. Of course. Mary tried to think straight, glancing nervously at the sleeping baby. Who had Holly gone off with? Bruno somebody? No. Rocco. Rocco without a last name. Or maybe he was just a ruse for Holly to get out and leave Jasper behind while Mary was still here.

Mary flipped through Holly's Rolodex until she found her sister Heather's phone number.

Heather answered right away, sounding as if she just woke up.

"Heather? It's Mary Baxter."

"Who?"

"Mary? I work with Holly?"

"Oh. Uh-huh," Heather said.

Mary wasn't convinced Heather remembered her, or even knew where Holly worked. "I need to find Holly. Have you spoken to her?"

"Yeah," Heather said through a yawn. Then, to someone else, "It's some lady looking for my sister."

"Heather?" Mary said impatiently. "Do you know where she is?"

"Aruba?"

"What!" Mary said. Then, hopefully, she said, "You're not talking to me, are you?"

"Yeah. I'm telling you. She went to Aruba. Or maybe Barbados. One of those islands. I get them mixed up."

That explained the light clothing she'd been wearing.

"Do you mean she's gone already?" Mary said.

She was practically shouting. Jasper stirred. He crunched up his face and she held her breath. But he just relaxed it again and continued to sleep.

"She met this guy a couple weeks ago and his friend has a house on the beach in like Tobago or somewhere," Heather was saying.

Mary sunk into the swivel chair, pressing the phone hard to her ear.

"Tobago?" she said.

Heather laughed. "Somewhere like that."

"Heather?" Mary said. "I'm going to give you my phone number, okay? I desperately need to talk to Holly. If she calls —"

"Do they have phones down there?"

"Yes, they have phones," Mary said. Knowing it was useless, she very slowly told Heather her number. "Can you repeat it back to me?" Mary said.

"Uh," Heather said. "Two-seven-three?"

"Two-seven-two," Mary said, clenching her jaw.

She repeated the number again, but before she could make Heather say it back to her, Heather said, "Got it. Bye," and hung up.

Mary placed the phone back in its cradle. When she glanced down at Jasper, he was awake. He stared at her calmly with his dark blue eyes.

She bent and unclasped the buckle on the safety strap, then lifted him out of the seat and into her arms. Mary felt his wet diaper against her arm. No diaper bag. No car seat. Nothing. Jasper was studying her as if he was waiting for further instructions.

"Okay, buddy," Mary said. "Let's go."

Settling the baby on one hip, she picked up the bouncy seat and tucked it against the other. Slowly, awkwardly, she made her way out of the office toward home.

A mother does not forget how to be a mother. Like riding a bicycle many years later, or the way your feet remember how to waltz, when a mother is handed a baby she knows what to do.

For Mary, this maternal memory came with an ache that had dulled somewhat over all these months. The heft of a baby in her arms, the acrid smell of baby wipes, the funny wet sounds a baby makes, the toothless grins, the way a baby's face crumples in on itself before he breaks into tears, all of it brought back memories of mothering Stella. And with those memories came the pain of loss all over again.

Still, she had to tend Jasper. Holly had left her no choice. She needed diapers, formula, baby things. Who knew how to take care of a baby? Without thinking, Mary picked up the phone and called Dylan.

He came right away. At first, they had stood awkwardly together in the kitchen. But when Mary held Jasper to her chest and Dylan made a list of what he needed to get, a sense of routine and familiarity settled over them.

At the door, the list in his gloved hand, Dylan paused to watch Mary with the baby.

"What?" she said harshly when she saw him still there.

"You look beautiful," he said.

She frowned at him. "Happy?" she said sarcastically.

"I'm not —" he began, but Mary turned from him. *Get out!* she thought, regretting that she had called him for help. She should have called Ellen. Or Scarlet. Or anyone.

While Dylan went to buy diapers and

bottles and formula, Mary played with Jasper and simultaneously tried to find Holly. Ridiculously, she left messages on Holly's home answering machine and cell phone. She called Heather, dialing her number again and again even as a busy signal beeped at her each time.

Before Dylan came back with any of the supplies, Jasper began to howl in that way that only babies have. He opened his mouth into a perfect O and wailed a shrill, siren-like wail that appeared to have no end.

Mary picked him up and walked him, pressed against her chest. Back and forth, patting his back, making soothing sounds he could not hear over his screams.

The phone rang, cutting through Jasper's howls.

"Mary!" her mother's voice shot into the room. "I want you to know I'm coming for Christmas. I'm coming to spend the holiday with you." She paused. "A mother should be with her daughter at Christmastime," Mamie said.

As if he understood the importance of what Mamie was saying, Jasper quieted for a moment.

"Mom," Mary began, but the word seemed to take on a new meaning and Mary was unable to continue.

"One more thing," her mother added, "Francisco is coming too. Remember him? The handsome doctor with the mustache? Don't worry. I already booked us a B and B on Benefit Street. See you soon, honey. *¡Feliz Navidad!*"

"Francisco?" Mary shot at the telephone.

Jasper began to scream again. "Stop crying," Mary said to Jasper. "Please."

Thankfully, Dylan came in with two big shopping bags.

"Diapers," Dylan said as he pulled a package from one bag.

Mary grabbed the diapers and immediately began to change Jasper's wet one.

"Wipes," Dylan said. "Onesies. And here's a rattle. A book. A blanket. A stuffed monkey."

Mary stopped, her hands firmly holding Jasper's ankles to lift his legs in the air. Dylan had handed Jasper a ring of bright plastic keys, and the baby shook them maniacally. The table was full of all the things a family needed to take care of a baby. Mary surveyed the toys and tiny onesies with the snaps up the inner legs and the bottles with the blue bears and red hearts and fire trucks. Then she looked at Dylan. He took a step toward her, and then another. Jasper shook the keys even harder, giggling.

The image of Stella as a small perfect baby filled Mary and she doubled over from its clarity.

"Ssshhh," Dylan was saying.

But if he was speaking to her, or the baby, Mary wasn't sure.

"We need to find Holly," Mary told Eddie.

He was wearing a weird Santa hat. Red felt, like most of them, and trimmed in white. But instead of rising to a pom-pommed point, the top of this hat was a red spring that wobbled every time Eddie moved his head. It made Mary seasick to watch.

"Maybe Jessica and I should take him," Eddie said.

Mary watched Jessica in the small group of guests at the Christmas party. She wore an elaborate sling that looked like something tribal. It held Waylon so that he faced out but could still hear her heartbeat. "Very important," Jessica had explained.

"I don't think that would work," Mary said.

"What the fuck was she thinking?" Eddie said, his hat bouncing.

"Holly? Thinking?" Mary said.

"Right," Eddie said.

They both looked down at Jasper. Dylan had bought him a red-and-white-candy-cane-striped onesie, and he lay in his bouncy seat, kicking his striped feet happily.

"I mean," Eddie said, "you just don't give someone a baby."

"We have to find her," Mary said again, trying not to sound desperate.

"Absolutely," he said.

On the night Big Alice's Sit and Knit was finally reopening, it was one week before Christmas, one week since Mary's Secret Santa gift had turned out to be Jasper, and still no word from Holly. The last time Mary had spoken to her, Heather told her that she was "ninety-nine percent sure" that Holly had gone to Cancún.

"Cancún?" Mary had said. "That's not an island. You said she went to an island."

"Curaçao?" Heather had offered.

Alice was having a knitting circle tonight, the first one in the new store. Scarlet was bringing a bûche de Noël and Ellen was making homemade eggnog. Mary's job was to bring paper plates and napkins and she had bought blue ones covered in white snowflakes.

"You sure you don't mind?" Mary asked Dylan as she gathered her yarn and needles.

Jasper was fussing in Dylan's lap, pulling on his glasses, poking his fingers up his nose.

"Maybe we could keep him," Dylan said.

"There is no 'we,' " Mary told him.

"Go," Dylan said.

The air had the sharp chill of winter. A black sky offered up a dizzying number of stars. Mary paused to search for Venus. She found it beside a white crescent moon.

A voice from the darkness said, "Hey."

Mary spun around to find Holly shivering in front of her. She had on that same denim miniskirt, no stockings, flip-flops.

"Holly," Mary said, her voice, her whole self, flooded with relief. "Thank God."

Holly's T-shirt had a picture of a pyramid on it and something in Spanish written below. An oversized man's jacket hung on her, unbuttoned.

Mary pointed at the shirt. "Cancún," she said.

"The Mayans rule," Holly said. She pulled the coat closed, her hands trembling. "I've been watching you guys. Through the window," she said. "You look like a real family."

"But we're not, sweetie."

"I like the striped thing," Holly said. "He looks cute."

Mary put a hand on Holly's arm. She felt the girl shivering.

"I did a good thing, didn't I?" Holly said. "Dylan came back."

"He's just helping out," Mary said.

Before she could say anything more, Holly fell into her arms and began to cry.

"You have to help me," Holly said. "Please, Mary."

When Stella died, Mary had been overcome by the way people had helped. Not just the lasagnas and the flowers, but how the laundry got done, the bills got paid, their small patch of grass got mowed. Friends sat by her side, offered advice, offered shoulders for leaning, for crying.

But until this moment, Mary had not been able to give to someone else who needed it. She remembered how she had stayed away from the hospital when Bridget was there. She had wanted to bring Ellen a jigsaw puzzle to help her pass time. She had wanted to be someone whose shoulder could be leaned on. But she was unable to face the pain in that room or to sit in a hospital and wait for news.

After Beth died, Mary had vowed to help her husband, to send cookies to her children, to go to their house one day and perform simple chores, like vacuuming or folding laundry. But her ability to give, like her ability for joy, was paralyzed.

Until now.

When she looked at Holly, something in Mary opened up.

"I can help you," she said. "I can."

Inside, Holly picked up Jasper tentatively. "You mad at me, Jazz?" she whispered.

The baby set his gaze on her as if considering his options.

Holly buried her nose in the nape of his neck. "Missed that smell," she said.

"I'm taking Holly to Big Alice's with me," Mary said.

Holly frowned at them. "The knitting lady?" she said.

Mary dug through her knitting basket until she found a skein of thick chunky chartreuse yarn. Maybe this was why knitters always bought yarn they didn't really need, so they could pass it on to someone who did need it. From her bag she removed two number sixteen needles and handed them and the yarn to Holly.

"By the time we get back, you'll have made a scarf," she told her.

Holly eyed the yarn suspiciously. "Nice color," she admitted.

The baby was fussing and Dylan bounced Jasper on his knee. Once again, Mary gathered her knitting supplies and the paper cups and napkins to leave. But before she could, the front door opened in a burst of rustling fabric and cold air.

"*¡Feliz Navidad!*" Mamie announced from the foyer.

She was wearing a complicated magenta shawl, wrapped and fringed, and she was carrying two oversized bags of Christmas presents, the gold and silver bows and ribbon poking from the tops.

"Francisco is snoozing at the B and B, so I figured I'd come over straightaway," she said.

When she walked into a room, she completely took it over. The small front living room filled with her as she talked and unwrapped her shawl and removed packages all at the same time.

"You said you were coming for Christmas, Mom," Mary said.

"I am," Mamie said, planting a kiss on Mary's cheek. She kissed Dylan and Jasper and Holly too, before she stepped back to study them. "I'm Mary's mother," she said to Holly.

"Wow," Holly said, clutching the yarn.

"I'm guessing this guy is yours?" Mamie said.

She lifted Jasper from Dylan's lap and made a funny face at him. Immediately, the baby started to cry.

Mary took Jasper from her mother and soothed him.

"We're just leaving," Mary said, sounding cross. She *was* cross. What the hell was her mother doing in her living room a whole week before Christmas?

"Are you going knitting?" Mamie said.

"Yes," Mary said reluctantly.

"At Big Alice's?"

"Want to come?" Holly said.

Mamie thought a moment. "It's been years," she said.

"I'm already late," Mary said, handing Jasper to Dylan again.

"So why are we standing around talking then?" Mamie said, wrapping her shawl around her with dramatic motions. "Let's go."

On the ride to Big Alice's, Holly and Mamie bonded over their love of Mexico while Mary seethed.

"Holly's been there once in her whole life," Mary mumbled.

"So romantic," Holly said, sighing. "The pyramids. The beaches. And it's so hot. I love the heat."

"Where I live, it's mountainous," Mamie was saying.

Mary focused on the dark road ahead of them. She didn't want her mother at the knitting circle. Imagining the fuss that would be made over her, the way she'd take over, made Mary want to turn around and go home.

The sign for Big Alice's appeared, lit, in the distance. Her mother and Holly were laughing together over something. Mary turned into the parking lot and stepped too hard on the brakes.

"Careful," Mamie said.

Mary grabbed her things and stormed out of the car, not waiting for her mother or Holly.

The new Sit and Knit smelled of just-cut wood, fresh paint, and the comforting familiar smell of wool. The rooms were larger, more open, and Alice had one entire room in the back just for the knitting circle.

As soon as Mary picked up her needles and began to knit, her anger dissipated. She was calmed by the motion of slipping one needle through a stitch and pulling the yarn onto the other needle, by the feel of wool in her hands, by the sound of everyone's knitting needles clicking.

At first, of course, her mother did take over. Her exuberant greeting of Alice alone made Mary consider leaving. But after the hugging and loud pronouncements, her mother bought yarn and needles and got down to the business of knitting.

Everyone was in their place. Her mother sat beside Ellen on a new sofa covered in chintz; Scarlet sat in an overstuffed chair; Lulu had her legs bent yoga-style in one corner of the couch where Harriet sat straight-backed and somber; and Mary rocked gently in a rocking chair salvaged, Alice told her, from an old seaside hotel. Across from her, heads bent together on a fuchsia love seat, Alice taught Holly how to knit.

"If you must know," Harriet said out of nowhere, "my son is seeing Roger."

Ellen grinned at her. "I can't tell you how happy that makes me. Roger deserves someone fabulous."

Harriet looked up, surprised. But then she immediately bent her head and continued knitting. She was making matching sweaters for Beth's kids. Already the smallest one was finished, folded neatly on the table beside her. Each sweater was a different color, but they all had white snowflakes across the yolk.

"David too," she said softly.

"What?" Ellen asked her.

Still not looking up, Harriet said, "David deserves someone fabulous too."

How far everyone in this room had come since that first knitting circle, Mary thought. Even she was a different person than that frightened woman who had sat with her scarf still on its needles, afraid to speak, to purl, to cast off.

Holly's face was scrunched in concentration. Mary watched her, marveling at how quickly she had learned. Already a scarf was taking shape. A feeling surged through Mary and brought tears to her eyes. In this quiet room, with these people, her grief had found comfort. She understood that it would never go away; that was impossible. But after these few years of coming together to knit, after hearing their stories, after all the hours she'd spent in this practice of making something out of series of knots, Mary realized that she would, after all, go on without her Stella.

Mary took a breath. She knit one more row. It was time, she knew, and so she began.

"We named her Stella because it meant star," she said. She was aware of her own mother's eyes on her, but she did not meet them.

"A star seemed fitting. She was our wish

come true. Our bright light. And think of all the kinds of Stellas there are in the world. Stella McCartney. Stella Adler. Even Stella Kowalski. She could grow up to be anything. Anything at all.

"Sometimes it feels like nothing came before her. Maybe that's because without her I sometimes feel like there is nothing left.

"But there was a life before her, an entire lifetime in San Francisco. Then one day I flew home to help my mother pack up our old house and move to Mexico.

"After she left, I stayed behind to clean the empty house. Sometimes I think I expected the walls to tell me things. But they were just quiet empty walls in need of paint. The last morning, I went to a Starbucks in a strip mall.

"All I wanted was a big cup of coffee and to fly home.

"I ordered a grande latte, emphasizing no foam. They always put too much foam in their lattes.

" 'Good call,' somebody behind me said. I turned around and there was Dylan. That's how we met. 'I know this,' he said, 'because sadly I have my morning coffee and dry baked good here every single morning.' He held up his left hand. 'Divorced. Recently.

Happily,' he added. 'Or not happily,' he said quickly, 'but decidedly.'

"He was so optimistic. So chatty. So hard to resist.

"When he asked me to join him, I did. He told me everything about himself: he was a lawyer, he had been married for six years, he had gotten married because it had seemed time to do it, but he had known immediately that although he was ready to get married, he had married the wrong woman.

" 'She wanted kids and so did I,' he said sheepishly. 'I just didn't want them with her.' He lifted his paper cup. 'So here I am, alone at Starbucks drinking foam.'

"After I got back to San Francisco, he called me from time to time, chattering on as cheerfully as he had that first morning. I started looking forward to his calls. His voice lifted my spirits somehow.

"When I went back to Rhode Island to close on the house I told him that I would never leave San Francisco. 'My life is just falling into place,' I told him.

" 'Mine too,' he said.

" 'I don't think you understand,' I told him, but he just grinned at me.

"I was never able to explain to my friends in California, or even to myself, how I ended up back here. I fell in love with

Dylan. He was easy to fall in love with. But to move back to a place I never even liked very much, at forty years old, leaving behind an entire life . . ." Mary shook her head. "It still baffles me sometimes.

"And it was hard at first. I didn't know anybody. Sometimes I'd run into people I'd known in high school and we had nothing at all in common. Dylan went off to a real job and stayed gone all day. The city felt too small and claustrophobic. I started to think I had made a mistake. Online magazines were flourishing and all of my writer friends suddenly had more work than they knew what to do with. The only work I could find regularly was writing brochures for local jewelry companies.

"I loved Dylan. I was certain of that, but I was reconsidering being here when I discovered I was pregnant. And my whole life immediately got better. This is why I'm here, I realized. Everything had happened in this way for one good, perfect reason: Stella.

"Before long my life was making sense. I got my job at the paper. I had friends at work, mommy friends, neighbor friends. I was always going somewhere. To take Stella to a birthday party or to the playground or to ballet class. I was picking up kids and bringing them to play at our house. I was making dinner every night. I was cutting cucumbers into perfect circles for snacks for Stella, and washing apples and cutting the skins from them in one continuous spiral. Everything I did for her brought me a hug and kisses. When I took her to school, she would choose a number, and that was how many hugs and kisses she had to give me before I could leave.

"We would have had another baby if it happened. But it didn't. And I wasn't disappointed by that because we had Stella.

"One day, I picked her up from school and the sun was shining brightly and she was in the backseat chattering about her day. She was like Dylan that way. She loved talking. I looked at that bright sun and listened to my daughter's voice and something came over me. Gratefulness, I think, for what I had. This child. This glorious day. This life. I was so overwhelmed that I had to pull over to the side of the road.

" 'Mama?' Stella said. 'You okay?'

" 'I'm just very very happy,' I told her.

"She sighed. 'I am very very happy too,' she said.

"I looked in the rearview mirror at her and she was grinning back at me.

"That day stays with me. You know how the Hmong make elaborate hats for their babies with flowers on the tops? So that when Death flies by and looks down at the earth, he mistakes the children for flowers and leaves them alone. That day I wonder if I tempted fate. Called attention to Stella and me and our happiness, you know?

"Because the very next day when I picked her up she said she had a tummy ache. I asked her all the usual questions. If she had eaten enough that day? Or too little? If she'd run too hard or too fast? But she shook her head, 'My tummy just hurts,' she said.

"When we got home, I gave her some Tylenol and put her on the sofa with her favorite blanket and let her watch television while I started dinner. I wasn't even a little worried. Her forehead was warm, and the worst thing I imagined was a touch of some bug or another. A deadline I had for the newspaper weighed much more heavily on my mind. Even though I went to check her a few times, I was really trying to shape an article I had to write. I needed a better lead. I needed a way to contain the story.

"I heard her call for me, and I went out to the living room and she looked really pale. I sat beside her on the couch. Her fever was so high that she burned through the blanket into me. Even then I wasn't worried. Kids get high fevers like that.

" 'Stay with me, Mama,' she said. Her eyes fluttered a little, then she seemed to sink into sleep. I did sit with her, stroking her forehead, smoothing her hair. When I took her temperature, it was one hundred and five. When I asked her questions, she didn't answer clearly. In fact, I couldn't quite rouse her. She forced her eyes open briefly, she mumbled replies, but something was definitely not right.

"It was almost seven o'clock. Too late to take her to the doctor. I could have called his service and waited for him to call me back. But for some reason I wrapped her in the blanket and took her in the car and drove straight to the emergency room. Fear was kicking in. I called Dylan, and he sounded calm. Was I overreacting?

" 'Stella?' I asked her.

"She mumbled again.

" 'Answer Mommy,' I said.

" 'Mama.'

"God knows what it took for her to say that, but I thought it was a good sign. I *was* overreacting, I decided.

"Then I was there, in the parking lot of the ER, bundling her up and running inside. Everything happened so fast. The way they looked at her and rushed us to a room. The way the doctor frowned as he examined her, shooting questions at me. I kept reciting the uneventful events of the afternoon. The tummy ache. The sleepiness. The rising fever.

"At some point, Dylan arrived. He was worried, I could tell. He kept calling people. His college roommate who was a doctor somewhere. Stella's teacher to find out if any other kid was sick. Then he'd come in and ask the doctor questions.

"The air in that room was full of tension. The doctor began to bark orders in a language I didn't speak. Nurses hurried in and out. Someone pushed me away from Stella and when I tried to reach her the doctor said roughly, 'Maybe you could step outside for a bit.'

"Dylan was gripping my arm and pulling me away. My own voice sounded foreign, distant. 'Something is very wrong,' Dylan said hoarsely.

I paced. I peered in the Plexiglas window of the room and watched the terrible scene unfold before me. At some point they had removed her clothes and they lay in a hot pink pile on the floor. A nurse stepped on them, then kicked them aside with the toe of her white shoe, and I pounded on the glass for her to pick them up. Stella had carefully chosen that top, those capri pants, from a catalogue, making neat circles in gel pen around all the clothes she wanted for spring.

"A round woman with a placid face and wire-rimmed glasses led us to a small room.

"She was a social worker and she had come to tell us how seriously ill Stella was. They had done a spinal tap, she said, and although the results were not yet in, the cloudiness of the spinal fluid indicated meningitis.

"I tried to make sense of the word. I remembered a local football team who had shared a water bottle all coming down with it. But they had survived and gone on to win the state championship.

"The social worker cast her glance toward the floor. 'There are two kinds,' she told us. 'This is bacterial.'

" 'Oh, God,' Dylan said.

"Later he told me about someone he went to law school with, a young man who felt fluish during Torts, lay down for a nap, and was found dead by his roommate that same night.

" 'They're doing everything they can,' the social worker said. She stood to go. 'Do you want me to send in the chaplin?'

" 'No!' I said. What the hell was going on here? I thought.

"Eventually, I went and sat by the closed door of the ICU, where they had moved her. Then I made my way inside and sat on the floor in front of her room. Until a nurse came and lifted me by my elbows and brought me inside. She gently pushed me onto a scratchy chair in one corner of the room.

" 'Stay there and don't get in the way,' she said.

"I stayed there for the next twelve hours, leaping to my feet every time a machine beeped or a nurse's voice took on an edge of panic. If there was a crack in the crowd that worked on my daughter, I found my way in and whispered for her to get better.

"Even now I don't want to talk about the tubes, the machines, the equipment in her and around her. Even now I don't want to talk about how she looked on that gurney. Or the way I heard a nurse call out that they were losing her. The sound of footsteps as doctors ran in. The feel of arms pushing me out of the room. The intercom calling for this doctor or that. The things that keep me up at night. The smells and sounds. The terror. The terror in my heart.

"I can only say what you all know. A mother should not watch her child die. A mother should not see the way life ebbs out of us, or what is left behind. A mother should not stand at her child's grave, or press her child's pajamas to her nose in the desperate hope that her scent is still there."

Mary struggled to say more. She had not spoken of Stella's death this way before. It was too much to say. Even now the words came out like bullets, sharp and painful. Perhaps by telling this story, she could finally heal.

"No mother should lose her child," Mary said.

And when she said it, her own mother jumped to her feet, dropping yarn and needles to the floor as she rushed to Mary.

"If I could only have kept this pain from you," Mamie said.

For the first time in a very long time, Mary let her mother take her in her arms. She let her mother cradle her. At last, the two women held each other and cried.

On Christmas morning, Mary woke to the smell of coffee and bacon. She pulled on her robe and went downstairs, where her mother stood at the stove, cooking.

"Are you a person who believes that it's never too late to start over?" her mother said without looking at Mary.

Mary tried to imagine the mother she'd

never known, the one who played with the little girl Susan, who laughed and found joy in her child. She could not yet see that woman. But Mary believed that someday, she might be able to.

"I am that kind of person," Mary said.

Her mother looked at her now, and Mary saw tears in her eyes.

"Thank you," Mamie said.

"Merry Christmas, Mom," Mary said. Then she added softly, "I'm glad you're here."

Mamie cleared her throat. "Let's not get all maudlin now," she said. "I'm making toads-in-the-hole. You always liked those."

Mary smiled. "My favorite," she said.

"I know," Mamie said, turning back to the stove.

20
THE KNITTING
CIRCLE

On Christmas night, after Mary played a long game of Scrabble with her mother and Francisco, then sent them on their way; after Holly and Jasper came by with a cake frosted green and sprinkled with coconut — "Like snow! Get it?" Holly had gushed — and opened all the presents Mary had bought for the baby; after Holly had said, "Hey, wait a minute. Nothing for me?" and Mary had told her that her gift was free babysitting, once a week for the rest of the year; after Scarlet and Lulu came by with champagne and poinsettias; after Mary went from room to room in her house turning off the lights; after a good Christmas was coming to an end, there was a knock on the front door.

Mary opened it and Dylan stood there, holding the divorce papers Mary had given him a few days earlier.

"A strange Christmas present," she said.

"But thanks."

She reached out her hand for them, and he gave her the papers.

Behind Dylan, snow started to fall, quickly dusting the street and the rooftops. The sight of him standing there made tears sting Mary's eyes. She turned to go back into the house, hoping he hadn't noticed.

"How was your day?" he asked, stopping her.

She looked back at him, the orange of his fleece vest bright against the darkness and the white snow.

"Good," she said. Then she added, "You know."

He nodded.

They stood apart like that in the hushed night for some time before Dylan spoke.

"By the way," he said, "they're not signed."

Mary took a step out the door.

"Why not?"

"Seeing you holding Jasper like that made me understand why I had to leave for a while."

"Awhile?" Mary said. She moved to step even closer to him, but stopped herself. Distance was better, she thought.

"And it made me understand why I need to come home."

"No," she said.

The weight of all that had come between them — Denise and her week with Connor, the frustrations, the grief; and the good things too — falling in love and having Stella, those brief years when the three of them made a family — the weight of all of it made Mary want to fall to her knees right here in the snow. She could not open her arms to possibility again. If she took Dylan back, these things would always be between them, and hurt and disappointment would hover around them, perhaps forever.

"I can't," she said, her voice small.

"Remember the day we met? At Starbucks?" he said.

"Let's not do this," Mary said, shivering in her thin white blouse.

"I fell in love with you that day," he continued. His hair was white with snow. "Remember when we moved in here?"

Mary swallowed hard. She had sat in their empty house and cried from happiness.

"That was a lifetime ago," she said. "It was."

"Mary?" Dylan said, as if he hadn't heard her. "Remember our beautiful little girl?"

"Go away," Mary said.

"We could adopt a baby, like Scarlet," he said. "Or we could try again. Or we could just grow old together, the two of us."

"Endless possibilities," Mary said.

"Yes!" Dylan said, taking a few steps toward her.

"The thing about possibility," Mary said, wrapping her arms around her shivering body, "is it can go either way. I don't know if I can risk it going bad."

"We have to take risks," he said. "If we don't, what's the point?"

"It's really cold out here," she said.

"Yes," he said.

"I'm going inside," she said, but she stayed right there. She looked at Dylan's face, marveling at how open it was. That ridiculous orange vest, the only bright spot out here.

"I don't know if I can forgive you," she said.

"Could you try?" he asked.

Mary looked at this man, her husband, the streetlight shining down on him, the snow falling fast around him.

He was coming toward her now, arms open. She could see the tears on his face. She could see him smiling.

"Can I come inside?" he was saying.

"Yes," Mary said.

The first wednesday night in October, Mary drove to Big Alice's for the knitting circle.

Mary's mind was full of plans for the blanket she was going to knit for Dylan for Christmas, a crazy combination of yarns and patterns, rows of zigzags, rows of purls, rows like waves. She needed thirty-five different yarns to knit it, all of them nestled in tight skeins.

Here and there, leaves had changed and Mary caught a glimpse of red and orange. The air smelled of autumn. At unexpected times Mary discovered that she still could experience joy. The first juicy peach of summer. Her husband's good-night kiss. The particular slant of sunshine out her window. The smell of rain in the air. Waves hitting the beach. The feel of new yarn in her fingers.

And yes, in the memory of her daughter. Stella's face upturned to meet Mary's lips. Stella asleep in her fuzzy red pajamas, her arms bent at the elbow, resting behind her head. Stella splashing in the tub, half hidden in bubbles, her hair wet and pushed off her face, her eyes sparkling. Her little-girl smell, a jumble of clean laundry, sweat, grape Chap Stick. Stella's smooth round tummy beneath Mary's mouth as she gave her a loud smack. The giggles that followed. Stella's voice, which sometimes in the quiet of evening or stillness of early morning

Mary could almost hear. *Mama.*

When she arrived at Big Alice's, Mary stepped out into the October night. She stood a moment, breathing in the cool autumn air. She stopped to look up at the dark sky filled with distant stars that glittered down on her.

When she opened the door, the knitting circle was in full motion. She stood there, her arms overflowing with yarn. Pausing, Mary let her eyes settle over each person.

There was Ellen, her lap filled with lime green yarn already in the shape of a sweater.

"I knit socks because they were small and didn't take very long," Ellen had told her last week when they met for a morning walk. "I was afraid to knit something that would take a lot of time because I didn't think we had a lot of time."

Scarlet's head was bent as she finished the small red sweater with the monogrammed white *L* on the front. In two weeks she would travel to China to bring home her daughter, Lily.

When she got the news a month ago, Mary threw her a baby shower. In the kitchen, refilling their champagne glasses, Scarlet had told her, "I am terrified to love someone again."

Mary hugged her friend. "It is terrifying,"

she said, thinking of those first tenuous months after Dylan had moved back. "But also exhilarating."

Lulu was scowling over a pointy-toed stocking in hot pink yarn with gold threads running through it.

At Scarlet's shower, she had announced that she had some news. She was going to move to Venice for a year. "Or more," she'd added tentatively. She had already sublet her apartment and rented one there. "If I don't do this, I'm afraid that I will spend the rest of my life alone and in fear." Mary had hugged her hard. "You'll meet a handsome Italian man," she predicted. "God help me," Lulu said.

"The book said this was easy," Lulu mumbled, pulling out a row of stitches.

"Slow down," Alice said.

"It's just knitting after all," Harriet said. "It's not brain surgery." Harriet had already begun this year's matching Christmas sweaters for Beth's children. Navy blue with flecks of white.

On the sofa beside Harriet, Roger and David sat together, both knitting rolled-brim hats. On Thursday evenings, when Mary went to the movies with Roger, they always had dinner afterward with David. He had moved into Roger's apartment above the

Sit and Knit Two after Labor Day, and worked at the store with him.

In the rocking chair, Holly sat with a skein of Rowan chunky yarn and her oversized needles, a long scarf hanging from them already. She only knit with these big needles, fast and furiously, producing a scarf or hat every time she came to the knitting circle.

Alice was teaching a new woman how to knit. Mary watched the concentration on the stranger's face beneath a tumble of dark curls.

"In college I knit a sweater for my boyfriend," the woman said apologetically. "A Lopi? On round needles?"

"I can bet you didn't marry him," Harriet said. "That's an Irish folk saying. Knit a sweater for a boyfriend and he'll never be your husband. Isn't that right, Ellen?"

"Something like that," Ellen said, winking at the woman.

"Now you've gone and dropped a few stitches," Alice said.

"Sorry," the woman said. "I'm too much of a wreck to learn, I think."

"Nonsense," Alice said. "I've taught people in all stages of emotional distress. They all learned. Every one of them. You will too, Maggie."

"I'll be the first failure then," Maggie said,

watching as Alice carefully picked up the dropped stitches.

"In knitting," Alice told her, "you can always correct the mistakes. Always."

Harriet put down her knitting and glared at Mary standing in the doorway.

"What in the world are you doing standing there like that?" Harriet said to her.

Unable to answer, Mary walked into the room and took the empty seat by the window. She had just finished knitting a scarf for Dylan. All she had to do was cast off and then she could begin her blanket.

"That's Mary," Alice told the woman. "In no time, she'll be teaching you to purl."

"I don't think so," Maggie said. "I can't even get the knitting down."

"Maggie," Alice said, "yes you can. Look at that perfect row there."

Maggie held up her knitting and examined her work. Then she started to cry.

"Sorry," she said. "I cry over everything these days."

Mary recognized something in this woman. A sadness, a grief that was yet too fresh to put into words. "I'm going to give you my phone number," she said, "and when you've finished that, call me and I'll teach you how to purl."

"I won't be calling you anytime soon,"

Maggie said. She bent her head. "My sister said knitting would help. As if anything could."

Mary knew that Maggie would call her soon. Tomorrow, or the next day. She would go home and knit and eventually the knitting would make the endless, painful hours somehow bearable. Mary knew this. But she said nothing. Instead, she began to cast off.

ACKNOWLEDGMENTS

Thank you to Hillary Day and Heather Watkins for telling me to use my hands; to Pam Young and Karla Harry for suggesting I learn how to knit; to Poo White for giving me Jen Silverman's name and phone number; and to Jen, who taught me how to knit. Thanks also to Stephanie, Nancy, Louise, and Alex from Sakonnet Purls, who picked up my dropped stitches and my spirits, over and over; Amy Lupica, who taught me how to cast off; Drake Patten, who drove every week one snowy winter to Tiverton with me; my knitting comrades Jennifer Becker, Nancy Compton, Ruth Rosenberg, Sarah Baldwin-Beneche, Laurie Eustis, Olivia Thacher, and Frances Carpenter; Mary Sloane, who is the best person with whom to spend a Friday evening of knitting and wine; and my mother-in-law, Lorraine Adrain, who brought me yarn and knitting advice. Of course, all my nonknitting friends deserve thanks for putting up with my obsession.

Many books were consulted in my pursuit of learning to knit and in the writing of this book to be sure I got the details right. These include: *The Knitting Sutra,* by Susan Gordon Lydon; *Zen and the Art of Knitting,* by Bernadette Murphy; *The Joy of Knitting,* by Lisa R. Myers; *Knitting Pretty* by Kris Percival; *A Passion for Knitting,* by Nancy J. Thomas and Ilana Rabinowitz; Elizabeth Zimmermann's *Knitter's Almanac;* and *The Complete Guide to Modern Knitting and Crocheting,* by Alice Carroll, which was published in 1942 and provided much of the knitting history and lore from that time for the character of Big Alice.

My special thanks to Helen Schulman, who would drive for hours to give me a hug when I needed it, accepted my knitted gifts, and whose love has no bounds. For reading and rereading, thanks to Joanne Brownstein, Marianne Merola, and my guardian angel Gail Hochman; my wise editor, Jill Bialosky; and the corporation of Yaddo for the space and time to write.

Finally, my family is my strength: June Caycedo, Gloria Hood, and Melissa Hood; Ariane Adrain; and the cousins: how did I get so lucky to have all of them? And my wonderful husband Lorne Adrain and son Sam Adrain, whose love for me is what gets me through. Thank you, too, to Annabelle Adrain for finding her way to us. Every day, when I knit, I am sending all my love to Auntie Angie, Auntie Rosie, my brother Skip Hood, my father Lloyd Hood; and most especially, my beautiful, smart and funny daughter, Grace Adrain.

ABOUT THE AUTHOR

Ann Hood is the author of seven novels, including *Somewhere Off the Coast of Maine* and *Ruby,* and the story collection *An Ornithologist's Guide to Life.* She has won a Pushcart Prize and a Best American Spiritual Writing Award, as well as the Paul Bowles Prize for Short Fiction. Her essays and stories have appeared in publications such as the *New York Times, Good Housekeeping, Bon Appetit, O* magazine, and *The Paris Review.* She lives in Providence, Rhode Island. To learn more, please visit her online at www.annhood.us.

The employees of Thorndike Press hope you have enjoyed this Large Print book. All our Thorndike and Wheeler Large Print titles are designed for easy reading, and all our books are made to last. Other Thorndike Press Large Print books are available at your library, through selected bookstores, or directly from us.

For information about titles, please call:
(800) 223-1244

or visit our Web site at:
www.gale.com/thorndike
www.gale.com/wheeler

To share your comments, please write:
Publisher
Thorndike Press
295 Kennedy Memorial Drive
Waterville, ME 04901